ONCE A RANCHER

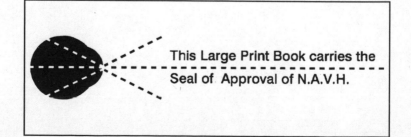

This Large Print Book carries the
Seal of Approval of N.A.V.H.

ONCE A RANCHER

LINDA LAEL MILLER

WHEELER PUBLISHING
A part of Gale, Cengage Learning

GALE
CENGAGE Learning·

Farmington Hills, Mich • San Francisco • New York • Waterville, Maine
Meriden, Conn • Mason, Ohio • Chicago

GALE
CENGAGE Learning®

LIBRARY OF CONGRESS CATALOGING-IN-PUBLICATION DATA

Names: Miller, Linda Lael, author.
Title: Once a rancher / Linda Lael Miller.
Description: Large print edition. | Waterville, Maine : Wheeler Publishing Large Print, 2016. | © 2016 | Series: The Carsons of Mustang Creek ; 1 | Series: Wheeler Publishing large print hardcover
Identifiers: LCCN 2016004936 | ISBN 9781410489043 (hardback) | ISBN 1410489043 (hardcover)
Subjects: LCSH: Large type books. | BISAC: FICTION / Romance / Western. | GSAFD: Love stories. | Western stories.
Classification: LCC PS3563.I41373 O53 2016 | DDC 813/.54—dc23
LC record available at http://lccn.loc.gov/2016004936

Published in 2016 by arrangement with Harlequin Books S.A.

Printed in the United States of America
1 2 3 4 5 6 7 20 19 18 17 16

For Paula Eykelhof
with admiration, gratitude and love

Dear Reader,

Welcome — or welcome back — to Bliss County in the great state of Wyoming, and to the town of Mustang Creek. This time you'll be meeting the Carson brothers, their various family members — and the women who enter their lives.

The Carsons are a long-established ranching family in the county. Slater, whom you'll get to know in this story, grew up ranching; now he's a documentary filmmaker, specializing in the history of the Old West. Drake keeps the ranch running (his story will appear in *Always a Cowboy*) and Mace, the youngest brother, is in charge of the vineyard and winery, their mother's pride and joy. (Mace's story is the third in this series, *Forever a Hero.*)

Each of these men is about to encounter a woman who challenges him in one way or another. A woman who's going to fall in love with him . . . and, of course, vice versa!

I think you'll like and admire Grace Emery as much as I do — and as much as Slater does. Grace is a former Seattle cop, now manager of the year-round resort near

7

Mustang Creek. She's also her teenage stepson's guardian, not the easiest situation to be dealing with. Grace is a woman who understands responsibility and isn't afraid of it.

One thing she and I both have in common with Slater is an interest in American history, especially the history of the West. Another thing (and I'm sure this is a belief you share, too, dear reader!) is a strong sense of the importance of family. And — no surprise — I share the Carsons' love of animals. I've also grown very fond of the cat Grace and her stepson adopt. And . . . I have a new cat of my own. Button is twenty years old, believe it or not, but looks (and acts) younger.

I hope you'll enjoy this first installment of the Carsons' saga. I'd love it if you joined me on my website, www.lindalaelmiller .com, to tell me what you think of the Carsons, to share your own experiences, to learn about contests, upcoming releases and more.

Much love,
Linda Lael Miller

CHAPTER ONE

Slater Carson was bone-tired, as he was after every film wrapped, but it was the best kind of fatigue — part pride and satisfaction in a job well done, part relief, part "bring it," that anticipatory quiver in the pit of his stomach that would lead him to the next project, and the one after that.

This latest film had been set in a particularly remote area, emphasizing how the Homestead Act had impacted the development not only of the American West, but also the country as a whole. It had been his most ambitious effort to date. The sheer scope was truly epic, and as he watched the uncut footage on his computer monitor, he *knew.*

160 Acres was going to touch a nerve.

Yep. This one would definitely hit home with the viewers, new and old.

His previous effort, a miniseries on the Lincoln County War in New Mexico, had won prizes and garnered great reviews, and he'd sold the rights to one of the media giants for a shitload of money. Like *Lincoln County, 160 Acres* was good, solid work. The researchers, camera operators and other professionals he worked with were the top people in the business, as committed to the films as he was.

And that was saying something.

No doubt about it, the team had done a stellar job the last time around, but this — well, *this* was the best yet. A virtual work of art, if he did say so himself.

"Boss?"

Slater leaned back in his desk chair and clicked the pause button. "Hey, Nate." He greeted his friend and personal assistant. "What do you need?"

Like Slater, Nate Wheaton had just gotten back from the film site, where he'd taken care of a thousand details, and it was a safe bet that the man was every bit as tired as he looked. Short, blond, energetic and not more than twenty years old, Nate was a dynamo; the production had come together almost seamlessly, in large part because of his talent, persistence and steel-trap brain.

"Um," Nate murmured, visibly unplugging, shifting gears. He was moving into off-duty mode, and God knew he'd earned it.

"There's someone to see you." He inclined his head in the direction of the outer office, rubbed the back of his neck and let out an exasperated sigh. "The lady insists she needs to talk to you and only you. I tried to get her to make an appointment, but she says it has to be now."

Slater suppressed a sigh of his own. "It's ten o'clock at night."

"I've actually pointed that out," Nate said, briefly consulting his phone. "It's five *after*, to be exact." Like Slater himself, Nate believed in exactness, which was at once a blessing and a curse. "She claims it can't possibly wait until morning, whatever *it* is. But if I hadn't been walking into the kitchen I wouldn't have heard the knock."

"How'd she even find me?" The crew had flown in late, driven out to the vineyard/ranch, and Slater had figured that no one, other than his family, knew he was in town. Or out of town. Whatever qualified as far as the ranch was concerned.

Nate looked glumly resigned. "I have no idea. She refused to say. I'm going to bed. If you need anything else, come and wake me, but bring a sledgehammer, because I'd probably sleep through anything less." A pause, another sigh, deeper and wearier than the last. "That was quite the shoot."

11

The understatement of the day.

Slater drew on the last dregs of his energy, shoved a hand through his hair and said, "Well, point her in this direction, if you don't mind, and then get yourself some shut-eye."

He supposed he sounded normal, but on the inside, he was drained. He'd given everything he had to *160,* and then some, and there was no hope of charging his batteries. He'd blown through the last of his physical resources hours ago.

Resentment at the intrusion sent a tremor through his famous equanimity; he was used to dealing with problems on the job — ranging from pesky all the way to apocalyptic — but at home, damn it, he expected to be left alone. He needed rest, downtime, a chance to regroup, and the home place was where he did those things.

One of his younger brothers ran the Carson ranch, and the other managed the vineyard and winery. The arrangement worked out pretty well. Everyone had his own role to play, and the sprawling mansion was big enough, even for three competitive males to live in relative peace. Especially since he, Slater, was gone half the time, anyway.

"Will do." Nate left the study, and a few

minutes later the door opened.

Before Slater could make the mental leap from one moment to the next, a woman — quite possibly the most beautiful woman he'd ever seen — stormed across the threshold, dragging a teenage boy by the arm.

She was a redhead, with the kind of body that would resurrect a dead man, never mind a tired one.

And Slater had a fondness for redheads; he'd dated a lot of them over the years. This one was all sizzle, and her riot of coppery curls, bouncing around her straight, indignant shoulders, seemed to blaze in the dim light.

It took him a moment, but he finally recovered and clambered to his feet. "I'm Slater Carson. Can I help you?"

This visitor, whoever she was, had his full attention.

Fascinating.

The redhead poked the kid, who was taller than she was by at least six inches, and she did it none too gently. The boy flinched; he was lanky, clad in a Seahawks T-shirt, baggy jeans and half-laced shoes. He looked bewildered, ready to bolt.

"Start talking, buster," the redhead ordered, glowering up at the kid. "And no excuses." She shook her head. "I'm being

13

nice here," she said when the teenager didn't speak. "Your father would kick you into the next county."

Just his luck, Slater thought, with a strange, nostalgic detachment. She was married.

While he waited for the next development, he let his eyes trail over the goddess, over a sundress with thin straps on shapely shoulders, a midthigh skirt and silky pale skin. She was one of the rare Titian types who didn't have freckles, although Slater wouldn't be opposed to finding out if there might be a few tucked away out of sight. White sandals with a small heel finished off the ensemble, and all that glorious hair was loose and flowing down her back.

The kid, probably around fourteen, cleared his throat. He stepped forward and laid one of the magnetic panels from the company's production truck on the desk.

Slater, caught up in the unfolding drama, hadn't noticed the sign until then.

Interesting.

"I'm sorry." The boy gulped, clearly miserable and, at the same time, a little defiant. "I took this." He looked sidelong at the woman beside him, visibly considered giving her some lip and just as visibly reconsidered. Smart kid. "I thought it was pretty cool," he explained, all knees and elbows and youthful angst. Color climbed his neck and burned in his face. "I know it was wrong, okay? Stealing is stealing, and my stepmother's ready to cuff me and haul me off to jail, so if that's what you want, too, Mister, go for it."

Stepmother?

Slater was still rather dazed, as though he'd stepped off a wild carnival ride before it was finished with its whole slew of loop-de-loops.

"His father and I are divorced." She said it curtly, evidently reading Slater's expression.

Well, Slater reflected, that was cause for encouragement. She did look young to be the kid's mother. And now that he thought about it, the boy didn't resemble her in the slightest, with his dark hair and eyes.

Finally catching up, he raised his brows, feeling a flicker of something he couldn't quite identify, along with a flash of sympathy for the boy. He guessed the redhead was in her early thirties. While she seemed to be in charge of the situation, Slater suspected she might be in over her head. Clearly, the kid was a handful.

It was time, Slater decided, still distanced from himself, to speak up.

"I appreciate your bringing it back," he managed, holding the boy's gaze but well aware of the woman on the periphery of his vision. "These aren't cheap."

Some of the *f-you* drained out of the kid's expression. "Like I said, I'm sorry. I shouldn't have done it."

"You made a mistake," Slater agreed quietly. "We've all done things we shouldn't have, at some point in our lives. But you did what you could to make it right." He paused. "Life's all about the choices we make, son. Next time, try to do better." He felt a grin lurking at one corner of his mouth. "I would've been really ticked off if I had to replace this."

The boy looked confused. "Why? You're rich."

Slater had encountered that reasoning before — over the entire course of his life, actually. His family *was* wealthy, and had been for well over a century. They ran cattle, owned vast stretches of Wyoming grassland and now, thanks to his mother's roots in the Napa Valley, there was the winery, with acres of vineyards to support the enterprise.

"Beside the point," Slater said. He worked for a living, and he worked hard, but he felt no particular need to explain that to this kid or anybody else. "What's your name?"

16

"Ryder," the boy answered, after a moment's hesitation.

"Where do you go to school, Ryder?"

"The same lame place everyone around here goes in the eighth grade. Mustang Creek Middle School."

Slater lifted one hand. "I can do without the attitude," he said.

Ryder recovered quickly. "Sorry," he muttered.

Slater had never been married, but he understood children; he had a daughter, and he'd grown up with two kid brothers, born a year apart and still a riot looking for a place to happen, even in their thirties. He'd broken up more fights than a bouncer at Bad Billie's Biker Bar and Burger Palace on a Saturday night.

"I went to the same school," he said, mostly to keep the conversation going. He was in no hurry for the redhead to call it a night, especially since he didn't know her name yet. "Not a bad deal. Does Mr. Perkins still teach shop?"

Ryder laughed. "Oh, yeah. We call him The Relic."

Slater let the remark pass; it was flippant, but not mean-spirited. "You couldn't meet a nicer guy, though. Right?"

The kid's expression was suitably sheep-

17

ish. "True," he admitted.

The stepmother regarded Slater with some measure of approval, although she still seemed riled.

Slater looked back for the pure pleasure of it. She'd be a whole new experience, this one, and he'd never been afraid of a challenge.

She'd said she was divorced, which raised the question: What damn fool had let *her* get away?

As if she'd guessed what he was thinking — anybody with her looks had to be used to male attention — the redhead narrowed her eyes. Still, Slater thought he saw a glimmer of amusement in them. She'd calmed down considerably, but she wasn't missing a trick.

He grinned slightly. "Cuffs?" he inquired mildly, remembering Ryder's statement a few minutes earlier.

She didn't smile, but that spark was still in her eyes. "That was a reference to my former career," she replied, all business. "I'm an ex-cop." She put out her hand, the motion almost abrupt, and finally introduced herself. "Grace Emery," she said. "These days I run the Bliss River Resort and Spa."

"Ah," Slater said, apropos of nothing in

particular. An ex-cop? Hot damn, she could handcuff him anytime. "You must be fairly new around here." If she hadn't been, he would've made her acquaintance before now, or at least heard about her.

Grace nodded. Full of piss-and-vinegar moments before, she looked tired now, and that did something to Slater, although he couldn't have said exactly what that something was. "It's a beautiful place," she said. "Quite a change from Seattle." She stopped, looking uncomfortable, maybe thinking she'd said too much.

Slater wanted to ask about the ex-husband, but the time obviously wasn't right. He waited, sensing that she might say more, despite the misgivings she'd just revealed by clamming up.

Sure enough, she went on. "I'm afraid it's been quite a change for Ryder, too." Another pause. "His dad's military, and he's overseas. It's been hard on him — Ryder, I mean."

Slater sympathized. The kid's father was out of the country, he'd moved from a big city in one state to a small town in another, and on top of that, he was fourteen, which was rough in and of itself. When Slater was that age, he'd grown eight inches in a single summer and simultaneously developed a consuming interest in girls, without having a clue what to say to them. Oh, yeah. He remembered awkward.

He realized Grace's hand was still in his. He let go, albeit reluctantly.

Then, suddenly, he felt as tongue-tied as he ever had at fourteen. "My family's been on this ranch for generations," he heard himself say. "So I can't say I know what it would be like having to start over someplace new." *Shut up, man.* He couldn't seem to follow his own advice. "I travel a lot, and I'm always glad to get back to Mustang Creek."

Grace turned to Ryder, sighed, then looked back at Slater. "We've taken up enough of your time, Mr. Carson."

Mr. Carson?

"I'll walk you out," he said, still flustered and still trying to shake it off. Ordinarily, he was the proverbial man of few words, but tonight, in the presence of this woman, he was a babbling idiot. "This place is like a maze. I took over my father's office because of the view, but it's clear at the back of the house and —"

Had the woman *asked* for any of this information?

No.

What the hell was the matter with him,

anyway?

Grace didn't comment. The boy was already on the move, and she simply followed, which shot holes in Slater's theory about their ability to find their way to an exit without his guidance. He gave an internal shrug and trailed behind Grace, enjoying the gentle sway of her hips.

For some reason he wasn't a damn bit tired anymore.

Having been a police officer, Grace had plenty of experience dealing with men. In law enforcement, still a male-dominated field even though women were finally making inroads, overexposure to testosterone was inevitable. She'd come to terms with the effect her appearance had on the male gender, not out of vanity, but because she was practical to the bone.

She wouldn't have described herself as beautiful; she got an instant update on her imperfections every time she consulted a mirror. She knew her mouth was a shade too wide. Her nose tilted up just a little, giving her an air of perkiness that was wholly unfounded, and she couldn't have gotten a tan in the middle of a desert. Her eyes were an almost startling shade of blue — she'd been accused of wearing colored

21

contacts — and she didn't even want to *discuss* the hair. Just call her Carrot-Top

It was ridiculously curly unless she wore it long, and the stuff could go clown-crazy if the humidity was high. Thankfully, Wyoming was drier than Seattle, so she didn't have to fight it quite as much now. The color was impossible to change, although she'd tried highlights and different treatments, but nature won out every time, so now she let it go its own way.

Slater Carson hadn't been turned off.

Quite the opposite, in fact.

Grace wasn't sure how she felt about her own reaction. Yes, she was jaded about men, but something was different this time. She was — okay, she could admit it — sort of *flattered*.

Recalling the slow, gliding assessment of those sexy blue eyes as they moved over her, she got a definite buzz. And Slater Carson wasn't hard to look at, either, with all that dark, wavy hair, a day's beard growing in and a lean, wiry build that said *cowboy*. He moved like one, too, with long, slow strides, and when he smiled at her as he held the back door open to a starry Wyoming night, there was an easy curve to his mouth, the hint of a grin, not in the least boyish, but confident, amused, knowing.

The message had been clear: he wouldn't mind if they met again.

Well, Grace thought, Mustang Creek was a small town, where everybody seemed to know everybody else, so they were bound to run into each other at some point.

If he expected more than a polite nod and a "howdy," though, he'd be disappointed.

Grace distrusted men like Slater — too good-looking, too privileged, too used to getting whatever and *whoever* they wanted. Yep, the illustrious Mr. Carson reminded her a little too much of her ex-husband, exuding confidence the way he did, certain of his success, of his place in the world.

No, thanks. Grace had been down *that* road before, and after all the excitement and the heady passion and the dazzle, she'd run smack into a dead end. In some ways, she was still reeling from the impact.

Feeling resolute, she got into her vehicle, which she'd parked in the well-lit driveway alongside the Carson mansion, and slammed her door, waiting for Ryder to stop dawdling and plunk himself down in the passenger seat.

This *wasn't* how she'd planned to spend her evening. Her vision had included downloading a movie, munching popcorn, generally vegging out on the couch with her bare feet propped up, wearing shorty pajamas and face cream.

Grace had had a long day at the resort; she'd dealt with a faulty air-conditioning unit and repairmen who couldn't seem to agree on what was wrong, a chronically late employee who was wonderful when he actually got there, by which time the rest of the staff was thoroughly and justifiably annoyed, plus guest complaints about the lap pool that ranged from too hot to too cool. Among other things.

Coming home to find Ryder about to nail a newly acquired and obviously expensive metal sign to one wall of his bedroom had immediately thrown her evening plans for a loop. Immediately suspicious, Grace had questioned the boy.

Never a good liar, he'd confessed.

Grace had figuratively grabbed the kid by one ear and dragged him to the Carson house.

Now he hauled open the door on his side and got in.

"I'm sorry," Ryder said. He didn't really sound sorry, and he didn't look at her, but sat staring out the windshield instead. His tone was stubborn, and the set of his mouth underscored his attitude.

Grace sighed inwardly.

Ryder was a good kid, and Slater Carson had been right earlier, when he'd said everybody made bad decisions now and then. "You know better."

"It just —"

She raised a hand to indicate she wanted him to stop. Now. "There's no excuse I care to hear. You stole something and we returned it."

Grace started the car, flipped on the headlights and turned around to head back down the driveway.

Ryder was quiet for a few minutes. They reached the county highway, which was practically deserted at that time of night, and, since both the ranch and the resort were well outside town, they didn't pass many cars.

Eventually, Ryder said, "He liked you."

Fourteen and he'd picked up on that, Grace reflected with rueful amusement, but he still couldn't pick up his underwear.

He liked you.

There was liking a woman, and there was wanting to go to bed with her. Grace was not inclined to explain the difference to a fourteen-year-old.

So she said briskly, "He doesn't know me."

"He thought you were pretty."

There were times when she wished Ryder

would talk to her more, and times, like now, when she wished he wouldn't. "I think it's just possible that he's prettier than I am."

That made Ryder crack up. "At least he tried to be subtle. He didn't, like, stare at your —"

He stopped abruptly, and Grace figured he'd be blushing right about now over what he'd almost said, so she cut the kid a break and kept her gaze on the road. "Mr. Carson was very polite," she conceded. "How's the science project coming along?"

Ryder jumped on the sudden change of subject, even if school wasn't one of his favorites. "Okay, actually. Turns out my partner isn't as geeky as he looks." He was quiet for a moment, then he went on. "I was wondering if he might come over to our place and hang out sometime. That okay?"

Grace felt a rush of relief. She'd been waiting for Ryder to stop rebelling against the move to Mustang Creek and make some friends, hoping and praying he would.

She was in over her head with this parenting thing.

And she didn't seem to be getting any better at it.

A few months back Grace's former father-in-law had called her one day, out of the blue. Haltingly, he'd explained that with his

26

wife so ill, they couldn't handle their grandson on their own. They hated to ask, but since Hank was overseas and all, they didn't have anyone else to turn to.

Hank, Grace's ex and Ryder's father, made a career of being unavailable, in her opinion, but of course she didn't say that.

She'd had no idea *what* to say, under the circumstances. Ryder's mother was remarried, with a whole new family, and for reasons Grace still didn't understand, the woman had never shown much interest in her firstborn, anyway. When she and Hank were divorced, she'd handed Ryder over without a quibble, not even asking for visitation rights.

The woman couldn't be bothered to send her son a birthday card, never mind calling to see how he was doing or firing off the occasional text to keep in touch.

The whole scenario made Grace furious on Ryder's behalf, and it didn't help that Hank was so emotionally distant, absolutely caught up in his military career.

In that respect, she and Ryder had been set adrift in the same boat, but Grace had had options, at least. She could divorce Hank — which she had — and move on. His son didn't have that choice.

So she'd said yes, Ryder could stay with

27

her until Hank's current deployment ended, and here they were in Mustang Creek, Wyoming, stuck with each other, both of them struggling to adjust to major changes.

Grace brought herself back to the present. "I think it would be great if your friend came over sometime. I could order you guys a pizza, how's that?"

Ryder nodded. "As long as it isn't like the ones they have at the spa, with goat cheese and whatever those green things are. I tried to like the stuff, Grace, but no way."

"Artichoke hearts," she supplied helpfully. "How about plain old pepperoni?"

Ryder grinned. "That would be great," he said.

"Okay, you're on. I just need your word that you'll stay out of trouble for five minutes." She feigned a narrow glare. "I didn't like facing Mr. Carson with what you'd done any more than you did, buddy."

Ryder's grin broadened. "Maybe not," he agreed, "but I think *he* sorta enjoyed it."

CHAPTER TWO

Beyond the tall windows of the breakfast room off the ranch-house kitchen, the Tetons soared against a morning sky of heartbreaking blue. Slater sat in his usual place at the table, coffee mug in hand, silently marveling. He'd looked out on that same vista almost every morning of his life and never once taken it for granted.

He was a lucky man, and he knew it.

The sound of boot heels on the wide plank floor alerted him to company.

"Hey, Showbiz." Slater's youngest brother, Mace, meandered in from the next room, pulled out a chair on the opposite side of the table and dropped into it, an easy grin surfacing. Of the three of them, Mace most resembled their dad, who'd been killed in a fall from a horse when Slater was twelve. Sometimes just the sight of his brother brought him a pang of grief.

"Hey, yourself," Slater responded lazily.

As nicknames went, he figured *Showbiz* was something he could live with; both Mace and Drake, his middle brother, used it often.

Mace reached for the carafe in the middle of the table and filled a waiting mug, adding a hefty splash of cream before closing his eyes, savoring that first sip and giving a blissful sigh. Next, he raised the lids on the metal serving dishes and helped himself to a heaping portion of scrambled eggs, bacon and sausage and three slices of buttered toast. He'd consume all of that, and most likely repeat the whole process.

Slater, a devout aficionado of home cooking, was continually astonished by the sheer quantity of food Mace could put away.

Finished with his own meal but in no particular hurry to head elsewhere, or to pad the silent spaces with talk, Slater replenished his coffee. He sat there, gazing quietly out the window, soaking in the special ambience of a country morning, content to be who he was, *where* he was.

Which was *home.*

When he needed a few minutes to digest the staggering view, like he did right now, he reined in his attention, absorbing his immediate surroundings.

He much preferred this simple but elegant space to the much larger and fancier dining room on the far side of the kitchen; the polished oak table was sturdy, seating six people comfortably.

The room doubled as a sort of butler's pantry, with two huge sideboards full of antique china and glassware. The liquor cabinet his great-grandfather had brought over from England towered against the inside wall, and the stained-glass panels in the doors gleamed with jewel-like colors. Even as a teenager, when he'd been tempted to raid the contents, figuring, as teenage boys sometimes do, that getting falling-down drunk would be a good move, he'd never actually carried out the plan. Prudently, his folks had kept the cabinet locked, and Slater hadn't been able to summon up the courage to risk damaging a treasured heirloom.

No, he'd swiped beer from the refrigerator instead and settled for a mild buzz rather than a full-on booze blitz.

"Nice morning," he said, watching as Mace did justice to the mountain of grub on his plate.

"Yep," Mace agreed. He was auburn-haired like their mother, with clear blue eyes, and he had a talent with anything that grew. That knack had manifested itself early in his life. When he was ten, their mother had given him a garden plot, a hoe and several packets of seeds for his birthday. While most boys wanted a new bicycle, he'd busied himself with tackling the GP as Slater and Drake called it (translation: the Garden Project), and they'd eaten green beans with supper every night until they'd finally begged for an ear of corn or even some spinach.

Slater wasn't a picky eater, but he wasn't a big fan of spinach, either.

A few years ago their mother, Blythe, had revisited her roots in the wine country of Northern California and decided to plant vineyards and produce a brand of her own. Mace had been the natural choice to run the operation. If a plant had leaves, he could make it grow — and thrive — in just about any soil.

"When did you get back?" Mace asked, serving himself up a second breakfast, now that he'd wiped out the first. Slater wondered if his brother's appetite would catch up with him one day, if Mace would pack a layer or two of fat over those lean muscles of his.

No sign of it so far.

"I got in last night," Slater answered. He'd slept like the proverbial rock, although he vaguely recalled a series of dreams involving a certain feisty redhead. No surprise there. Grace Emery was the last person he'd seen before he'd stripped off his clothes, showered and fallen face-first into bed. Meeting a woman like that was bound to be a memorable experience, even for somebody half-dead with fatigue.

Mace nodded.

Slater, not usually given to idle chitchat, kept talking. "The production went well and we wrapped early, which almost never happens. Not by much, but early is still early."

"Sweet." Mace picked up a piece of toast. "Now you go into the cutting and editing thing, huh?"

"The director will handle most of that."

"What comes next?"

He'd been thinking about that; on some level, he was *always* thinking about the next project. "I've been playing with the idea of doing a history of Wyoming — how it was settled and all that — but what it also is today. Too many people seem to believe the whole state is barren, except for a ski resort or two and a couple of million sheep. I figure it might be time to update the image a little."

Mace nodded again, his expression thoughtful. "You could throw in some stuff about the ranch — you know, about Dad's family and the railroad money his grand-father inherited and then used to establish the ranch. You might even include the estate in California Mom's people founded." He was warming to the idea, visibly picking up steam. Trust Mace to find a way to work the winery angle, never mind the logic of highlighting California history in a movie about Wyoming.

Slater smiled — and listened. His brother was on a roll, and some of his ideas were good.

"And what about this place?" Mace went on. "How many historic Wyoming ranch houses were specifically designed to look like something out of *Gone with the Wind*? There's a story there, don't forget."

There was indeed a story. The mansion had been built, back in the day, to assuage the homesickness of their great-grandmother, a young Southern bride, far from home and yearning for the plantation of her childhood.

By now, Mace was so caught up in the impromptu brainstorming session that he waved his fork in enthusiasm. "I think it would make a great project. You could call it 'The Carson Legacy: One Family's Journey in the Great West.' "

Slater smiled again. "Okay, the Carson

clan made its mark, I'll grant you that. But there were a lot of other pioneers, too."

Mace grinned back at him. "I wouldn't mind seeing myself immortalized on film," he said.

That was when Drake wandered in, yawning, probably not from lack of sleep but because he'd been out tending horses since the crack of dawn. "Now why, little brother," he asked, "would anybody want to *immortalize* the likes of you?"

Drake was built like Slater and Mace — tall, lean and broad through the shoulders; unlike them, he had dark blond hair. He looked like a cowboy, could handle a horse like no one Slater had ever seen and was just plain born to be outdoors. He yawned again, swung a leg over his customary chair and sat, reaching for the coffee. He scowled at Mace and grunted to underscore his previous remark. "Why should you be immortalized? You're not all that special, except in your own opinion."

Mace tried not to seem affronted. "Look who's talkin'," he drawled.

Drake flashed that cowboy grin of his. "The voice of reason, that's who," he said affably. He nodded at his older brother. "Hey, Slate. Heard you were home. I would've said hello before now, but we're moving a herd to the south pasture, so I've been at it for a while. Anyhow, it's good to see you back."

It was good to *be* back.

"Mace has been doing his damnedest to inspire me." Slater drank the last of his coffee. "Says I ought to include our family's history in the next documentary."

"Oh, jeez." Drake rolled his eyes and sipped from his mug. "Plenty of skeletons rattling around in *these* closets. If you're planning on turning them loose, well, I'd appreciate it if you left my name out of the script."

Mace raised his eyebrows, nudged Drake with a light jab of his elbow. "You could do a feature on our fascinating brother here," he suggested drily. "Focusing on his love life. The title could be 'Boring on the Range.' "

"Ha-ha." Drake shot his younger brother a glare. "That's a brilliant idea," he said. "Oh, and by the way, I was up and around long before you finished getting your beauty sleep. Now, I'm thinking maybe you should go back to bed for a while. You obviously need some more shut-eye."

Slater slid back his chair and stood, empty mug in hand. "You two need to drum up some new insults," he said. "If I can change the subject — Mace, aren't we supplying wines for the Bliss River Resort now? How's that going?"

His brothers exchanged glances — and grins.

Mace said, "I was right! Big Brother *did* find a way to get her into the conversation. You owe me ten bucks."

Drake made no move to pull out his wallet. "Damn," he agreed, "that *was* fast, Slate. You have some special radar or something? 'Beep, beep, pretty redhead within range. Sound the alarm. Man your battle stations.' "

Okay, so he hadn't been as subtle as he'd thought in bringing their discussion around to Grace Emery.

Slater decided to brazen it out, anyway. "You mind telling me what you two loco cowboys are talking about? All I asked was how the deal with the resort was going." God knew he couldn't have asked Grace the night before, with her all worked up the way she'd been. He sat down again, grabbed a sausage link from what remained of Mace's double breakfast and took a bite. Harriet Armstrong, the Carsons' longtime cook and housekeeper, mixed the ingredients herself. Yet another reason there was no place like home.

He'd eaten in some fancy restaurants, but whatever Harriet put on the table would do just fine. She ran the house with the same kind of no-sweat finesse. He and his brothers referred to the housekeeper as "Harry," because that was Blythe's name for her. Harry was like a second mother to all of them, and she'd never had a problem calling bullshit when they tried to put anything over on her.

Mace apparently felt it was incumbent upon him to elaborate on the wager he'd made with Drake. "I bet that if you took one look at Grace Emery, you'd be getting acquainted right quick. You'd be all over that." He shook his head. "It's a mystery to me how you did it so fast. You arrived after supper last night and now it's breakfast time. Every guy within a hundred miles of Mustang Creek suddenly feels the need for a spa visit, just so they can get a look at her, and you, brother, you somehow figured out how to get her to come to *you.*"

His assistant, Nathan, must have told one of them about Grace's visit, Slater concluded with a degree of resignation. Fine. He wasn't going to tell them why she'd stopped by; the business about the swiped sign was between him and Ryder. As far as he was concerned, the matter was settled.

"What's her story?" he asked.

Mace seemed to relish answering the question. "She's divorced. The kid lives with her because her ex-husband is some sort of hotshot military type. He's deployed at the moment." He paused, then added, "From what I've heard, she's doing a great job at the resort. The owner hired her personally."

Not much news there. Grace had told him most of those details, along with the fact that she'd been a police officer at some point. As brief as their encounter had been, though, Slater could well imagine the memorably lovely Ms. Emery meeting any task head-on. Of course the transition from cop to hotel manager *was* quite a leap. Obviously, there was more to her story, and he wanted to hear it. "Interesting."

One thing about his brothers — they weren't inclined to poke their noses into other people's business, and when he didn't divulge Grace Emery's reason for stopping by, they left it alone.

Mace said matter-of-factly, "To answer your other question, our wine arrangement with the resort seems to be going well. On another subject, I've been doing some research, and I'm getting some new info on what vines we ought to put in. As you know, Mom wants to expand the operation, take it national. Anyway, the clients at the resort select different wines than the ones the liquor stores order from us. The higher-end lines go over better with the spa guests — they want the full-bodied, well-balanced reds or big, oaky chardonnays, while on the retail level, the customers seem to prefer fruity, lighter varieties. We're entering a few competitions this year to see if we can get more press." He paused, but only long enough to take a breath. Once Mace got talking about the vineyards and the wines they produced, it was hard to shut him up. "The trick here is dealing with our weather and finding vines that can handle the winters and still produce the quality of fruit and yield we're after. Right now we buy most of our grapes from other states. That's not unusual, but I'd like to swing the pendulum our way."

Slater enjoyed his younger brother's passion for the wine business because he knew this venture was their mother's dream as much as it was Mace's. They were three very different people, he and Mace and Blythe, but he could identify with both of them, since filmmaking and running a successful vineyard were both artistic pursuits. Drake, however, couldn't have been less interested, down to earth as he was — always active, always on the move. It was almost comical the way animals and kids gravitated toward him. Slater had seen his middle brother at many a picnic or cookout with a toddler on his lap and three dogs belonging to someone else at his feet. He'd be talking away with friends, evidently oblivious to the Doctor Dolittle phenomenon.

"I don't know much of anything about making wine," Slater admitted, addressing Mace, "but that sounds like a plan to me. I can grow mold on a piece of cheese in the fridge, and that's about it. Speaking of wine and cheese, I need to throw a shindig for the investors. They deserve a celebration. I'm thinking the resort would be the perfect venue."

Both his brothers laughed, and Drake reached into his pocket and pulled out a few bills. He selected one and handed it to Mace. "You win," he said. "Here's your ten bucks."

Grace peered at her computer screen, blinked a couple of times to make sure she wasn't seeing things. The booking had come in just as she was thinking about taking her lunch, and it was major. Slater Carson's production company had reserved fifteen of the resort's best rooms as well as the private dining room, and had requested gourmet menu suggestions and comprehensive spa privileges for its top executives and a number of investors.

The bill would amount to tens of thousands of dollars. Grace was new enough to the resort-management field to be impressed, although she supposed such expenditures were common in the corporate world.

Not that Slater struck her as the corporate type; she couldn't really picture him wearing a suit, giving speeches in some boardroom. He'd looked like a denim and custom-made boots man to her, but then she'd met him only once, and under distinctly awkward circumstances at that. So maybe she'd missed something.

Still, Grace had good instincts where people were concerned; as a cop, she'd learned to depend on her gut.

She'd certainly noticed Slater's easy air of command. He was clearly comfortable with himself, and he was assertive but not overbearing. Otherwise, he would've been a lot tougher on Ryder the night before.

It was a safe bet that Mr. Carson had a clear idea of what he wanted and seldom, if ever, hesitated to go after it.

She couldn't help making a few comparisons — and there were undeniable similarities between Slater and Hank, her ex-husband. Both men were strong, single-minded and ambitious.

There were undeniable differences between them, too.

Hank, in fact, was not merely ambitious, he was driven, a trait that could seem sexy at first glance; power usually *was* sexy. She'd been drawn in quickly, despite the practicality that had served her so well on the force. Trouble was, she'd sadly miscalculated her place in the pecking order. On the list of Hank's priorities, she came in last.

Even Ryder was low on the figurative totem pole. Hank's career was number one, and both she and his son were basically distractions. Afterthoughts.

She'd been wounded by this realization, and she'd been cautious ever since. One major mistake was forgivable; two would constitute disaster.

Okay, so she didn't know Slater well enough to write him off as a player, but she'd learned to be wary of his brand of charisma.

If he saw her as a conquest — she'd run into that attitude before *and* after Hank — he was riding for a fall that would bruise his masculine ego big-time.

Count me out.

She looked past her computer monitor, took in her surroundings. It was an old trick, a way of grounding herself in the real world when her mind wandered.

Grace loved her spacious second-floor office, overlooking the pool and the gardens. There was a small balcony, complete with a couple of ornate deck chairs and a small, glass-topped table.

Not that she had time to sit out there and enjoy it all.

This morning, though, she had the balcony doors open, and a cool, soft breeze wafted in, scented with a tinge of pine and the lush flowers crowding the gardens.

The resort was a terrific place to work, her salary was generous and so far, she'd gotten along beautifully with the guests as well as the staff. In short, she'd finally gotten her life unstuck, and no complications would be tolerated.

Specifically, the tall, dark-haired, good-looking cowboy sort of complication.

"Did you see that booking I forwarded?"

The question came from her assistant, Meg, who was standing in the doorway, smiling broadly. Meg was young, energetic and fresh out of hotel management school, but inexperienced. The resort owner,

44

George Landers, was an old friend of Grace's father's. He had reliable instincts when it came to hiring key people. In time, Meg would develop the necessary air of confident authority required to run one of his resorts, but for now, she was still "wet behind the ears," to quote George.

Grace herself had a degree in the hospitality field — which she'd obtained part-time while she was still a cop — but no real experience, and she wasn't positive that confidence was her strongest suit, either, given some of the choices she'd made in the past. She was skilled at handling difficult situations, however, and the boss knew that because he knew *her.* She'd been trained to function under intense pressure, but in reality, she didn't actually run the resort as much as she supervised the *staff* who ran it.

The exact instructions she'd received: *Just make sure everybody's doing what they're supposed to do. I trust you to take care of whatever comes up.*

Thank God *somebody* believed in her abilities.

Or maybe she'd just gotten lucky.

George Landers had gone to college with her father, and the two men had played golf together ever since, every Wednesday afternoon. When George learned that Grace might be looking for a change of scene, he'd punched her number into his cell phone, invited her to his office and offered her the job on the spot.

She'd jumped at the chance. No, she hadn't realized Ryder was going to jump with her, but she could cope with that. After all, she was crazy about the kid.

"I was actually just looking at it," she answered belatedly, smiling at Meg. "Very nice."

"The Carson name carries considerable weight around here." Meg, wearing the fitted jacket and skirt the company required, crossed the threshold and laid a set of invoices on the desk. "They've also recently opened a winery. That Ranch Hand Red on our wine list in the dining room is one of our best sellers."

This was valuable information. "The Carsons own Mountain Vineyards? Hmm." Grace tapped a few keys and their website popped up. The winery building itself was picturesque, a restored barn or bunkhouse, perhaps, rustic but sturdy, attractively weathered, with a shingle roof and tall windows. The mountains provided a staggering backdrop.

Oh, yes. The place was the epitome of Western charm. "I wonder if they'd consider doing tours and a few wine-tasting events for our guests," Grace went on, musing aloud. "We could add that to some of our packages, since not everyone comes here to hike or ski. The spa is a big draw in its own right, and wine-tastings ought to fit the mood."

"It won't hurt to ask them," Meg announced brightly. She was, as usual, brimming with enthusiasm. "It would be fabulous if we could get a few more gigs like this one, right? And this is such gorgeous country — ideal for a corporate getaway."

Meg's buoyant spirits might have been irritating, if they hadn't been completely genuine. Grace had liked her from the moment she'd first walked through the elaborate glass doors downstairs.

Thoughtful, she tapped her pen against her desk blotter. "I wonder," she murmured, "if Slater Carson would consider using the resort in one of his films. As I understand it, he's only made historical documentaries so far, stuff about the Old West. Maybe he'd be interested in some kind of joint promotion."

Meg sank into a chair, her eyes wide. "That's a stretch," she said honestly, "but like I said before, it can't hurt to ask. I mean, what if it actually worked?" She

47

paused, bit her lower lip. "Would you like me to draft a preliminary proposal?"

The idea *was* a stretch — but the good ones usually were. *Nothing ventured . . .*

Of course she'd eventually have to make the pitch in person, face-to-face with Slater. Still, it made sense to plant a seed, get him thinking about the possibilities. After all, Mustang Creek was his hometown; surely, he cared about the local economy.

"Do that," she decided aloud. "And let him know we'd be willing to offer some leeway on the cost of the event he just booked and any other business he sends our way in the future. Mention the winery connection, too."

"Consider it done," Meg said. She was an attractive young woman, with shiny brown hair that fell gracefully around her shoulders, eyes the color of warm honey and a friendly smile. Secretly, Grace envied her assistant's less dramatic coloring a little, her own being . . . well, a bit on the flashy side.

Inwardly, Grace sighed, reminding herself of her mother's oft-given advice: *Be yourself and keep putting one foot in front of the other.*

Then Grace was all business again. "I want the head chef in the kitchen for this event," she said. "And whether he likes it or not, we'll offer a simple menu — one seafood dish, one poultry, one beef, one pork and one elegant vegetarian option. No fancy ice sculptures, nothing with flames." She grinned at Meg, who grinned back. "Stefano gets carried away sometimes, as you've probably noticed. I've tried to rein him in, but as he's pointed out numerous times, I'm not a chef."

"No," Meg said, "but you *are* the boss."

"Indeed I am."

"Will there be anything else?"

Grace waited for a moment, then made the leap. "Invite him to dinner," she said. "Next Thursday night, if he's free."

Meg looked mildly confused. "Who? Stefano?"

Grace shook her head. "Slater Carson," she answered. "I'll give him the proposal then. I'd call him myself, but I want this to be formal, just business."

Meg gazed at her curiously, no doubt wondering if Grace knew the legendary filmmaker and if so, how. And too smart to ask.

"It's a long story." Grace waved a hand in casual dismissal, although, in truth, she didn't *feel* casual, not where Slater was concerned.

Meg nodded and left the office, closing the door quietly behind her.

Once Grace was alone, she found her thoughts turning in another direction.

She was uneasy about Ryder; he'd crossed an alarming line, stealing from Slater Carson.

Okay, so it wasn't armed robbery or drug trafficking, and she didn't want to make too big a deal of it. Still, she'd seen too many kids head down the wrong trail in her last job, and the trouble often began with some small infraction.

Theft was theft.

Ryder was a decent kid with loads of potential, but that didn't mean he wouldn't keep right on screwing up, because he was *also* a confused and lonely kid, and with his dad so far away and his mother permanently disinterested, he was especially vulnerable.

Well, Grace resolved for about the hundredth time since Ryder had moved in with her, if the boy *was* destined for a life of crime, it wasn't going to happen on *her* watch.

Except that she had only so much influence over Ryder.

The hard truth was, Hank needed to man up, take responsibility for his son, give the kid some love and guidance. Yes, he provided financial support, but that was far from enough.

Ironically, though, if Ryder went downhill from here, Hank would blame *her,* not himself.

Did she care about Hank's opinion? No.

But she *did* care, very much, about Ryder.

She smiled. The boy put on a convincing tough-guy act, but there was more to him, thank God. A *lot* more.

For instance, she knew he was secretly feeding a stray cat that had showed up on their patio a few days ago. She'd glimpsed the poor creature a couple of times, saw that it was thin, matted and skittish. When she'd tried to approach, the animal shot into the bushes and hid there, but Ryder had fared better. He'd set out pilfered lunch meat or a bowl of milk and then wait, crouching, almost motionless.

And the cat would come close enough to eat a few bites or lap up some of the milk.

That image of Ryder, that display of kindly patience, gave her hope.

Later, when she was officially off duty, she drove into town, visited the supermarket, planning to fix Ryder's favorite meal, spaghetti and meatballs. She added potatoes to her cart, then vegetables for a green salad, a stack of canned cat food, and some of the dry kind, too — along with a couple of ceramic bowls.

Back at the condo, which was part of the resort complex, she thought about how lucky she was to have this job. It was demanding, sure, but besides her salary, she had health insurance and a decent retirement plan, and she didn't have to cover rent or mortgage payments.

Plus, nobody shot at her or yelled abuse simply because she wore a badge.

She paused in the parking lot to admire the place. The condo boasted three sizeable bedrooms, one of which she used as a home office, two bathrooms, a nice sleek kitchen and a Wyoming view that faced the scenic Bliss River. She'd decorated with a few antiques she'd inherited from her grandmother — an English case clock, a pewter pitcher she'd set on the mantel, a beautifully framed and very old charcoal drawing of horses standing in the snow, their manes ruffled by the wind. She'd also splurged and bought a new chocolate-brown couch, with scarlet velvet pillows for accent.

The low, square coffee table was new, too.

Feeling domestic, Grace carted in her briefcase, purse and one bag of groceries. Ryder abandoned the video game he'd been absorbed in and jumped to his feet.

"Need some help?" he asked, with a shy grin.

"Yes," Grace answered, pleased. "There's more in the car."

Ryder rushed out the door, all legs and elbows, and when he returned, he was carrying the bag of cat kibble under one arm. The expression on his face made Grace double-glad she'd decided to cave on the adopt-a-pet question.

"What —" he began, looking down at the heavy bag clutched to his side.

Grace smiled, took the bags from his other hand and set them on the counter. Then she rummaged through them until she found the bowls. "I know what you've been up to, bud," she said.

To his credit, Ryder didn't try to dodge the issue. "He's so hungry, Grace. Scared, too. There are things out there that could get him —"

Grace nearly choked up; she was so moved by the tenderness in Ryder's young and so often sullen face, but she kept smiling. *There are things out there that could get him.*

Was that how Ryder felt, too? Alone in a big, dangerous world?

Probably.

Grace swallowed hard, forcing back the tears. "There are a few rules here," she warned. "We'll take the cat to the vet as soon as possible. He can't come inside until he's been checked out. He'll need shots and neutering, and you're going to have to do a few extra chores around here to pay me back. I'll buy his food, but the rest is your responsibility, Ryder — and that includes cleaning the litter box. Do we have an agreement?"

Ryder's eyes were wide with disbelief. "You mean it, Grace? We can keep him?"

She laughed, wanting to hug the boy, but sensing that the timing was off. So she gave him a light punch to the shoulder instead. "Did you hear anything I said just now?"

How many times had this child been promised something and then been disappointed?

"I heard," Ryder said, very softly. "Thanks, Grace. I mean, really, thanks."

"Make sure you're picking up what I'm saying here," she said with mock sternness. "This is *your* cat, not mine. He'll be dependent on you, and that's a big responsibility." She softened her tone. "Take good care of this little guy, and you'll have a faithful friend for the duration. Can I count on you, Ryder? Can he?"

Ryder's voice was hoarse when he replied, and his eyes glistened slightly. "Yes," he said, and then cleared his throat.

He was growing up, Grace thought suddenly.

Or just *growing.*

When had he gotten so tall? She needed
to take him shopping for new clothes, and
soon.

"All right, then," she said, turning to
unpack the other groceries so he wouldn't
see that her eyes were moist, too. "Go feed
your cat." A pause. This was the best conversation she and Ryder had had so far, and
she didn't want to let it go. She blinked and
glanced back over her shoulder. "What's his
name, anyway? Has he got one yet?"

Ryder's grin practically lit up the room.
"Bonaparte."

Definitely unexpected. Grace raised an
eyebrow. "Interesting choice. Any particular
logic behind it?"

"Sure," Ryder said, plunking down the
bag of kibble and opening the top to scoop
out the cat's dinner. "Napoleon Bonaparte
started from humble beginnings and became one of the greatest generals the world's
ever known. *And* he declared himself em-
peror." He took the second bowl to the sink
and filled it with water. "I think that's pretty
awesome."

"And there's a connection between the
general and the cat because —"

Ryder headed for the patio doors, bowls in hand, sloshing water on the floor as he moved. "I guess I just liked the story," he said. "Look at it this way, Grace. I've been paying attention in history class." He used one elbow to open the glass slider. "I told you I was going to try harder, remember?"

Grace's throat felt tight again. She nodded, watching as Ryder stepped out onto the patio, dropped to a crouch and set the bowls down. He turned his head to meet her eyes.

"I didn't want to come here," he reminded her cheerfully. "But now I'm actually starting to like it — a little."

Grace chuckled.

That was progress, anyway.

"Bonaparte's a great name," she said.

She wasn't sure if Ryder had heard her, not that it mattered. By then, the cat had come slinking across the flagstones on the patio, too scared to get close, but too starved to stay away.

CHAPTER THREE

The stallion, charcoal-gray with a black mane and tail, was the living definition of the word *wild.* He stood, majestic, almost a part of the early-morning sunlight blazing around him like an aura, while his harem of mares grazed nearby.

Despite the distance, the animal seemed to know he was being watched; Slater noted the creature's raised head and direct gaze, the forward slant of his ears, the muscles in his powerful haunches as he readied himself for fight or flight.

Slater gave a low whistle of grudging admiration as he handed the binoculars back to his brother. "That," he breathed, "is one hell of a horse."

Drake's response was a disdainful grunt. "He's a bold son of a bitch, I'll say that for him." He lifted his hat long enough to shove a hand through his hair in a gesture of barely contained frustration. "I was planning on breeding at least one of those mares with that stud Tate Calder bought last year — the black one with the look of a Thoroughbred? I've even paid the damn fee." The hat came off again, and Drake slapped it against one thigh to emphasize his point. With a slight motion of his head, he indicated the stallion, along with the band of prize mares, every one of them either bought and paid for by him, or bred and raised right there on the ranch. "Now, thanks to that thieving bastard out there, I'll have to shit-can the whole idea."

Slater suppressed a grin. There were times when it was fine to needle Drake, and times when a misplaced word could have the same general effect as tossing a lighted match into a stand of drought-yellowed grass.

And while Slater enjoyed a good brawl as much as the next man, he didn't have the energy for that kind of drama. So he nodded slightly in the stallion's direction and said, "He's quite a specimen himself, that horse. Bound to sire some mighty respectable foals."

Drake's eyes narrowed, but he was calming down. He seemed to be fighting back a grin of his own, although Slater couldn't be sure. "You think he's going to bring those mares over to the barn, drop them all neat and tidy, so we can see that they get proper prenatal care? Hell, Showbiz, you've been on the road too long if *that's* what you're expecting. Either that, or you've been watching too many old Disney movies."

Slater chuckled, took back the binoculars and scanned the horizon for the stallion and his four-legged admirers. Smiled to himself. The animal had lost interest in his observers by then, and who could blame him, with all those mares at his beck and call?

"You get in touch with the BLM?" Slater asked, lowering the binoculars. He hadn't watched a Disney flick recently, and while he did spend more time away from home than he wanted to, he belonged to the place as much as Drake did. The ranch was his legacy, too, and his future, in all the ways that counted.

At the mention of the Bureau of Land Management, Drake finally cut loose with a chuckle of his own. "*Yes,* I called the BLM," he replied, with terse good humor. "Let's just say that between the wild donkeys and the mustangs, they've got their hands full. In other words, if we've lost a few fancy mares, well, in their considered opinion, that's *our* problem."

Slater raised one shoulder in a shrug. "I reckon it *is* our problem," he said. "We could get some of the hands together, saddle up and ride out, see how many of those mares we can rope and lead home."

Drake sighed heavily, shaking his head. "Priorities, brother. We're missing some calves, too, so just about everybody's out there trying to track 'em down. Not having much luck, since it hasn't rained in a while. Whoever or whatever is rustling beef isn't leaving any kind of trail." He paused, looking genuinely worried now. "If I had to venture a guess, I'd say we're dealing with wolves or a big cat. In which case I'll have to dust off one of my rifles."

Briefly, Slater rested his left hand on Drake's shoulder. He knew his brother was feeling bleak. He loved animals, *all* animals, and he had a rancher's respect for the natural order of things. To a hungry wolf pack or any other predator, a calf was food, plain and simple. He understood that. Still, it was his job to protect the herd.

"Need any help?" Slater asked quietly. He had about a dozen urgent phone calls to make, and there was paperwork, too, but he'd put it all aside if Drake said the word. He was a filmmaker by trade, but first, last and always, he was a Carson.

A rancher.

But Drake shook his head again. "We'll

take care of it," he said. Then his mouth formed a tired grin. "You've got enough to do back at your office." He paused, gestured, the motion of his hand taking in the mountains, the range, the broad and poignantly blue Wyoming sky. "This is *my* office," he said, with a note of grim pride. "Not perfect when it's dead cold in the winter and the wind is gusting at sixty miles an hour and hurling snow in your face like shrapnel, or when it's so hot you feel the heat shimmer up from the ground and your shirt is stuck to your body. But hey, it suits me just like being Mr. Showbiz suits you."

Slater nodded an agreeable goodbye and walked back toward the house, thinking Drake had a good handle on his place in the world. His brother tackled life head-on and waded right in, got things done.

As for their youngest brother, Mace, he tended to operate by intuition.

Slater smiled when he went up the steps and found his mother watering the plants on the wide front porch. She glanced up and smiled. Blythe Carson was still slim and youthful at seventy, wearing jeans and a loose cotton blouse, and she'd caught back her thick hair in a clip as usual. She had a natural beauty that didn't require embellishment, but she was like steel under that soft, feminine exterior. Maybe she'd been born resilient, maybe she'd developed the quality after giving birth to three unruly sons, losing the husband she'd loved early on and, finally, inheriting a ranching business she knew little or nothing about.

But if a challenge came her way, she pushed up her sleeves, both literally and figuratively, and dealt with it.

In fact, his mother's unbendable spirit was a big part of the reason he'd become interested in making historical documentaries. Those stalwart pioneers had so many stories to tell, and she represented, to Slater, anyway, how women had handled the challenges and discomforts of settling the West. It was all about the *journey* in his films, where you started and where you ended up, and that same strength of character — what country people called "gumption."

"What's on your agenda today?" Blythe asked.

"Work," he said. "I offered to lend Drake a hand out on the range, but he's got it covered."

"He's *always* got it covered," she said mildly. "Finds it hard to accept help — like a few other people I could name."

She was, of course, referring to all three of her sons.

"Hmm. Wonder where we get that particular trait," he said.

Blythe made a face at him.

He paused before opening the side door to enter the house. "Want to walk over to the winery with me later? You and Mace could give me the tour. I haven't been over there since you added the new cellar."

"I'd love that. Call my cell when you're ready. Better yet, text me." Not usually demonstrative, Blythe reached out and touched his cheek in a brief, tender gesture of affection. "I'm so glad you're back."

Call my cell. Better yet, text me. Slater smiled to himself, remembering how hard it had been to persuade his mother to get a mobile phone in the first place. Now she was adept at high-tech communication. "Sounds like a plan."

He went into the house and through a foyer with a chandelier that should have been in a museum somewhere. The piece wasn't original to the house, but went back much further, probably to the turn of the nineteenth century; according to family legend it came from a grand Southern hotel. A beautiful creation of flawless crystal, it seemed incongruous — and yet oddly natural — in a ranch house set among mountains and prairie.

By now such things were part of the landscape to Slater. His family was eclectic, to say the least.

He entered his office, formerly his father's study. He was comfortable there, among the belongings of generations — polished bookcases and a vast collection of volumes, most of them having some flavor of the Old West. There were classics and plenty of nonfiction, a smattering of epic poetry and high-brow philosophy, but a generous sprinkling of Zane Grey and Louis L'Amour, too.

Slater settled into the old leather chair and booted up his computer. As he'd expected, a slew of emails awaited him, the majority sent by various crew and staff members wrapping up last-minute details on location.

He took care of those first, and it was, as usual, a time-consuming task.

There was a message from the resort concerning the dinner and meeting he had booked that morning, confirming the date he'd chosen — still almost a month out — but it was the second email that really got his attention. He was invited, in a briskly businesslike way, to have dinner the following week with the resort manager — none other than Grace Emery herself — so they could discuss "possible joint endeavors and promotions."

A slow grin spread across Slater's face as he considered, just for a moment, a few possible joint endeavors he might be able to suggest.

I'll be damned, he thought, smiling.

Recalling last night's brief and testy exchange with her, he marveled at — okay, *celebrated* — the fact that the lovely Ms. Emery wanted to see him again. For *any* reason.

Grace had been furious at her stepson, yes, and she'd virtually forced the boy to apologize. But she'd also taken an apparently instant dislike to Slater. Now, all of a sudden, she wanted to talk business? Over dinner?

Since there was no one around to see, Slater punched the air with one fist and muttered, "Yes!"

Ideally, the meeting would be one-on-one. No assistants. No heads of this department or that.

Just Grace and him.

But life was rarely ideal.

Warning himself to rein it in, not to read too much into the unexpected invitation, Slater printed out the confirmation for the other event, his company gathering, filed it and sent the notice to his guests, indicating the time and place — one month from this coming Saturday.

That done, he carefully composed his RSVP to the second get-together.

Of course the email would go straight to Grace's assistant, someone named Meg, but surely she'd see it, too. He rested his elbows on the desk, that smile still lingering on his mouth, although most of his triumph had subsided, turning into something more fragile, like hope.

He'd sensed, despite the bristling body language and snappy retorts of the night before, that the attraction between him and Grace hadn't all been on his side.

But maybe he was wrong on that score. Maybe the invitation was exactly what it appeared to be — strictly business.

Slater paused, leaning back in his chair, reflecting. Going by what his brothers had told him about Grace, she'd already given plenty of eager cowboys the brush-off. She was, after all, a busy woman with a demanding job, plus dealing with a troubled teenage boy. While Ryder seemed like an intelligent kid, the smart ones were often the hardest to manage. Throw in a move from one state to another and a career change, and it was no great leap to figure out that romance might not be all that high on

Grace Emery's to-do list.

Come to think of it, getting involved wasn't really on Slater's agenda, either. He loved his work, enjoyed dating a wide variety of women, most of whom he met on location, spent as much quality time with his young daughter, Daisy, as possible, and helped his brothers with the ranch and the winery. He figured that was more than enough for one man. And he subscribed to the if-it-ain't-broke-don't-fix-it theory. Nope, he wasn't looking to complicate matters.

Still, some of the best things in life were unplanned.

Like his daughter, Daisy, for instance.

Pensive now, Slater picked up his phone, scrolled down his contact list and hoped he'd catch up with Raine this time around. He'd left two messages already, but his ex-girlfriend, who happened to be the mother of his only child, kept eclectic hours, and her somewhat free-spirited lifestyle often made communication difficult. When she answered, she said with a little laugh, "Well, I guess trouble's back in town."

Slater smiled. He'd thought he'd loved Raine, back when they were together, and he knew she'd believed she loved him. And yet they'd always been more friends than lovers. Yes, the sex had been stellar, but they'd both been young and healthy, so it made sense that they'd enjoyed making love. They'd finally realized that they didn't have what it took to get married and stay that way. "You guess?" he countered mildly, snapping out of his reflective mood. "I've sent you a couple of emails and called a few times. Some people would interpret those things as clues to my return." He spoke in a relaxed tone, used to Raine and her legendary ability to focus on her work, when she chose, to the exclusion of everything and everybody around her — except for their young daughter. "Fortunately, Daisy bothered to get back to me, and we've been plotting against you. What are you doing for dinner tonight? I haven't seen my daughter in two months, if you don't count that flying visit so I could see her in the school play. And according to Mom, Daisy's playing softball this summer, so I'll want to be at as many of her games as I can." A pause. "Obviously, I have some catching up to do in the father department."

There was a lilt in Raine's voice. Predictably, she'd let most of what Slater had said pass. "Dinner?" she echoed. She'd probably been thinking about some project she was working on. "I guess it depends on whether or not Harry's doing the cooking. Our being available, I mean."

"Harry is doing the cooking," Slater confirmed, amused. He'd already worked out an arrangement with the housekeeper. "Unless you'd rather go to a restaurant."

"And miss one of Harry's incomparable meals? No way, José."

He laughed outright, warmed by Raine's friendship. Their relationship, long over in terms of romance, had been an interesting chapter in his life, an illustration of the old adage that opposites attract. Slater believed in roots, family, tradition, while Raine took a more whimsical approach, but they usually managed to agree on the basics.

Usually.

Slater felt a twinge, remembering. They'd already gone their separate ways, quite peaceably, and been apart for six months or so when Raine had come to see him after a lengthy visit with some New Mexico cousins. She'd been eight months pregnant when she turned up on his doorstep and, while the prospect of becoming a father had brought him up short, once the initial shock was past, he'd been delighted.

Raine was fiercely independent and when she'd discovered she was pregnant she'd never questioned, not for one second, that she wanted the baby. They hadn't discussed parenthood during their time as a couple, except in the most hypothetical way. Yes, they both liked the idea of having a baby — later. Some vague, undefined *later*. Maybe that was why she hadn't informed Slater when she found out, but he'd never once doubted that the child she carried was his.

He'd asked Raine to marry him.

She'd smiled and punched him in the shoulder and said, "Don't be silly. It wouldn't work, and we both know it."

So there'd been no wedding.

And while Slater and Raine had never lived under the same roof, they'd become a sort of family, the three of them. Slater supported Daisy, spent as much time as he could with her, loved her as deeply as any father had ever loved a child. And Raine was equally committed to motherhood.

It was an innovative setup, no denying that, but Slater wouldn't have changed anything, even if a do-over had been possible.

He'd fought it for a while, had wanted to take the traditional approach. In the end, he knew Raine had been right all along. Daisy was a happy, well-adjusted child. She got excellent grades in school, had numerous friends, was healthy in every way. She had a solid home — two of them, actually — and parents who loved her.

So far, so good.

"Slater?" Raine's voice was like a friendly poke in the ribs. "Are you still there?"

"I'm still here," he replied quietly.

"So what's on the menu? For dinner, I mean? Not that I care, because everything Harry makes is delicious."

Slater snapped out of his momentary distraction for the second time in two minutes. He grinned. "I have no idea what Harry's planning to whip up, but *she's* cooking it, not me. So are you going to be here or what?"

"We'll be there," Raine said. "Usual time?"

"Yeah. You know Harry and her schedules. This place runs like clockwork."

"We'll be prompt. The last time I was late, she claimed the dishwasher was broken and made me do up the whole works while she supervised. Remember?"

He did. "Served you right," he said.

"Never any sympathy," Raine accused him. "In fact, you laughed."

Slater had to laugh again, recalling the incident. "I've warned you over and over, sugarplum. Punctuality's important to Harry. Nobody holds up the program and gets away with it."

"Well," Raine said, "her one-of-a-kind garlic mashed potatoes are important to me, so let's hope she's serving up a batch of those. Daisy and I will be there at six sharp."

When Slater ended the call, he texted his mother, which seemed ridiculous since they were in the same house, but such were the oddities of modern life.

Ready to go to the vineyard?

The response was almost instantaneous.

I can't wait to show you the changes we've made. Meet you out front.

Slater stood, his thumbs working on the phone's keyboard.

By the way, Raine and Daisy will be here for dinner tonight.

We'll keep it short then. I'll run into town for ice cream as soon as we're done.

Walking, Slater keyed in a couple of smiley-face icons, followed by:

I was hoping for those lemon bars Harry bakes.

Already on the menu. But Daisy loves chocolate ice cream, and thanks to your brothers, we're always out of the stuff.

Here's a concept. Why don't we discuss this in person?

Blythe immediately replied with an icon of her own, a smiley face sticking out its tongue.

Slater groaned and dropped his smart — or *smart-ass* — phone into his shirt pocket.

This was going to be a good day, and an even better evening, spent with the women he loved — young, old and in-between.

Raine was still on his mind as he headed for the front of the house. The last time he'd seen her, her shining dark hair bounced around her shoulders, but considering how impulsive she was, she might've had it cut short or dyed it green in the interim. She had mischievous hazel eyes and an infectious laugh; it had been that laugh that had caught his attention in the first place, when they'd met at a party a little over a decade ago, the beginning of a six-month affair. A talented graphic artist, Raine also designed websites and had recently done a stunning one for the winery.

His thoughts shifted, once again, to Daisy.

From the very beginning, she'd been a member of the Carson clan; they'd instantly embraced her. In fact, they completely spoiled her. There'd been the pony from Uncle Drake, the custom dollhouse from Uncle Mace, the fit-for-a-princess bedroom their mother had designed for the little girl's frequent visits to the ranch. Slater had finally had to ask them, politely of course, to stop one-upping him all the time.

Yeah, *that* had worked. The Christmas he'd given Daisy a bicycle, she'd received two more — one from each of her uncles.

But these were small glitches to Slater. Early on, he'd been afraid Raine might decide to leave town, move somewhere far from Mustang Creek to pursue big-city work opportunities, taking Daisy with her. But that fear had been put to rest when he and Raine had signed a joint custody agreement.

He'd bought her a house in town, and she'd established herself as a valued member of the community.

Raine had also been the one to suggest that Daisy take the Carson name.

Slater stepped onto the side porch, really more of a veranda, and saw that his mother was waiting, chatting with one of the hands, who held the reins to two saddled horses.

The older man's eyes lit up in his weathered face, and when Slater got close enough, he received a hearty slap on the back as welcome. If he hadn't been expecting it, he might have staggered under the blow.

"Slate, good to see you, son." Red — named after the river — was a true tough-as-nails cowboy, the old-fashioned variety. He was like a human barometer, and Slater didn't check the forecasts when he was home; he just asked Red, who would squint at the sky and give him an accurate prediction every time. Slater could swear the man had worn the same hat for the past thirty years, but maybe he just liked the style and actually bought a new one now and then.

"Good to be home," he said, meaning it. "When I come back, I always wonder why I left to begin with."

"I wonder the same dang thing." Red patted the neck of one of the horses, a restive bay. "This here is Heckfire," he told Slater. "I know you miss old Walter, but Drake and I thought you might like this young fella."

The horse was a sleek beauty with a glossy coat, and he tossed his head against the rein. Slater sensed that it wasn't so much rebellion as the fact that he wanted to get moving. *All this yammering is boring. Let's run.*

There was no question that Slater missed

his gelding, a horse that had been a gift from his father. But his four-legged friend had been nearly thirty years old, and when Slater had said goodbye on his last visit, he'd known it was for the final time.

He ran his hand down the length of the horse's muscled neck and was rewarded with a nicker and an investigative sniff as Red handed over the reins. "He's a show-stopper. But . . . Heckfire?"

"We call him Heck. The name comes from Drake. Even as a colt, this critter was causing trouble, and we hadn't named him yet and your brother said, 'Heck, he's full of fire.' " Red paused, cleared his throat then glanced at Blythe and blushed. "Well, he didn't exactly say 'heck,' " he clarified. "Anyhow, we, uh, adapted the name, and it stuck."

Blythe rolled her eyes but said nothing. Red was an institution on the ranch; he'd worked for the family longer than Slater had been alive. A widower, the old man had never gotten over his long-dead wife. He still placed flowers on her grave every Sunday afternoon.

Slater merely waited, nodding once, because it was obvious Red had more to say. "You'll have to teach this stubborn cayuse a few manners," the old cowboy said, rubbing his grizzled chin and assessing the gelding solemnly.

"You know I like a challenge," Slater said. "Once he and I come to an understanding, things will be fine." With a sidelong glance at his mother, he threw in another observation. "Just like women."

Sure enough, Blythe elbowed him in the ribs. Hard.

Since he'd been prepared for her reaction, Slater barely flinched.

Red chuckled. "Now, there I'll have to disagree with you, son. No man *ever* understood a woman. They're a whole other species."

Blythe cleared her throat and folded her arms. "Excuse me? I — a woman, as it happens — am standing here listening, or have you two bone-headed males forgotten that?"

"Mrs. Carson, ma'am." Red touched the brim of his hat, still grinning irreverently, and politely held her horse while she mounted. Slater swung into his old familiar saddle, felt another pang at the loss of Walter, but was pleasantly surprised by the fluid smoothness of the bay's gait as they cantered down the drive. The old cowhand was right; the horse ignored subtle commands like an irritable teenager, but basically behaved himself. Slater had been around horses since early childhood, and he knew a fine animal when he rode one. He applauded Drake on this particular choice.

— They slowed once they reached the first row of vines, which to his admittedly inexpert eye seemed to be doing well. "Mace put in an irrigation system that cost a staggering amount of money," his mother told him as they walked alongside their horses. "But you know, when it comes to anything with leaves and branches, I trust him. He's made several trips to the Willamette Valley, visited your uncle in California for hands-on harvest demonstrations several years in a row, and he's really getting a feel for it. He's grafted some varieties with surprising success, and if he can produce just the right grape, we might be in a position to stop ordering most of our fruit, like we do now, and produce enough ourselves. Certainly the apple wine he made last year was a big seller on a commercial level, but he's tried a bit of everything, including cranberry and peach. Plus different varieties of red, from merlot to zinfandel, and whites from chardonnay to Riesling. You name it. He loves experimenting."

"I'm sure he's having fun. He's like a mad scientist," Slater said. "I still remember when he was in college and he started making his own beer. His apartment looked — and smelled — as if he'd hijacked a still from the hills of Kentucky or something. I went there to visit him once, and he persuaded me, against my better judgment, to take a swig. The stuff tasted okay, but I don't remember one damn thing about the rest of the night. As I recall, I slept upright in a chair, still fully clothed, and come morning, I had a crick in my neck you wouldn't believe. I declined to repeat the experience. He thought it was funny."

Blythe sent him a mischievous grin. "I've heard that story a time or two. I hate to be the one to break the news, but he still repeats it."

"If he values his health, he'd better not do it in front of me." Slater meant it. Adding insult to injury, he'd awakened with a vicious headache that memorable morning. Worse, he'd felt like seven kinds of fool.

"Ah, there's nothing like having three boys." Blythe's tone was wry.

"Except having a little girl who's getting to be not so little. Daisy's eleventh birthday is coming up. Any ideas?"

"Yep, but it's every man for himself, Slater. Both of her uncles have asked me the same question. I didn't help them, either."

"I'm her father. That's different."

His mother gave him a pointed glance he recognized. Drake and Mace were equally familiar with the expression, no doubt. "Don't you think it's time you got married and had a few more children?" she asked. "For Daisy's sake, of course."

CHAPTER FOUR

No pressure.

At all.

Grace sipped her morning coffee, checked the time on the computer in her home office and felt as if she hadn't seen the light of day except through a window all week. She needed to go for a long walk to clear her head.

Ryder was in trouble at school. It wasn't a big deal, just some roughhousing during gym, but he'd been sidelined and suspended from PE class for a full week. The worst part was that he hadn't told her about it. The coach had called.

This situation was troubling, to say the least, and she felt totally inadequate. Walking the fine line between being likable and being any kind of disciplinarian was proving to be a real challenge, but here she was, doggedly doing her best.

Maybe — maybe — Ryder was doing his

best, too. It was one thing to be a single parent; it was another to be the single parent of a child who wasn't your own. She loved Ryder. That wasn't in question and never would be. But the boy clearly had issues, and little wonder, since he'd been neglected by both his parents for most of his young life. How had that problem, one she hadn't created, wound up being hers to solve?

More frustrating still, Grace realized Ryder's mother was never going to do anything to help, and Hank was off who knew where — no one was *allowed* to know — and it had become *her* dilemma. The worst part was that Ryder was a bright kid, so he was perfectly well aware that none of this was supposed to be up to her, a stepmother with no legal authority over him whatsoever. Naturally, he was resentful as hell. The poor kid needed *somebody* to be mad at, some way to vent all that adolescent emotion.

The whole mess just about broke Grace's heart.

There was a scratching sound at the back door of the condo, and Grace left her office, crossed the small kitchen and looked out through the screen. The cat, perched primly on the welcome mat, peered in at her and meowed. Bonaparte, so recently rescued, was filling out nicely, now that he was getting regular meals and plenty of love.

He was completely black except for a white patch on his chest, had startling emerald eyes and had yet to allow Grace to pet him, although she'd seen Ryder sit down and coax the cat onto his lap numerous times. The roughness of Bonaparte's fur was already smoothing out and he was friendlier, but she did wonder how they'd ever get him into a pet carrier so they could take him to the veterinary clinic for a checkup, neutering and shots.

Disregarding her own rules, she opened the screen door, fully expecting the little creature to run away. But when she stood back to allow him space, he timidly came inside, taking one careful step at a time as if he were asking *do I really live here?*

The sight gave Grace another twinge of pain, because it reminded her so much of Ryder. Wary, uncertain of his place in the world, grateful, even eager, for acceptance, but hesitant, too. Never quite knowing where he belonged, or with whom.

"I'll leave you alone until you're ready," she told the cat in a gentle voice. "Ryder will be home soon."

Then I have to yell at him, Grace thought

83

miserably. *Which I don't want to do, but I have to file it in the folder labeled* For Your Own Good.

Bonaparte investigated the baseboard and then sat down. His unwinking green eyes watched her every move.

The cat and Ryder really were kindred spirits.

No question the cat was malnourished and scrawnier than he should've been, but he was making progress. "If you were me," Grace asked Bonaparte, in need of a sounding board, even if it had four feet and fur, "what would you do? Would you ground Ryder? Or will that only make everything worse?" She fingered a strand of her hair. "See this? Well, it's true what they say about redheads. I'm notoriously outspoken. I get mad, and I get over it, but I do get mad."

Her cell phone pinged, indicating a message. She glared at it, let out a measured breath and tried to decide if she wanted to look. A group of executives for a high-end Fortune 500 company was scheduled to stay the weekend, and some of the requests had been on the ridiculous side, but she knew it was part of the job. She'd apologized for not being able to supply a brand of scotch not available within a hundred miles of Bliss County. She'd hired a full-time bartender for the evening and was paying the kitchen staff overtime. She'd checked all the rooms herself and arranged the resort's signature Welcome Baskets for each one. She couldn't imagine what might go wrong, but considering how her day was going, anything was possible.

Ryder was late coming home from school. She hoped he didn't have detention or something like that. It occurred to her that the text could be from him, so she snatched up her cell and saw with relief that it was.

I was talking to some guys and I missed the bus. Be there soon.

The number was unfamiliar. The school had cracked down on students bringing cell phones. If a kid was caught with one, it was confiscated and a parent could come and pick it up from the office. If a kid was caught twice, it wasn't returned. Grace understood the policy; it would be difficult to teach anyone anything if all your students were playing on their phones during class. But at times like this, it would be nice not to be frantic with worry.

Be there soon? Some parent must be giving him a ride, because the resort and condo complex was a fair way outside Mustang

Creek. As it was, the bus dropped him off at the end of the drive and Ryder had to walk a good three quarters of a mile to get home. Most of the condos were rentals for hikers in the summer and skiers in the winter, so he was the only kid his age who lived there full-time.

Grace yanked open the door when she heard the car pull up, so she could profusely thank the parent, whoever it was, before she got Ryder inside and ripped into him for fighting at school.

Not a car but a truck. Moreover, it had a familiar sign on the side. As Ryder opened the passenger door and hopped out, the driver emerged, too, the sun shining on his dark hair. Vivid blue eyes, those striking features — straight nose and sensual mouth . . . Slater Carson. He was dressed differently than when she'd seen him last, more businesslike in a tailored shirt and dress slacks, but he still wore cowboy boots, and his slow smile matched his stride as he came around the truck. "I found something I thought you might want back. Picked it up along the side of the road."

She gave Ryder *the* look. "Thank you, Mr. Carson. I'll admit," she added for Ryder's benefit, "to being worried half out of my mind. Ryder, go feed your cat, and if you have homework, don't even *think* about video games or watching TV. And clean your room, too."

Ryder obviously had some sense of self-preservation there, because he didn't argue, just bolted through the door.

Slater Carson chuckled. "Guilt. Good strategy. My mother always used that one on me. Actually, she still does. Hey, the kid missed the bus. It happens."

"The kid," Grace informed him in a tight voice, "got into a fight at school and was suspended from his gym class but didn't mention it to me, and now he's so busy goofing off with some of the *guys* that he misses the bus. To tell you the truth, I'm a little annoyed with him right now."

"I can see that." Slater's eyes were amused but sympathetic. "So did he, judging by the way he hightailed it inside. He's probably already hauling out the vacuum cleaner. Oh, and my name is Slater. Mr. Carson is reserved for my bank manager."

"And you can call me Grace," she said with a little more composure. "I really do appreciate you bringing Ryder home, Mr. Car— I mean Slater."

"No problem."

She should do *something.* Why was she tongue-tied? That never happened to her.

"Can I offer you a glass of iced tea?"

Okay, kind of lame as Ryder would put it, but better than nothing.

"I'm actually headed to the resort for drinks with a friend who's there for a small conference this weekend. That's why I spotted Ryder hoofing it along the road."

His *friend* must be one of the executives — or an important investor. She guessed she'd find out soon enough.

She gave him a straightforward look. "I take it that we owe you for a good chunk of our corporate business. I noticed a number of the guests are from California. I assume that has to do with your connections in film and finance."

He didn't confirm or deny. "This area is off the beaten path. It's hard to relax in the middle of traffic and everything else that comes with a big city. Care to join my friend and me?"

Grace was more than a little unprepared for the invitation. True, she had to go back to the resort now that she'd located her errant stepson, although there was a conversation they still needed to have, but she hadn't expected to have a drink with Slater Carson — at least not tonight.

On the one hand, it was good public relations.

On the other hand . . . it might be dangerous for private relations.

He was taking a gamble.

When Slater had recognized Ryder Emery
trudging along the side of the road, head
down, he'd pulled over and offered him a
ride. The young man — almost man — had
seemed very relieved. Slater understood that
Ryder's situation was a difficult one; Ryder
lived with his stepmother, he was going to a
new school, leading a new life. But he also
needed to grasp a few realities, most of
which involved the fact that he was both
unlucky and very lucky. Slater didn't know
anything about the kid's parents except that
his dad was military and they weren't here,
but Grace was, and that, as far as he could
tell, was extremely lucky.

Slater, Drake and Mace had lost their
father way too early. Not lucky. But they'd
been left with their mother and Harry, Red,
and a few other people who'd eased their
pain, so that was *very* lucky. He was waiting
for Daisy to ask him why he and Raine had
never gotten married. He was going to tell
her the truth. That they liked each other
but weren't a good match, and not making
the mistake in the first place was better than
a divorce. Remaining friends seemed a great

solution and they both loved her.

Oversimplified, perhaps, but true.

Slater had seen the relief in Grace's eyes when she realized the boy was safe, so affection wasn't the problem. She'd been worried, that was all. Like any parent would.

"Listen, Grace, whether he could have prevented it or not, I don't think Ryder meant to miss the bus deliberately."

She hadn't responded to his invitation yet. He watched her and couldn't deny that she looked just as beautiful as when he'd first seen her, and just as hopping mad. This afternoon she wore some kind of lacy sleeveless top and a navy skirt, and both complemented her vivid coloring. "Are you always going to take his side?" she snapped.

Always? The word had obviously startled her as much as it had him. She stopped and visibly steadied herself. "Sorry. I meant, this is the second time he's really messed up in the last few days. You're being very understanding, when I'm mad as hell because he can be so thoughtless. Part of me wants to ground the kid until he's eighteen, and another part wants to ask him how he feels, but I know he won't answer that. Anyway, yes to the drink. Thank you. If I stay here, I'll probably end up chewing Ryder out — again." She paused. "Let me get my purse.

90

Okay if I drive with you? I can walk back later."

She turned in a swirl of long red-gold hair and outrage and stalked into the house. Nice long legs and firm backside. He liked the view. Slater also agreed that the irate redhead and the truculent teenager should probably be apart for a little while before they had their next conversation. Ryder had seemed tense in the car, and Slater had left him alone. First of all, it certainly wasn't his business, and second, he remembered how he'd dealt with life at that age. A knee-jerk reaction to criticism had been his default setting back then. In the end, after thinking it over, he'd usually decided that maybe his parents weren't complete idiots after all.

Now, as a parent himself, he was well aware that his opinions might be scorned first and reluctantly respected later.

Grace reappeared with a black leather bag over her shoulder and a more relaxed demeanor. "He apologized," she said as Slater opened the passenger door. "That's something. All I told him was that I was going back to work. He apologized on his own."

"You just won the lottery of boyhood maturity markers." He closed the door and went around the truck, sliding into the driver's seat. "There's an unwritten rule in the land of teenage boys that you don't ever apologize for anything until you're willing to admit you were wrong. I think I was about thirty when I crossed that line."

What was it with him and how a woman laughed? The sound of her laugh was . . . well, it might be a cliché, but *musical* was the word that came to mind. Her response made him grin, and his groin tightened. Or maybe it was the way she crossed those sexy legs. Or the way her breasts were nicely outlined by her blouse when she leaned forward.

It had been a long time since he'd felt as interested in a woman as he was in this one.

Maybe long enough to qualify as never.

That thought set him back.

It was only lust, he reminded himself as he backed out of the driveway. He barely knew her so the attraction was mainly physical. But fate did seem to be tossing him in her path. Or perhaps it was the reverse. She was no less aware of him . . .

He wondered about her life as a police officer and could only imagine some of the remarks she'd heard, since law enforcement didn't usually deal with the finest society had to offer. He asked conversationally, "So, how long were you a cop?"

"Eight years." To his disappointment Grace tugged her skirt down a little. She raised her shoulders in a shrug as she said, "It was an interesting journey. I thought at one time, with the usual starry-eyed optimism, that a degree in criminal justice and a belief in right and wrong enabled a person to make a difference."

"I'm guessing the optimist turned into a cynic?"

She considered that for a moment. "Actually, no. She's still around — the optimist, that is — but older and wiser. She learned about the world we live in, and about people in general, and not all of that was good. But the stars are still there, winking in the night sky."

Slater laughed. "I see them, too, once in a while. I think you'll like Mick Branson, by the way. The friend we're meeting, that is. He's a major investor, as well as a good buddy of mine. Be warned that he could be the most self-possessed, understated person I've ever met. The sense of humor lurking there is so dry, it's easy to miss, and I've been tempted to ask him if he's ever lost his temper. I'm going to assume he has, but nobody could tell that by looking at him. Or talking to him . . ."

Grace's lips curved, and he couldn't tell if

it was a grimace or a smile. "He sounds interesting. I think my assistant's talked to Mr. Branson on the phone. She seemed unclear about whether he was pleased by the arrangements or not. I'll be glad to meet him in person and get a clearer sense of the situation."

"Good luck with that. Mick's more of a read-between-the-lines sort of person." The resort was only maybe half a mile from the condo complex, and Slater pulled into a parking spot. "But he'll like you, I know that. Confident women are definitely his thing. Confident, *beautiful* women, it goes without saying, are even more his thing."

Mick had better not like her too much, Slater thought — then felt like a fool.

"That's a well-done compliment," Grace remarked.

"Just telling the truth."

"Yet you invited me to meet him, anyway," Grace said serenely as she unbuckled her seat belt. "Have I mentioned that confident men are *my* thing?"

"Not yet." He got out and went around to open her door. "Must be convenient to have the office so close by."

"Sometimes it is, sometimes it isn't." She accepted the change in subject as she stepped out. "I'm not like you, traveling all over. In fact, I never really leave the office."

"Advantages to both." For the first time he touched her, placing one hand lightly on the small of her back as they walked to the resort's main entrance. "This is your territory. I've been here before but never to the Diamond Trail Bar. You lead and I'll follow."

"That's the way I like it."

Her arch glance gave him pause. Flirtation? He couldn't come up with a swift response to the possible sexual innuendo, although he rarely found himself at a loss for words. Especially in *that* kind of situation. Slater accompanied her into the foyer, inwardly shaking his head, and wondered if he was making a wise move or just being an idiot.

He expected a vote would grant him the idiot award. Grace Emery was on the prickly side; obviously her life was complicated if she was raising her stepson, and his was complicated, too, between Daisy and his job.

But . . . nothing good in this world, his mother had often pointed out, came easy.

The Diamond Trail was on the side of the building facing the mountains, with big windows and raised walnut tables, a huge river-stone fireplace and an elegant bar, which stood near a small infinity fountain that matched the obsidian stone of the counter. When Grace walked in, the bartender waved, so she went over, murmured a greeting then rejoined Slater. "I don't drink when I'm at work. Will you be offended if I have water?"

"Nope, but as someone with a vested interest in a winery, please tell me you enjoy a glass now and then."

"I love wine," she said. "And I love the wines from Mountain Vineyards. Especially the pinot noir and the chardonnay. Your brother is very talented."

"I'd like to think it runs in the family," Slater said smoothly. "Talent, I mean. I'm not talkin' wine in my case. There's our table. Mick beat us here. As I said, I think you'll like him."

She looked up at Slater, laughing again.

Mick stood when he spotted them, his dark eyes holding that glimmer of understated amusement. He was from New Mexico, and there was a Latin grace about him. Most likely a legacy of the old Dons, the aristocratic families who'd come over from Spain and settled in the Southwest four centuries ago. He somehow *looked* aristocratic and maybe it was a mistake to introduce him to Ms. Emery, but Slater had the feeling she liked *him* well enough that he

96

was safe.

If he had to call it, he'd venture a guess that she liked down-home cowboys more than high-powered executives.

Or was that wishful thinking?

There'd been no mention of the dinner invitation he'd received in his email that morning. Slater decided not to let that worry him. Yet.

"Pleased to meet you, Mr. Branson." Grace shook Mick's hand and sat down. "I'm the resort manager. I know you've spoken to my assistant, Meg, on the phone. I hope everything's going smoothly."

"So far, absolutely. Pretty place." Branson sat down, as well.

"I'm glad you think so."

Slater took a seat next to Grace. He wasn't implying any kind of personal relationship . . . well, maybe he was. There was no doubt that most men looked at Grace just as Slater did, with pure male appreciation. "Mustang Creek is off the beaten path, which makes it a great place to relax and do business without distractions."

Mick looked out the window at the spectacular view of the Tetons, and then deliberately back at Grace. "I don't know. The gorgeous scenery is a little distracting."

"Nice line," Slater said drily. "I'm going

out on a limb here and saying the lady's heard it before."

Branson smiled his enigmatic smile. "You're probably right," he conceded.

Grace laughed and shook her head at the two of them, but a small smile played on her mouth.

Mick turned to Slater. "So tell me, now that the project's wrapped, what direction do you want to take next?"

Slater was seriously contemplating that Wyoming angle, the one his brother had suggested. After a young man came to take their order, a beer for him and a bourbon on the rocks for Branson, then left again, he answered. "What would you think of a saga about the pioneers who settled this area? The locale is gorgeous, as you just pointed out, and there are quite a few people I know personally with family stories to tell. So far, most of the films have focused on historical events and they've had what I'd like to think is a sweeping view of American history. What about a focus on how a small Wyoming town was settled and how it survived, changed, modernized, and what it's like today?"

"You mean Mustang Creek." Mick appeared thoughtful, rubbing his jaw. "That's an interesting idea. And certainly your family has a lot of history here. I like the personal angle. If you'll come up with a proposal and include a few visuals, I'll look at it and present it to my associates for consideration." Mick, as it turned out, ran a sizeable investment firm, specializing in film and music.

That was all Slater could ask for. At present, the vision in his head was just a starting point, a scant outline of what the production might become, but this was how projects began. "Sounds good."

"For someone like me who's relocated here, that would be very intriguing," Grace chimed in as their drinks arrived. She took a sip of water. "You know, the resort was built about fifteen years ago, but before that there was an old hotel here, as I'm sure Slater remembers. The owner told me that although he'd thought about renovating, it actually made more sense from a business standpoint to tear it down and build a modern facility that would accommodate a spa. However, there are loads of boxes down in the basement with pictures of famous guests, the former hotel itself, antique skis, even the old bar, which would be a beauty if it was refinished. There are also clippings from newspapers as far away as Denver, Helena and, of course, Cheyenne. I just glanced at them, wondered why he hadn't donated them to the historical society, and got out of there as quickly as possible. They built this right on the same spot and even used the original foundation. Dark as a dungeon applies, believe me. It has lights, but the space is so big that you have to turn them on as you go. If any of that interests you, I'll ask my boss if you could check it out. I doubt he'd mind. As a matter of fact, he'd be thrilled about the publicity." She drew a deep breath then shuddered dramatically. "Count me out of the exploration part, though. Last time I was down there, I came eyeball to eyeball with a spider I swear was as big as my hand. I went straight up and called an exterminator."

Slater was fascinated by the research material she'd just described. He was also amused by what she'd revealed about this unexpected phobia. "Grace, you used to be a cop. I assume you carried a weapon and apprehended bad guys. A spider? Really?"

"Really," she replied firmly. "I don't love snakes, mice or stinging insects, so I avoid them. My attitude is you stay away from me and I'll stay away from you. But spiders send a chill up my spine."

Mick gazed at her, obviously enthralled. "You used to be a cop?"

Slater found the expression on his friend's face slightly irritating. It said, *Hey, you can put me in handcuffs anytime.*

"In another life," she said. "Like I told Slater, I loved it in the beginning but the job can burn you out pretty quickly. When you work in law enforcement, just about everyone you come in contact with is unhappy, both the victims and the perpetrators. Here, I take care of minor glitches, but a lot of the people I interact with are on vacation and, therefore, in a good mood. I love to see smiling faces and hear that our guests had a wonderful time."

"I can understand that."

She rose. "Speaking of which, I need to go see if there is a crisis like a broken ice machine or housekeeping forgot new towels for someone's room. It was a pleasure to meet you, Mr. Branson. Oh, the drinks are on me." She took a twenty from her purse and set it on the table.

Slater objected immediately. "I invited you. No way."

"You'd be doing me a favor if you'd pay for the drinks in cash and save the receipt. Please don't get all gallant and pay for it yourself with a credit card. I'm conducting an internal investigation involving cash transactions." Her voice was pleasant but there was a certain steely undertone. "Good night, gentlemen."

They both watched her walk away. "I wouldn't mind her investigating me," Mick murmured with a slight smile. "But not, shall we say, in a law enforcement capacity."

Slater nodded. "Yeah, I'm not surprised. I wondered about introducing you two." A pause. "I like her, Mick."

Mick swirled the bourbon in his glass. "That came through loud and clear, my friend. I'm decent at reading people and I predict you have a shot." His voice became businesslike again. "Her information about the hotel is a valuable contribution. I'm really starting to like this idea."

CHAPTER FIVE

Slater Carson was trying to drive her crazy.

A few days after their impromptu meeting with his friend Mick, he'd called and asked if he could take Ryder to a college football game. Not one nearby, either. Oh, no. They were going to *fly* out to Laramie with a friend of his and would be back that night but maybe a little late. Private plane and an experienced pilot, he promised. His friend Tripp Galloway had once owned a charter company and had been given the tickets by a friend and former client. Coveted fifty yard line seats. Did she mind?

Not a bit. Grace really needed the break, and she figured Ryder did, too.

First, Ryder had gotten into trouble for fighting at school. Now she'd received an email from the principal concerning an incident in English class. Apparently he'd been rude to the teacher, making some inappropriate, smart-aleck comment during a grammar lecture about the conditional tense. (No doubt his new friends had guffawed in great approval.) So, in one way she absolutely *didn't* want to reward Ryder when he'd misbehaved; in another way she suspected he'd be safer at a distance.

From her.

School had just started and she already had notes? The kid needed to shape up now or he'd be struggling the entire semester, maybe the entire year.

She hoped the tight-lipped silence she maintained as she drove Ryder to the ranch conveyed what she wanted to say. She could've recorded a full box CD set just on the importance of turning in his homework. It would be easier if she didn't care and could shrug and point out that he wasn't even her son. But she *did* think of him as her son. And she *did* care.

A lot.

Too much, maybe.

No, she acknowledged, there was never too much caring when it came to a child. And Ryder was still a child, whether he'd agree with that or not. Yes, he was starting to look like a man and she'd gone ahead and bought him an electric razor, which he certainly didn't need yet, at least not every day, and she knew that somewhere in her future lurked the discussion they'd have to have about safe sex. Not that the school system didn't do a fairly good job with sex education — he'd come home snickering about it one afternoon — but the two of them needed to sit down, one-on-one. Hank would owe her for that, although, frankly, she wondered if Ryder would even be willing to listen to his father, should he suddenly put in an appearance and *act* like a father.

Understandably, Ryder was damned angry with *both* parents. His mother should be here for him now, not Grace. And, as for Hank, his unswerving loyalty to the army and to serving his country was admirable, but his son was paying a high price for that devotion. Just as *she* had, while she and Hank were married.

"I hope you realize the only reason I agreed to let you go on this trip is that although I'm disappointed in you right now, I'm not out to punish you. I need your word, Ryder, that you'll try harder in school." She paused. "Wait. Let me rephrase that. I need your word that you'll try *at all.*"

For a long moment Ryder just stared out the passenger window without speaking. Grace was about to scream when he finally said in a defensive voice, "Grace, I suck at

English. Even when I try I get really bad grades, so I quit trying. Why do it for nothing? I was flunking, anyway."

"So that's why you were rude to the teacher? And that's why I heard from the principal?"

He didn't respond and had gone back to staring out the window.

She turned onto the country road toward the Carson ranch. Cattle grazed in the pasture, and the afternoon sun gave the scene an almost mystical glow. "This seems to be an ongoing discussion between the two of us. If something's wrong, don't you think you should mention it to me? I can't solve a problem if I don't know it exists in the first place."

"It's *my* problem." His expression had that sullen cast she disliked.

She slowed for a cattle guard. "It will be when you wind up flipping burgers for a living instead of going on to college because you failed English. How about a tutor? If someone can sit there with you and you can point out what you aren't getting about a subject, that person can help."

She'd do it herself, but she had a feeling that would only cause more friction, and she was often gone in the late afternoon and early evening as it was.

"I'm not stupid. I just don't like English."

"I don't remember calling you stupid, Ryder. I didn't, I wouldn't, and you're aware of that. Quite the opposite. I'm more frustrated because I *know* you're smart and could do better."

At least that point wasn't argued. "Maybe," he muttered, and it sounded like an apology.

Luckily, that was when they pulled into the ranch drive and drove under the large curved sign with the Carson emblem — a giant C and two racing mustangs — over the entrance. Grace carefully guided the car down the lane and changed the subject. "I hope you remembered to put on sunscreen."

She probably deserved the look of disgust he gave her and she stifled a wry laugh. "What? Real men don't get sunburns, is that it?" she quipped, hoping to lighten the moment.

Slater was just coming out of the house with a small cooler and waved as they drove up. The only other time Grace had been there it was dark, so she studied the place as she parked and got out of the car. First of all, the house was huge. She could understand why all three Carson sons still lived on the ranch. With red brick walls and white pillars, the place would've been at home amid giant trees trailing Spanish moss instead of framed by the mountains, but it was certainly a beautiful old house. Steps led up to a wide veranda with a row of rockers on one side and an ornate glass-topped table with chairs on the other. Pots of brilliant blooming flowers gave a splash of color, obviously Mrs. Carson's touch. Grace couldn't quite picture the rancher, the winemaker or the film producer out there wielding a watering can.

"Right on time. That's great," Slater said. "We're due at the airstrip in half an hour. Thanks for letting Ryder come along with us, Grace."

"I appreciate your thinking of him." She said it primly, and his response was a slow smile and a hint of laughter in those oh-so-blue eyes. The man was in full cowboy mode, with denim shirt, jeans and boots, hat in place.

Just then a young girl dashed out of the house, flew down the steps and grabbed Slater's hand. She wore pink jeans, a floral shirt and little plaid tennis shoes. Young, still in grade school, maybe nine or ten, Grace guessed. Her voice was excited. "Daddy, are we leaving *now*?"

Daddy?

"Yep, in about a minute. Daisy, this is

Grace, and the tall one next to her is Ryder."

Slater's daughter was the very image of him, with thick dark hair and long-lashed eyes the same vivid shade of blue. She smiled shyly. "Nice to meet you."

Grace automatically smiled back, not sure why she felt so unnerved. Slater was in his midthirties, so it was hardly shocking that he might have a child. It was just that he'd never mentioned being married or (more likely) divorced — or that he had a daughter. Then again, she'd met him only a few times, three in total, and he was hardly obligated to relate his life story. "You, too, Daisy."

Thankfully, Ryder was polite enough to say hi without prompting.

Slater correctly interpreted Ryder's expression. "Don't worry, the ladies aren't going to the game. Daisy and her mother are going out to eat and do a little shopping. Their interest in football is on a level with mine for malls and ice cream parlors."

A woman came out of the door just then, fumbling in her purse. "Sorry, I left my cell in Daisy's room by accident when we were going through her clothes."

Instantly, Grace sized her up. Stylishly cut dark hair that fell to her shoulders, hazel eyes, high cheekbones, willowy figure . . .

She was strikingly attractive.

Slater said drily, "I've given up on you ever being punctual. That's why I pad arrival and departure time. Grace, this is Raine McCall. Raine, Grace Emery. I'll introduce you to Ryder when we join him in the truck. We all set?"

His ex or whatever she was smiled at Grace apologetically. "I'm afraid Slater's right. No matter how hard I try, I'm late for everything." Raine fairly twinkled with uncomplicated friendliness. "Drake and Mace both told me you were a looker, and they sure weren't kidding. I'd kill to have your coloring." She gestured at the truck. "If you want to come shopping with us, hop in."

"I, er, can't." Grace was taken completely off guard. "I have a dozen errands to run, but thanks for the invitation."

"Some other time, then. I'd better hurry or Slater will strangle me." With a wave Raine hurried toward the truck, the kids ahead of her. Moments later they were all aboard, and the rig's engine roared to life. Grace got back in her own car and followed the cheery little group down the driveway, feeling surprisingly unsettled. She wasn't interested in a relationship with anyone, much less another man who was gone most of the time, a man who reminded her more than slightly of her ex-husband. Not only that, Slater apparently came with baggage.

She had enough of her own.

So why did she care whether he had a child and a beautiful ex? (Assuming she *was* his ex, of course.)

That was a question she needed to ask herself over a glass of iced tea, once she'd gotten the oil changed in the car, gone to the dentist for a routine visit, went to the bank and dropped by the quilt shop she'd seen in town. She'd decided she wanted to treat herself and brighten up her bedroom, and a colorful quilt might be just the thing.

So she certainly hadn't lied about her full afternoon. She didn't get much time off, and when she did, she had to make it count.

After all that, she might sit down and read the "new" novel she'd picked up three months ago and then left sitting, unopened, on the coffee table. She'd actually had to dust it the other day.

With her luck, the story's hero would have memorable blue eyes, wavy dark hair and an unforgettable smile.

They got to the arena just in time for kick-off.

Slater could tell Ryder had enjoyed the

ride in the sleek private plane, and he didn't blame him. Taking a charter was infinitely better than flying commercial airlines, and Wyoming's incomparable scenery made it even more of a treat. It was breezy that day, so the flight was hardly smooth, but they'd landed safely, and the car sent by Tripp's friend was there to take them to the field. Slater had called ahead to arrange a rental car for Raine and Daisy.

This was turning out to be a sweet deal; they had a luxury suite, with a clear view of the whole field. Even a teenager's normal feigned boredom with just about everything was set aside, for this afternoon, anyway. Ryder had talked to Daisy a little bit on the ride in from the airport, just short sentences, mostly in answer to her incessant questions, but he hadn't been unfriendly or condescending. Tripp had let the boy sit up in the cockpit for a while before landing, and when Ryder had returned to his seat, he'd been wearing a big grin.

It wasn't hard to guess that a fourteen-year-old boy who flew in a private plane to a college football game and then sat in a suite couldn't wait to tell his friends at school. Maybe Slater would get a nod for being a film producer and Tripp for being a pilot. Ryder seemed like a kid who might

112

benefit from some personal attention, especially some adult male attention.

He'd have to ask about Ryder's mother sometime if he could ever get Grace alone for a private conversation. When he'd spoken to her assistant, Meg, she had made it pretty clear that the dinner invitation was to talk business concerning the resort. He'd resigned himself to the fact that the conference manager would join them because he was asked if he cared to bring his assistant along. He normally would, but Nate had flown home to Boulder to see his parents and get in some well-deserved time with his girlfriend. Slater hated to break it to him that he'd already come up with another project so soon, one he was excited about starting.

"Oh, man, that was close. It was nearly intercepted." Ryder was practically bouncing in his seat but caught himself. He wasn't missing a play. "Were either of you guys on the football team in high school or college?"

Tripp nodded. "Both of us. We were ranch kids, so we also did rodeo. When you get to high school next year, you'll find Mustang Creek has a rodeo team. Between rodeo seasons, we played football. Basketball and baseball, too."

That distracted Ryder's attention from the

game for a moment. "You mean you rode bulls and broncs and that stuff? That's *way* cool."

Slater said, "No bulls — those were too dangerous. But yes, we did some bronc riding, calf roping, steer-wrestling, that sort of thing. I went on the circuit two summers in a row right out of college, but several broken bones later, I decided I didn't like hobbling around on crutches or waking up in the morning and feeling like a truck had backed over me."

"Never ridden a horse. Always wanted to, though." Ryder sounded matter-of-fact.

Tripp and Slater looked at each other in consternation. To them, that was the equivalent of never riding a bike.

A roar from the stands brought their attention back to the action on the field. The teams were evenly matched, so it was an okay game in Slater's opinion, fast-paced and with some exciting plays. He could swear Ryder ate four hot dogs, but he and his brothers had certainly been a wrecking crew at the table in their teens, and they still managed to put it away like a pack of ravenous wolves, according to Harry. He texted Raine in the last few minutes of the final quarter so she could meet them at the airplane, and she replied with:

We'll be there. My feet hurt, but not as much as my bank account. My credit card might need an aspirin, too.

He didn't doubt that last part. Although Raine loved to prowl through antiques stores and artisan shops, she knew Daisy loved malls, so they usually hung out there.

When they reconnected, the rental car was piled with bags and boxes, and Daisy, she of the boundless energy, looked tired. She'd brought Ryder some sort of oversize cookie, and Slater shook his head as the kid began munching away on it well before they took off. He waited until the cookie had disappeared into the proverbial bottomless pit before he asked, "Did you mean it about wanting to learn how to ride a horse?"

Ryder looked up from the remains of his cookie, crumpling the package. "Well, yeah."

"Horses are critters you have to learn about from the ground up. It so happens that my brother's been grousing about being short a stable hand. It would be grunt work like cleaning tack and mucking out stalls, just warning you, but if you want a job for a few hours after school, we could arrange to go out riding afterward. I usually try to take at least a short evening ride. Of course Grace has to agree first."

"She might not. She's mad at me." Ryder lowered his eyes. "I'm getting a really bad grade in English this term. I tried to tell her, I'm no good at it."

Raine, who'd been listening to the conversation, piped up. "Hey, Slate, maybe you could ask your mother to take a look at Ryder's homework for an hour or so before he starts working. She's far more patient with Daisy than I am when it comes to that sort of thing. Right, Daze?"

Daisy yawned. "Right," she agreed. "I was having trouble with spelling, and she helped me understand better."

It was the first Slater had heard of any spelling problems. Was that because he'd been away so much? A pang of guilt struck him, but he powered through it and nodded at Raine. Her idea was probably a good one, since Blythe had been a teacher at one time, and she'd sure seen him and his brothers through their share of homework-related trauma. Math had been Slater's personal nemesis, but his mom had finally managed to get the basic concepts across to him, and he'd gotten much better grades after that.

"I'll talk to my mother and Grace," he told Ryder, "but only if you're truly interested."

Ryder's response was, if not enthusiastic, certainly positive.

CHAPTER SIX

Grace was used to nasty situations, thanks to her years wearing the badge, but she still hated firing people. The department managers usually handled hiring and firing in their own divisions; theft was a different matter since she, as general manager, had the final say over whether or not to pursue criminal charges.

The particularly vindictive attitude of the employee being let go didn't help her stay levelheaded about her decision.

David Reinhart, normally so affable that he bordered on obsequious, slammed his name tag and apron down on her desk with a force that nearly toppled the vase of fresh flowers she'd purchased at the supermarket. "You red-haired bitch," Reinhart spat furiously. "I do a great job! The customers love me!"

"You are chronically late. Pam has given you two formal warnings already, and our policy is three strikes, and you're out," she said, keeping her tone even. "I agree — the guests love you. But I'm letting you go, just the same."

"So I run a little behind every once in a while." His voice was thick with anger, his fists clenched at his sides. Grace wondered idly if she'd need her well-honed self-defense skills before the interview was over. "I work my ass off when I'm here!"

"Your inability to show up on time aside, you've been adjusting transactions at the end of almost every shift," she said, getting to the bigger and more substantial issue. "How you got the manager's code, I'm not sure. You're only taking cash, which in this day and age is not the preferred method of payment, fortunately, but more of it changes hands in the bar than in the dining room, and you must've figured that out early on. You got careless." She waited to let her words sink in, then went calmly on. "Pam mentioned to me that it was a relief not to be making so many cash drops. That was a red flag, and I started having her track how many transactions she actually logged in every night, and guess what? That number didn't match up with the cash on hand. Every single time it was off, you were working."

"I work five friggin' nights a week." Rein-hart's manner was still aggressive, but he was beginning to look a lot less sure of himself. He loosened his tie with a nervous jerk of one hand. "And I have news for you. Pam can't handle her workload and besides that, she's just plain stupid. She forgot to do what you asked. It's that damn simple. I say, prove it."

It was true that the older woman got flustered now and then when it was busy, which was the main reason Grace wasn't pressing charges against David Reinhart. All that had to happen to get him off the hook in court was for Pam to admit that she'd forgotten the task even once.

She wasn't through. "A few customers have called to say their credit card numbers might've been used without their authorization. The purchases are all at the spa, but they're expensive things you could — and I'm sure you do — sell online. You under-estimate the few people who meticulously check their bills." She took a shaky breath. "All of this really reflects poorly on the resort. I could fire you for the tardiness alone, so I don't have to prove the theft un-less you push me. If you're foolish enough to do that, you can bet I'll pin you to a wall with steel spikes. Shall I go on, Mr. Reinhart, or are you going to do the smart thing and walk out of here while you can?"

It was a shame, really. Reinhart was tall, young, nice-looking, personable, and he was right, the patrons liked his facile charm. But she'd met criminals like him before, and although the previous manager — who'd since retired — had hired him, Grace became suspicious. As a result she did a thorough background check and had to conclude that he'd faked his references. This wasn't his first rodeo. The long string of jobs he'd abruptly left triggered her curiosity. She also discovered that he'd been expelled from college, which didn't prove he'd steal, but wasn't exactly a character endorsement, either.

"The tough cop." His eyes held a certain glint she didn't like but had seen countless times. It said she was too feminine, too soft, to defend herself.

If that was what he thought, he was dead wrong.

For a long moment, they glared at each other.

And then someone knocked on the door.

Reinhart lifted his hand from the desk with an unpleasant smile. "I guess I was leaving, anyway."

When he wrenched the door open, Slater

Carson was standing on the other side.

Slater watched as the young man rudely brushed past him. When he turned back to Grace, he asked, "Is this a bad time?"

Grace shook her head. "Pretty good timing, actually. Our business was concluded, but I have a feeling the interview wouldn't have been over without a few more threats, and I was about to be called worse than a red-haired bitch."

Slater's blue eyes suddenly took on a dangerous gleam. "Wish I'd been around for that. I'll be right back." He swung around.

"Carson, stop!" Grace rose, touched but exasperated, and used her best cop voice. "In your tracks. I mean it. I used to be the person who was called to break up fights between big strong men, remember? It's handled. Now, I assume you stopped by for a reason?" She waited, willing him to listen to her. "Ryder seems to have had a wonderful time at the game. Please tell me he behaved himself."

Slater stopped, turned around. Reluctantly.

She wondered if he'd come by, intending to give her another restless night's sleep. She'd had an unbelievably erotic dream the other night, and even though Slater was dressed in jeans and a plain white T-shirt that emphasized his wide shoulders, thanks to the dream, she had no difficulty imagining what the relentlessly sexy Mr. Carson looked like naked.

Good. Too damn good.

She really hoped she wasn't blushing. With her fair complexion it was always noticeable.

"Ryder did fine. And I'm glad he had a good time. We all did."

So, Ryder hadn't acted out; that was a relief, anyway.

Just then the phone on her desk lit up — the front desk was calling. "Excuse me for a moment. I have to take this." She indicated a chair. "Please, sit down."

Slater sat, but not in one of the comfortable plush chairs in front of her desk. Instead, he hitched himself onto the edge of the desk itself; the motion was smooth, and it brought him way too close. Grace handled the small problem conveyed over the phone (concerning a staff scheduling issue), and fought the urge to scoot her chair back to put some distance between them. She rolled the chair away an inch or so, hoping he wouldn't notice how jumpy she was.

He did. She knew that from the hint of amusement lifting the corner of his mouth.

122

Slater was well aware that he affected her and just *how* he affected her. "How did you happen to land this job?" he asked.

Great. A relatively normal, if somewhat blunt, question. One she could answer, unlike some he could have asked, such as, *Why are you looking at me like that? As though — if there was a convenient horizontal surface — you might consider . . .*

"I majored in criminal justice, but I did a minor in business. My dad was a police officer in Seattle. He's retired now, but back then he was at the top of his game. I admired him, so I followed in his footsteps. After about five years on the job, I decided to get a master's degree in hospitality management on the evenings I was off duty. I'd taken a hotel management class as an elective while I was an undergrad, because I thought it would be an easy A. It wasn't, not at all. Still, I kept thinking about it, and I wondered if down the line I might want to change careers. Plus, by then, my marriage was getting rocky, and I needed something else to think about."

Slater's expression indicated that he understood. Maybe he did.

She turned the conversation back to him. "So, since the subject came up, why a film producer?"

He shrugged, his expression casual. "Same story to a certain extent. Took a film production class on a whim and got hooked. I worked various jobs as I was learning, including sound, cameras, even helped put up sets and that's a physical job, so it suited me. All of it suits me. I grew up out of doors and that's mostly where we film." He paused. "And that's a perfect segue as to why I'm here. I promised Ryder I'd run this by you. I hope I'm not putting you on the spot, but I talked to him about doing some chores on the ranch. Only if you agree, of course."

She wasn't sure what to say. He *was* putting her on the spot. If she said yes, Ryder might get hurt or find new ways of getting into trouble. If she said no, and the boy had his heart set on doing this, she'd be the ultimate villain.

As often happened, Slater seemed to know exactly what she was thinking. "If you want to teach that kid real discipline, stick him in a stall with a pitchfork and a wheelbarrow. It's hard physical work, and he'll have to learn how to deal with the animals. Ryder told me he wants to ride, so part of his compensation would be riding lessons. My mother will also check his homework regularly, and she's the most demanding yet gentle critic I've ever run across." He shifted slightly on the desk. "Feel free to get second and third opinions from Mace and Drake on that score." A pause, another shrug. "Look at it this way. It'll keep him busy."

Grace figured there were several additional ways to look at that offer. There was, for instance, the deliciously dangerous possibility that Slater was trying to get to her through Ryder — but, alas, her highly developed instincts said otherwise.

Still, his intentions toward her were precisely what she'd imagined in that dream; she was sure of it. But she was equally sure that Slater wasn't using Ryder to get there. The cowboy code wouldn't have allowed that.

"I hope your mother's up for a challenge, because my stepson will definitely be one." She might have spoken forcefully, but she was already caving. After all, part of Ryder's problem was a lack of supervision. She worked too many evenings.

It wasn't her fault, or Ryder's; it was just life.

At least now he had Bonaparte to keep him company, but the cat couldn't be expected to nag him into doing his homework. Couldn't provide what Ryder needed most — a strong masculine influence in his life.

Slater eased his hip off the desk. Stood. "Mom raised three rowdy boys. Mace and Drake were a handful, always arguing over something. They haven't changed much, to tell you the truth."

"You, I suppose, were an angel," Grace remarked, raising her eyebrows.

He grinned. "No comment," he said. "Anyway, if you're okay with this, Ryder can take the bus to the stop closest to the ranch and walk the rest of the way. It isn't far. In bad weather he'll just have to do what we did and bundle up. I'll expect him to do a good job, of course, but I think he understands that. Once he's through with his chores, the riding lesson and the homework stint with Mom — and Harry's crammed him full of supper — I'll bring him home."

She wouldn't even have to cook? Surely, Grace thought, there had to be a downside to this generous offer.

"Harry is a woman, I presume?" she asked.

Slater nodded. "Housekeeper and second mother." He headed for the door. "See you soon."

Just like that, he walked out as if the whole thing was settled, although technically, she

126

hadn't said yes.

How the heck had all of this happened so fast? she fretted silently. And did Slater Carson *always* get his way?

If that was the case, and she suspected it was, she was in *big* trouble.

Slater warmed the bit in his hand, and Heck fought it for only a minute or so before he accepted it, and the bridle could be fastened into place. Once Slater had checked the cinch, he swung into the saddle. Drake was waiting for him, none too patiently, just outside the stable doors, mounted on his favorite horse, an Appaloosa gelding called Starburst.

They rode out at a trot, past the fenced pasture near the house toward the far north section, before urging the horses into a faster pace.

It was truly a beautiful evening; the mountains reflecting a ruby-red sunset streaked with indigo, snow already on the peaks, and the air had a crisp tang to it like a fine wine. If Mace could bottle that atmosphere, Mountain Vineyards would make a fortune, Slater thought as he and Drake and their horses covered some ground.

Minutes later they came to the edge of a crystal-clear creek and splashed through at a walk. The aspens were turning, Slater noted, tinting the landscape gold. Winter was on the way, but that was fine. Christmas was special around Mustang Creek, and he enjoyed the changing seasons.

"See that stand of pine over there?" Drake pointed. "We found a good-size doe there a couple of days ago, and she'd been mauled. Badly. I doubt there's anything left of her by now, but it was a fresh enough kill that the hair stood up on the back of my neck. I took out my rifle, could've sworn I was being watched. You know I don't get nervous easily, but I had a real nasty feeling. And those missing calves — well, we haven't come across so much as a hank of hide or a bone fragment."

Grim as it was, things like that happened on ranches now and then. Slater took an educated guess. "Wolves?"

"Maybe." Drake pushed his hat up a little, his expression pensive. "Except something had dragged the carcass of that doe quite a ways, and it wasn't all that small. I've seen wolves relay a deer, taking turns running it until they wear it out, so they know how to work as a team. But I'm not ruling out a big cat."

Like most ranchers and farmers, the Carsons didn't romanticize wolves. They were expert predators.

"Did you move that prize bull in from the far pasture?" Slater asked, after swallowing the bile that scalded the back of his throat.

Drake frowned. "I've considered it. Fact is, that critter is hell and gone scarier than any mountain lion, but he gets even more aggressive if we move him. Got away last time we tried to bring him in, and all hell broke loose. We had a one-bull rodeo that day." A slow grin replaced Drake's glum expression. "I reckon he's fundamentally opposed to change of any kind, and I confess, I admire him for the strength of his convictions."

Slater was always impressed by how well Drake knew just about every animal on the place. He chuckled at his brother's choice of words. "Poor old feller," he said. Then, with a shake of his head and a quick adjustment of his hat, he observed, "Only you would worry about the preferences of a half-ton bull."

Drake's answer was wry. "Poor *me,* you mean. The day ol' Sherman went on a tear, all the hands were laughing as I left a trail of apples, like Hansel and Gretel leaving their bread crumbs, trying to coax that testy s.o.b. up the ramp and into the back of a cattle truck. Red about split a gut, watch-

129

ing." Drake paused to resettle his own hat. "I kept hoping the old coot would laugh so hard he'd fall off his horse. Would've served him right."

Slater tried not to show how much he was enjoying the tale. "Wish I'd been here," he said.

Drake studied him then sobered again. "Not to change the subject, but how's the quest going?"

"What quest?"

"Grace Emery."

Slater went for a noncommittal reply, leaning over to pat his horse's neck. "I don't know that she can be defined as a quest."

"What is she, then? A nice lady you could invite over for a cup of tea? I was under the impression that you'd like to further your acquaintance with her through some conversation. Namely, pillow talk."

"You know," Slater retorted, "you're not half as funny as you think you are." All of a sudden, he was losing it, he realized, and there was no call to be so touchy. He and Mace and Drake had always said what they thought. So he tried again. "I like Grace," he said moderately. "I won't deny that. She isn't just beautiful, she's smart, not to mention generous, taking on her ex's son, raising him with no hands-on help from his dad, as far as I can tell." His temper ratcheted down another notch or two. "And I appreciate you agreeing to let the boy do some work around the stables. When our dad died, we could take Mom's support for granted, and the support of Harry, Red and everyone else around us. Ryder doesn't have that. He can count on Grace, of course, but his own parents aren't even there for him. He probably figures he has to feel grateful for practically everything that anyone, including Grace, does for him. It isn't a bad life lesson to figure out that things don't always go smoothly, but that doesn't mean it's easy to learn, either."

Drake was silent as he walked his horse around a hole in the trail they were riding. After a few minutes he said, "When Dad died, I remember lying in bed and thinking over and over — what are we going to do? I was scared half to death. It wasn't that I didn't trust Mom. It was just that without Dad —"

"You weren't the only one who felt that way," Slater reminded his brother. He'd experienced the same sense of panic and insecurity — despite the love and support of all the people around him. "I thought Dad was indestructible, I guess. Superman in chaps and a Stetson. And I was wrong, of course — because none of us is immortal. Can you imagine what it must be like for Ryder, knowing his father is in some hostile, dangerous place?"

"No, I can't imagine." Drake's profile was outlined by the rays of the setting sun.

"You being on board with hiring him is damned generous."

"Please, Slate. Did you ever doubt I'd want to help the kid? Besides, it isn't as though the hands are falling all over themselves to muck out stalls. They'll be happy to show him the ropes, if only because it means they don't have to do the job themselves." He mulled it over for a few hoof beats, the way he tended to do. "I'd get Red to break him in, but that old duffer might just talk the poor kid to death on day one."

They both laughed.

"I think Ryder'll be a fairly quick study." He hoped so, anyway. The boy was bright enough, but he didn't *have* to scoop and shovel and walk a mile from the bus when the wind was whipping up. He had a cushier option — going home to a comfortable condo on the grounds of a well-equipped resort, watching television, playing on the computer, goofing off.

"Damn it, look at the ridge up there." Drake exhaled audibly as he pointed toward the tree line. "I swear that horse is gonna turn my hair white before my time."

Slater followed the direction of his finger and drew in a quick breath. With the setting sun and the shadows moving in, the gray horse stood in stark contrast to his surroundings, almost ghostly in the fading light of day, and the mares and foals were nowhere to be seen.

The animal snorted in warning, gave a ringing whinny, shrill enough to raise gooseflesh, and then whirled on his hind legs and pounded off through the long grass.

"I do believe that stallion just told you to go to hell." Slater had to tighten the reins on Heck, who clearly wanted to beat feet in the opposite direction.

"I saw it, all right," Drake growled, yanking off his hat to slam it against one thigh in sheer annoyance. "And I got the message."

Slater shifted in the saddle, thinking how much he'd like to film that stallion. "Yeah," he agreed with some admiration. "He told you that this is *his* territory and he'd be obliged if we'd make ourselves scarce. Permanently."

Drake was still gazing up at the empty ridge. Glaring was more like it. "Yup, that came through loud and clear."

"I have to admit I'm looking forward to seeing his foals," Slater said.

Drake didn't disagree, just rested his hands on the saddle horn and continued to gaze broodingly at the place where the horse had been seconds before. "I don't mind telling you I was hoping he'd moved on by now. I can't have him kicking down our fences. It's enough of a job to keep them in good repair as it is, and I sure don't want him stealing any more of our mares." He turned with a lifted brow and a small grin. And just like that, he changed the subject. "Hey, Slate," he said cheerfully, "maybe that's the tactic you should take with your pretty redhead. Break down her door, toss her over your shoulder and carry her off." He indicated the vanished stallion with a jab of one thumb. "Works for him."

"That idea is *so* not politically correct," Slater pointed out. "Besides, she'd probably shoot me." He'd seen Grace mad several times now, and while he'd enjoyed watching, he knew she could handle herself better than a lot of men. "I think I'll try finesse before I get drastic. We have a dinner date coming up — it's business-related, unfortunately — but I'm hoping to parlay that into a drink at her condo afterward." He remembered Ryder. "The hell of it is, we still wouldn't be alone."

Yep, even that would be a challenge.

He lived at a big busy ranch, and she had a teenage roommate. He'd considered asking her out for dinner on a strictly nonbusiness date, but that wasn't as easy as it sounded, either. The resort probably had the best restaurant food in the area, unless you counted the killer burgers at Bad Billy's. But Grace worked at the former, and the latter was a little on the raucous side for a romantic dinner out.

Privacy would be ideal, but that might take some doing.

His brother turned his horse with a slight tug of the rein and just a tightening of his knees. "You'll figure it out. I haven't ever noticed you having any trouble with females. Come on, I've been itching to see how Heck does against Starburst in a flat race."

The big bay must have understood because he whirled around so quickly that Slater, who was a more than competent horseman, was almost unseated. Then the gelding took off so fast Slater lost his hat.

But Drake lost the race.

CHAPTER SEVEN

That evening, Grace was running late.

This was the night of her business dinner with Slater. The way things had turned out, it was going to be just the two of them . . . Which made her feel excited but also nervous. Without the buffer of other people, there'd be nothing to keep them from acknowledging — or even acting on — their mutual attraction. Well, nothing except her stepson's presence, of course.

Luckily, all she had to do was put the chicken in the oven, set the table and change. She'd cheated and had the chef at the resort prepare his famous salad with arugula, feta and dried cranberries; the scallion vinaigrette was a house favorite, and all she had to do was toss everything together. The twice-baked potatoes were from her mother's recipe collection, and if she could just shed her business suit and put on something casual, run a brush through her hair — and relax, she'd be fine.

When the conference manager had called that morning with apologies because her daughter was ill, Grace had made an executive — and possibly idiotic — decision. She'd phoned Slater and informed him that they'd be having dinner at her condo instead. Alone.

He'd agreed immediately, which had been flattering, but now she had to pull herself and dinner together. That was when she saw a pair of — no doubt dirty — socks on the living room floor, thanks to her stepson. There was more cat hair on the couch, and she was afraid that if someone opened the door to the laundry room, clothes would come tumbling out of the basket. As Grace discovered when she picked up the socks and tried to toss them in, that wasn't a theory, it was physics.

Laundry cascaded out at her, avalanche-style.

Grace took a deep breath, calmed down and started a load of wash. While that was chugging away, she took a lint roller to the couch, clearing away cat hair, and when she'd finished *that* appealing task, she opened the cupboards to take out some plain, square plates — white but not pretentious — and set the table. She still had just enough time to change out of the linen suit she'd worn to work that day and into jeans and a sleeveless pink blouse. She brushed her teeth, and, as a finishing touch, applied lip gloss to her mouth.

Ryder was going to be a happy camper, since the kitchen staff all had a weakness for him and had sent along a tasty meal, which was a menu item he'd recently encountered when she'd brought home leftovers from her own lunch, old-fashioned beef and noodles. That was what she'd told him, but it was really Beef Stroganoff. Straight from the spa menu, with lean filet, organic mushrooms and Greek yogurt instead of sour cream, all ladled over handmade buckwheat noodles.

Realizing her feet were bare, she slid them into leather sandals.

She'd let Slater select the wine from the limited supply she kept on hand.

Was she sending him a message? Could be. It would be helpful if she knew exactly what that message was, but at the moment she didn't care.

She was warming garlic bread in the oven when Slater pulled up. It had come from the bakery at the spa that afternoon, an artisan bread that would make her look as if she cooked like a genius, when in fact, though competent, she was no chef. If people were being robbed, she could jump in and sort things out, but if their hollandaise sauce curdled, they were on their own.

Ryder came through the back door in a whirl of earthy scents that hinted at horse and manure, and said without preamble, "I'm gonna shower." He did kick off his running shoes and throw them out on the front porch. She suspected he was following Slater's instructions, and was grateful for that.

Slater himself followed at a more leisurely pace. "A domestic goddess at work, I see. Smells great. Can't say it hurts my feelings any that we're having dinner here. I like the resort, but I'm more jeans and boots than white shirts and ties." He paused to look down at his feet, and his eyes were twinkling when he met hers again. "Don't worry, they're clean. Ryder did all the dirty work."

Grace smiled, feeling ridiculously nervous. "How's he doing?" she asked.

"All in all, he's doing fine. He'll catch on once he gets used to the job. And it does take some getting used to, shoveling sh— manure, but Ryder's still enthusiastic and that's a good sign. As for his homework, I know he did it, and he and my mother sat

139

down and talked it over." He grinned. "I didn't comment. Seems to me, the fewer people who pester him about it, the better he's going to respond."

Around Grace's place, homework discussions invariably ended in a sullen silence from Ryder and some muttering from her.

"Sounds good," she said.

Slater walked over and set two bottles on the counter. "I'm bringing this as an offering from my brother, who wants us to try them. You and I are sort of a focus group. That doesn't mean he expects lavish reviews. It just means he needs unsuspecting fools who are willing to try his latest concoctions. He wanted to know the menu. I didn't know, so he sent a medium-bodied red and a dry white. I'm not sure what I'd pair with either one, probably baked beans out of a can if left to my own devices, so that's going to be up to you."

This was where she could try to sound highbrow, but that wasn't her. "I marinated some chicken and there's a sauce everyone at the restaurant raves about. They made some for me, plus their signature salad. I'm out of baked beans, sorry about that, but my mother makes this cheesy potato dish that probably has a zillion calories, so that'll have to make up for it. As for how to pair the entrée with a wine . . . I say we crack them both and go sit on the back patio for our business meeting."

Slater wore a soft gray cotton shirt tucked into his jeans, and his wavy dark hair was long enough to give him a bad-boy aspect, but there was no hint of a five-o'clock shadow this evening. The last time she'd seen him, he'd obviously put off shaving for a couple of days. He'd looked sexy, actually, but Slater would probably look sexy slathered in mud. He drawled, "If all business meetings were run by women as pretty as you, I'd be up for a lot more of them. I usually avoid meetings if I can. Corkscrew?"

After that unexpected lead-in, it took Grace a few seconds to make sense of his one-word inquiry. "Top drawer, to the right of the sink."

Embarrassed, she headed outside with a small tray of appetizers and two wineglasses, the cat, Bonaparte, following hopefully behind. To his credit, he wasn't begging. Or maybe that was to *her* credit, since she'd pointed out to him in no-nonsense terms that sort of behavior was not going to be allowed. The feline listened better than Ryder ever did and had accepted her edict.

Grace sat in a chair near the glass-topped table and watched Slater deftly close the screen door with his elbow. He glanced at the creamy red pepper dip on the tray, a plate of veggies and delicate water crackers next to it. "White was a good choice, then?"

"At the moment a good choice will be whatever you put in my glass."

"Long day?" He carefully poured her wine but certainly didn't miss it when she leaned back and crossed her legs. The man could multitask.

She nodded and murmured a thank-you when he handed her the glass. "I had to help set up the monthly luncheon for the local chapter of the Audubon Society today. Believe it or not, they bicker and argue loudly enough that the manager who usually handles it reserves the room farthest from the regular dining room. Apparently, certain species of hawks and western bluebirds inspire great — and, shall we say — rowdy — passion in a group of otherwise dignified people. I was in and out of there, just keeping an eye on the service, but let me tell you, when someone introduced the topic of pileated woodpeckers, the subject shifted to whether the ivory-billed variety still exists. Mayhem ensued."

Slater laughed as he settled into a wicker chair and stretched his legs. "If memory serves, it was thought to be extinct for over half a century until about a decade ago, when someone supposedly spotted one — in a Louisiana swamp. Since I don't cruise swamps because I feel about alligators the way you do about spiders, I'm not likely to validate that sighting, but I am an amateur bird-watcher."

She wouldn't have guessed he was afraid of anything. Then again, she sensed there was nothing simple — or predictable — about Slater Carson. "You do travel a lot, so I imagine you get to see quite a variety of landscapes. Are you still contemplating the film set around the settlement of Bliss County?"

"Just about every waking moment right now," he admitted, studying his wineglass and taking a tentative sip. "Hey, that's pretty good. I don't like anything too sweet, but this has a nice balance. Mace said he used chardonnay grapes and left it unoaked." Grace sampled the wine and he was right; it tasted light and crisp but still had character. "It gets my vote, for what that's worth. I'll recommend it to our buyer for the list at the resort."

"My brother's taken on this winemaking thing full speed ahead. When you meet him, you'll see that for yourself. Mace has a degree in horticulture, and his choice of career didn't surprise any of us. Drake thought about becoming a veterinarian, but he was already starting to run the ranch, so he opted to go for ecology. Not surprising, either. He's all about the balance of nature, which is an interesting path sometimes, considering what he does."

"You all sound very different."

"We are. No doubt about that." He raised his glass. "What about you? Siblings?"

Dusk was lowering, sending a few slanting shadows onto the small patio. "One older brother. He lives in Dallas. He's an accountant. We keep in touch by phone and email, and see each other at Christmas. He has two little girls and I really like his wife. Our parents live in Seattle." Grace was finally starting to relax, and she was a little surprised to realize she'd been so tightly wound. Doing the jobs of two people, getting ready for this dinner, hoping Ryder was going to handle his job at the ranch, worrying about his schoolwork . . .

She should probably take a minute or two every day to inhale deeply . . .

Like now, having a nice glass of wine with an intriguing man, her feet in airy sandals, the evening beautiful and quiet. Perfect.

Until Bonaparte decided to jump up and curl himself on her lap with a small rusty purr, twitching his tail before he shut his eyes for a nap. Incredible, considering he hadn't allowed Grace to so much as pet him before this sudden display of affection.

Maybe it was the wine and her stressful day fading away, but Grace just said what she'd wanted to say ever since the day she'd dropped Ryder off at the ranch to fly to the football game. "Tell me about Raine."

What about Raine?

Cautiously, Slater asked, "What do you want to know?"

"Are you married, divorced, separated?"

Married? Was that what she thought? Time to set the record straight.

Maybe it was a testament to growing up in a small town that Slater assumed Grace knew what had happened between him and Raine, since it was hardly confidential information. He needed a second because he was caught off guard, but then shook his head. "None of the above. We dated for a few months, about twelve years ago." His smile was wry. "Well, obviously more than dated. I was off on location for most of her pregnancy and she was away visiting relatives, so I had no idea I was about to have a daughter. I only found out about a month before Daisy was born. It was . . . an

145

interesting moment in my life. The good part is that Raine and I agree it would never have worked if we'd gone the traditional route. As it is, we get along fine and my family loves her, and our daughter is spoiled but seems well-adjusted to me."

"I wondered." Grace's expression was hard to read, but her words sounded like an admission. The dying sunlight caught her shining hair. "Raine seemed nice, and she struck me as an interesting person."

"She's the quintessential artist," Slater explained, "unconventional and someone who definitely goes her own way. That's Raine. She's a terrific mother and a fine friend." He tried to decide if he should be blunt. Why not? he decided. "You said you wondered because of my obvious interest in you? I would never do that if I was married or even involved." He watched her, speaking gently. "Just so we have that straight."

"I didn't think you would," she said, looking him in the eye, "and neither would I since we're getting everything *straight.*"

He grinned, enjoying the view of her shapely feet in those strappy sandals. "Are we going to butt heads over how ethical we both are?"

She smiled, just a glimmer that also reached her eyes. "Maybe. I have to warn you I'm easy to stir up."

Uh, *yeah,* he thought. "That sounds promising." He held his glass halfway to his mouth, studying her over the rim.

If there was one thing Grace couldn't seem to do with any consistency, it was control that blush of hers. He found it endearing, especially since she was so self-assured and businesslike otherwise. She shot back, "I didn't mean it *that* way."

"More's the pity." Slater shifted downward in his chair in a relaxed sprawl. "Shall we get on with the business portion of the evening? You want to feature Bliss River Resort and Spa in the credits at the end of the next film, correct? With maybe some footage of the original hotel. This would be in exchange for reasonable rates on accommodations for the crew when we're filming near Mustang Creek."

Grace looked flustered for a moment but quickly recovered her composure. "That's about right, yes. I talked to the owner and he also requested that if you use some of the artifacts from the old hotel, including the historic photographs, you mention the resort's current name. Nothing big. Maybe just an acknowledgment that the original building's been replaced with a modern resort and spa. You could show a picture of the previous structure and then flash the new one. If we have a deal, you can help yourself to anything you want."

Slater knew she was referring to the artifacts in the hotel basement, but he couldn't hold back. The opening was too irresistible. "Anything?"

"In the basement," Grace clarified pointedly, although there was amusement in her eyes.

"And you won't set foot down there, so I guess I'm out of luck."

"I doubt you believe that. The out of luck part, I mean," she murmured.

Again, promising. She wasn't the sort to play games, and he appreciated that. The chemistry between them was strong, and she seemed to be sending some very positive signals his way.

Grace lightly stroked the cat sitting on her lap. "We have a deal?"

There was no downside for Slater, so he promptly agreed. "Deal — as long as Mick lines up the backers as he usually does and the movie happens. I have no doubt he'll succeed, since he's excited about it, but I never make promises I can't keep."

Her lashes lowered. "Good to know."

"So can we call the business part of the evening concluded?"

The breeze lifted a lock of curly red-gold hair to tease her cheek, and she brushed it away. "You won't get an argument from me. I already give the resort a lot of my time as it is."

"So the rest of the evening is all ours." He held her gaze.

"And the cat's. Bonaparte's." She petted the cat again and smiled ruefully as the sound of the refrigerator being opened came through the screen. "*And* a teenage boy in starvation mode." She deposited the animal gently on the brick patio and said to Slater, "Excuse me for a minute while I head off the inevitable peanut butter sandwich and give Ryder a real dinner."

"Take my word for it," Slater said with amused emphasis, recalling the football game. "He can eat both."

"True. I think the local grocery store's business has doubled since we moved here. Try the dip and come up with something I can tell the chef who made it. Like your brother's wine, it's a new recipe."

When Grace disappeared inside, the cat — Bonaparte — eyed Slater's lap speculatively, but wasn't quite trusting enough to make the leap and instead curled up under Grace's wicker chair. When she came back out, he immediately started to purr so

149

loudly, he could hear it a few feet away. "You have a not-so-secret admirer," Slater observed. "And you can tell the chef the dip is outstanding."

"Good. We have a different chef for the spa than we do in the main dining room, and they are both high maintenance. They're fairly competitive and don't particularly get along. Anything that makes either of them happy makes me happy."

"You have a stressful job." Slater could relate. Production schedules — not to mention the dueling egos of various artistic types — sometimes made for long, trying days. "What does Ms. Grace Emery do to relax?"

"Read." She curled her legs comfortably under her. "Listen to classical music. Take walks. Yoga a couple of times a week at the spa."

Somehow, her answer didn't surprise him. "I have another suggestion."

"I'll bet."

He couldn't help laughing at the sarcasm in her voice. "Well, yeah, that. But what I was really asking was, do you ride?"

"Horses?" She shook her head, her hair brushing her shoulders. "I'm afraid not. I have once or twice, but I think I was about thirteen at the time."

"Want to give it a try? This is some beautiful country, and there's no better way to see it than from the saddle." He used his most persuasive tone. "I'll pick out a well-mannered horse, I promise. Nothing lets me unwind like an evening ride."

Any woman he was truly interested in — and despite the usual misgivings, he was *very* interested in this one — needed to be able to ride a horse.

She looked dubious. "I'd have no idea what to do."

"I'm teaching Ryder. I could teach you, too. Think about it."

The timer on her phone pinged and she tapped the screen and stood up. "Dinner's ready. Lucky for you — although I'd say I'm a decent cook when I have the time — I had lots of help tonight."

He was on his feet just as fast, and before she could take a step, caught her hand. "Grace."

She turned, inquiry in her blue eyes, and he tugged her closer, sliding his arm around her waist as he pulled her up against him. He said softly, "I'm not interested in the awkward good-night kiss at the door. And, as you may have noticed, I'm impatient by nature. I'm dying to do it right now. Hope you don't mind."

And apparently, she didn't. He lowered his head and brought his lips to hers. Any thoughts of making it a soft romantic kiss evaporated when Grace responded, at first slowly, but then with an uninhibited enthusiasm that told Slater she'd be everything he'd imagined in bed and then some. Untamed. Not just beautiful but passionate. His body tightened in all the predictable places, and since he could feel the hardening tips of her breasts through the thin material of her blouse, she seemed to be having a similar reaction.

It was gratifying to know, with absolute certainty, that the attraction wasn't one-sided. An off-the-scale kiss was a very good start. He took his time about it, enjoying the feel of her in his arms.

"Grace, I . . . Oh, jeez. Sorry. I didn't . . . I mean . . ."

At the sound of Ryder's voice, they broke apart. Grace's cheeks were flushed, but her voice was steady as she turned toward the door. "No problem. What is it?"

Slater wasn't happy about the interruption, either. Still, he took pity on the kid. "Everything okay?" he asked.

"Just . . . just talked to my dad," Ryder said through the screen, still stammering.

"He's got some leave coming up. He's going to come here, if that's okay."

CHAPTER EIGHT

It really, *really* wasn't okay.

Grace was still off balance from that devastating kiss and now *this*?

Just what she needed — her ex-husband in Mustang Creek. Hank hadn't been happy about the divorce, and she was pretty sure he still thought she'd "come around" if he poured on the charm. Typical.

Hank had liked coming home to a convenient bedmate, someone who took care of the house, the bills, did all the cooking, bought gifts for his family on the appropriate dates — something *he* should have done — and even mowed the lawn. All while *she* was working, too.

Oh, yes, and if she wouldn't mind raising his son in her spare time, why, he'd be ever so grateful. It was the kind of mundane responsibility neither of Ryder's parents could be bothered to handle.

Who but Hank Emery would've had the

gall to crash into her carefully reconstructed life with practically no warning at all?

Grace felt as if her back was against the wall. She couldn't tell Hank not to come; Ryder needed to see his father.

"I'll get him a room at the resort." Her tone was sharper than she'd intended, so she modified it. "I'm sure he won't mind a short walk. I do it all the time."

"I thought he could have my room," Ryder was quick to say. "It's just for a month, and I can sleep on the couch."

A month? She had to struggle not to look as unhappy as she felt. She was not sharing her home with Hank for a month, period. And she absolutely wasn't going to share her bed. "Then I can stay at the resort," she said with a small sigh. "Heaven knows I'm always there, anyway."

Ryder's jaw stuck out at a stubborn angle. "This is *your* house, Grace. He's not kicking you out of it just because he's pretending he wants to hang out with me. We'll see how long he lasts."

She could let that go, especially since she had the feeling he could be right about the duration of his father's stay — but he was also wrong.

"Ryder, he's not pretending." Hank was all about Hank, no question, and yet she knew he loved his son. He was just never cut out to be a parent, in her opinion. The day they got married, he'd happily relinquished all parenting duties to her, and before that, Ryder had been more or less living with his grandparents. She chose her words carefully. "He's a busy man with a lot of responsibilities. He's made sacrifices to do what he does, but unfortunately you and I did, too. However, if he says he wants to spend a month of his leave with you, I believe he means it." Slater hadn't said a word during her conversation with Ryder, which she appreciated. This was her problem, and interference would not be welcome. She'd spent eight years with male counterparts trying to "protect" her when she could take care of herself just fine. Other than the incident with firing David Reinhart, Slater seemed to be good at keeping his mouth shut and backing off when she asked.

Ryder looked as though he might want to argue some more, but she cut him off with his favorite distraction, namely food. "Hey, there's some beef and noodles in the oven for you. Have you fed Bonaparte?"

That cat was uncannily smart. At the sound of his name, or maybe it was the word *fed,* he emerged from under the chair and came to the screen door, looking hopeful. Ryder still stood there for a second, but then he opened the screen to let the cat in and opted out of saying anything else.

"Well done." Slater raised his brows when she turned around. "I know for a fact he ate two pieces of chocolate pie during his tutoring session."

"Sounds like a rough life."

"It can be. You haven't met Harry. She likes things to run the way she likes things to run."

Grace sighed. "I hope the look on my face didn't show how I feel about Hank descending on us. I don't want to hurt Ryder's feelings — this *is* his dad, after all. But I'm sure you figured out that I don't want my ex moving in with us for a month."

Hank's parents were good people; they were attentive grandparents to Ryder and exchanged emails with Grace on a regular basis. Why couldn't Hank stay with *them*?

"That message came through, yes." His reply was droll. "I'm hardly an expert, but it seemed to me that Ryder isn't sure how to feel about it. If I had to venture a guess, it would be that he's secretly hopeful it'll go well but he isn't counting on anything."

She walked over and dropped back into her chair, reaching for her wineglass. "He and I had a similar reaction, then."

Slater settled back into his chair, as well. "We can talk about it, but we don't have to. Up to you."

Her smile was probably full of weary cynicism. "If you don't mind, I want to think about it first, discuss another time."

"Fine with me."

"You're being deliberately charming."

There was a glint of amusement in his eyes. "An astute observation. You have to watch me every second because I'm an opportunist. When your ex-husband's here to stay with Ryder, would you consider going away with me for a weekend? I need to scout some locations for the new film."

Not subtle, but she didn't think that was his goal. Charming, yes, subtle, no.

She liked that he was straightforward about his request, so it worked. "If I can manage it, that sounds like a possibility," Grace responded neutrally. She might *need* to get away. Plus, that had been one very nice kiss.

A hot, skillful kiss that promised if she wanted the full Slater Carson experience, she wasn't going to be disappointed.

He added, "I was already planning to ask you before this latest development, so don't think I'm working an angle now."

"I'd be kind of disappointed if you weren't." Grace flashed her best teasing smile under the circumstances. It wasn't as if she hadn't expected Ryder's father to reappear now and then; it was more that she was getting used to their family being the two of them.

Oh, and Bonaparte. Three. A family of three. Which reminded her — they had to get him to the vet in the next little while. She'd make an appointment tomorrow. As it was, she'd broken her own rules by allowing him inside without having the requisite checkup, shots and neutering.

Still, they were a family of three.

Not quite like the tight-knit Carson bunch, but they were holding their own. Dinner, taking out the trash, even if Ryder grumbled about it, homework, small arguments, occasionally watching a movie together, sharing the growing but cautious affection of the cat . . .

She'd imagined that Hank would want Ryder to fly out to Seattle, not the other way around. She'd heard, through her ex-in-laws, that he'd put their house on the market, so maybe it had sold. While she'd loved that house, Hank hadn't shown much sentimental attachment to it, although, to be fair, he was hardly ever there. She

159

could've taken it in the divorce, except that by then she'd already made the decision to move someplace more peaceful than a big city.

"I'd better get our dinner out of the oven," she told him, determined to enjoy the rest of her evening.

Surprisingly, she did.

The evening's success was helped by the fact that the food was delicious, thanks to the communal effort involved. She wasn't sure how Slater managed to stay so fit when he ate like a longshoreman after a hard day.

They drank decaf coffee on the patio afterward, and to her disappointment — true to his word — he didn't attempt a good-night kiss. After he'd left, she went into her home office and sent a quick email to George Landers, the resort owner, informing him that the meeting had gone well. Then she scrolled through her messages and found one from Hank. Brief and to the point, but that was him.

Thanks for agreeing to put up with me. I'm currently in Washington, DC. See you soon.

As far as her personal life was concerned, this was bad timing on several levels. Of course, it wasn't as if one business dinner constituted a real date with Slater, but an invitation for a weekend trip was a different story.

"Grace?"

She turned to see Ryder hovering in the doorway, wearing pajama bottoms with moose patterned all over them and a black T-shirt with the logo of one of his favorite video games. Despite his gangly height, he looked very young. A lock of hair flopped over his brow. She'd chosen to let him wear it however he wanted — Save the Arguments for Important Things was her current motto — but she had a feeling Hank would cart his son off to the barber immediately.

"Is it okay if I still go to the ranch after school even while my dad's here?"

That was a fair question. "Yes, I think so. It would be the responsible thing to do. When you agree to take on a job, that's an obligation you need to fulfill. If anyone should understand that, it would be your father."

He looked relieved, which told her about his uncertainties over this coming visit. She felt some trepidation herself.

Maybe she should address that kiss. Hesitantly she began, "Slater and I —"

"Like each other. That's not exactly a secret. Give me some credit, Grace. I pretty much figured that out the night you dragged me into his office at the ranch."

It was a relief not to delve deeper into a subject that might make a teenage boy squirm in discomfort, but then he added, with devastating maturity and insight, "My dad's not going to be on board with that. I think he's coming here to see *you* more than he's coming to see me."

The paperwork was always his least favorite part of the job, so he tended to leave it to someone else, but Slater was reading through his email when a knock interrupted him and he glanced up.

His mother stood in the doorway. The thing about Blythe Carson was that she looked and sounded deceptively mild-mannered; while she called you *honey* and *sweetheart,* she rearranged your schedule and adjusted your life. It didn't help that she was right 99 percent of the time, but still . . . he was a grown man and he knew that expression of hers. She had something to say.

"Am I disturbing you?"

"Of course not." He rose to his feet, instantly wary.

She was dressed for bed, her favorite blue robe over cotton pajamas patterned with tiny pink roses, her auburn hair, lightly streaked with gray, hanging loose. She sat on the small leather couch he sometimes used for reading. "You came home rather early," she said. "How was your date?"

He swiveled the desk chair to face her and sat back down. "It wasn't a date," he explained mildly. "Ms. Emery had a business proposal involving the resort and the production company. So, it was a business meeting that included dinner."

And a satisfying kiss that would've been even better if they hadn't been joined by the kid, but he could hardly blame Ryder for that. Not only did he live there, Slater also had the impression he didn't get to talk to his father very often.

His mother smiled. "Ms. Emery? Ryder told me you have quite a crush on Grace."

His brows went up. "I think at my age the term *crush* is hardly applicable."

She gave an airy wave. "My term, not his. I think he said you have a 'thing' for her. Mace and Drake were joking about it the other day, as well. True?"

"I thought you were helping him with his homework, not sitting around gossiping about my personal life."

"I'm your mother, so naturally everything about you is important to me." She didn't act the slightest bit repentant. "There's no such thing as a Carson secret. My spies are everywhere. I'm not nosy, just interested because I love you. Now then, when are you seeing her again?"

"Between her picking up Ryder here or me dropping him off at her place, I'll probably see her fairly often."

"Raine said she's very attractive. Harry told me the same thing. And Daisy said she's really pretty."

"Harry?" He didn't recall them meeting.

"Naturally, she looked out the window when Ms. Emery dropped Ryder off for the football game excursion."

That he believed. It had been impossible to get away with anything when he was a kid because Harry seemed to have eyes in the back of her head. "I won't answer that on the grounds that it might incriminate me."

A small dimple in her cheek deepened as she smiled. "I want you to invite her to dinner. I need to meet her."

Alarm flickered through him. "And force her to run the Carson gauntlet? What surer way is there to send a woman hightailing it right out of Bliss County? Or maybe leave

164

the state of Wyoming entirely?"

"Oh, we aren't that bad, honey." She rose and came over to pat him on the cheek. "I'll tell your brothers to settle their current dispute, whatever it is, before we sit down to eat."

"Good luck," he muttered. "A new one'll just pop up. I'm not sure Grace is ready to take on the Carson Clan experience."

Or if she even wanted to tackle it in the first place. She had a stressful job, a teenage boy to manage, a new life, and now her ex-husband was going to complicate the situation. This wasn't the time to pressure her. He was about to start a new project and soon would be in full-blown production mode, which meant working twelve-hour days. None of that was conducive to a successful romantic relationship, and to be honest, he didn't quite know what he wanted, either. He had a daughter, a close-knit family and a satisfying career. Female companionship wasn't hard to come by, either, so . . .

But she'd basically agreed to the weekend away and he was already looking forward to it.

When his mother went off to bed, he decided he'd had enough of paperwork, and maybe cool night air would be a good idea.

There was something about a starlit sky and the silhouette of the mountains, especially with the tang of fall in the air. It held a special aura that might or might not be unique to this part of the world, but he'd never experienced it anywhere else. He walked out on the porch and leaned on the rail, listening to a nighthawk's cry.

"Fine night."

He hadn't realized Mace was there, lounging in a chair, feet propped up. His brother tipped back a beer and grinned. "Tell me, in order of importance, how was your delicious redhead, and then how was the wine?"

Slater wasn't convinced that Grace was *his* in any way. One kiss hardly sealed the deal. "It was a good evening and good wine." He rubbed his jaw. "What is it with this family and probing questions?"

"The redhead is personal, the wine is research. As the creator, I *want* it to be good, so I'm not impartial. Was it? Honestly?"

"It really was. Grace is going to suggest it to her staff for the wine list."

Mace pushed to his feet and ran his hand through his hair in evident — and amusing — relief. "You're sure she liked it?"

"Hell yes, I'm sure," Slater said, inwardly laughing. "You think I'd make that up?

When did you develop all this insecurity, brother? The wine was excellent and Grace loved it."

His brother turned away for a minute and then audibly exhaled. "I've been busting my ass trying to make this vineyard a going concern. Every success takes me one step closer. I tossed the dice on not oaking that chard. Everyone told me people pick up a chardonnay and expect that certain taste."

Slater rested his elbows on the rail. "Here's a thought. Ask Grace to let you host tasting parties at the resort. Maybe offer to print a wine list that features Mountain Wines. Raine could do some fantastic graphics. You'd be giving some of it away for free, but the publicity would be worth it."

Mace's eyes gleamed in the starlight. "I'm game. You care to run the idea by her? I reckon you've got some influence."

"I'd like to think so." Slater shook his head. "But I can't promise I do. That is one very independent female. She doesn't need me. She doesn't need the Carson legacy. She doesn't need anyone but herself. Her assistant suggested she might be interested in wine-tasting tours here for their guests, so the rest is up to the two of you."

As usual, Mace broke everything down to

its basics. "You might *think* she doesn't need anything, but we all need something. Plants need soil, sunlight, nutrients, rainfall . . . Human beings need family, friends, shelter, food, and maybe I've been around Mom a few years too long, but love is a good thing, too."

"Ever been?" Slater shot his youngest brother a questioning look.

"In love? Nope. Still waiting for her. Like a fine wine, you can't rush it. You?"

He took in a deep lungful of clean air and considered his answer. "I'm in love with this place, with the spirit of it. I felt a certain kind of love with Raine, but we were both finding our way around life then, trying to make sense of things. We can agree on one matter, anyway — we both love Daisy."

"That's obvious to everyone, and it's also obvious that if you were meant to be with Raine, you would've moved heaven and earth to make it happen. Is Grace Emery a possibility?"

Was she? He was interested in her sexually; that was undeniable. Just the sight of her bare feet had turned him on big-time, so what would the bare rest of her do to him? He'd give a lot to find out. "That's way too profound a question this early on. She and I hardly know each other."

168

"I thought love was a little like being struck by lightning," Mace said.

Slater recalled the evening Grace had stalked into his office, dragging Ryder with her, furious and determined to set things straight. If that was lightning, it was heat lightning, and it *was* like being hit and hit hard.

"Could be," he commented lightly.

"Slate," his younger brother said sagely, "I'm gonna tell you what your problem is. It's always been your problem."

Hell, he couldn't wait to hear this. Criticism wasn't his favorite thing, and no good comment ever followed *always been your problem.*

"Like what?"

"Of the three of us, you're the true Romeo." Mace held up his hand, palm forward. "Shut up and let me finish, because I know you're going to argue, but it's true. Drake and I want the same things you do, but we're more grounded. We deal with plants, horses, cattle — the weather today, not a hundred years ago . . . We're not re-creating the past."

"Documenting the past," he corrected.

Mace laughed quietly. "Okay, you win that one, but you aren't off the hook. For lack of a better way to put it, although this sounds like Valentine card drivel, you have a romantic soul. That's why history interests you so much."

"Shouldn't I be lying on a couch in your office, Dr. Carson? Let's leave my soul, romantic or otherwise, out of this discussion." He shrugged. "Grace is beautiful and smart. I know for a fact that I'm not the only man who finds her attractive. Let's see what happens. We both have a lot going on right now. For one thing, her ex-husband is coming to see Ryder and wants to stay with them. She didn't seem all that thrilled about it."

Mace gave him a speculative look. "You don't, either."

"No comment."

Just then Drake appeared, walking up the shadowed path to the house, his shoulders slumped with weariness, two of the herding dogs, a large German shepherd named Harold, and his slightly smaller female counterpart, Violet, trotting behind him. His clothes were dusty, and when he took off his hat as he climbed the steps, there was a smear of dirt across his forehead. As he reached the porch, a long distant howl rose in the background, answered almost immediately by another wolf.

Mace said sardonically, "Hey, Drake, I

think they're singing you a lullaby."

"I hear 'em. Luckily, I'm bone-tired so the happy reminder that they're out there, probably scouting our cattle, won't even keep me awake."

The sound made the dogs restless, though. Slater put his hand on Violet's head and she calmed down, but Harold was on full alert, nose in the air, hackles up.

"They know what's going on out there."

"Hell, yes. Those dogs know everything. Back to what's going on — how was your date?"

Slater had had enough and got to his feet. "This is the nosiest damn family in the world. I'm going to bed."

"What's up with that?" Drake took his now-empty chair.

As Slater reached the door, he heard Mace say casually, "Don't mind him. He's the dictionary definition of a lovesick fool."

Pure Drake, his brother retorted, "Like you'd recognize a dictionary if it bit you on the ass."

Despite his annoyance, Slater had to laugh. *Let the games begin.* He'd be surprised if they weren't still sitting there arguing when he strolled out with his cup of coffee in the morning.

CHAPTER NINE

Her tire was flat.

Not a big deal, Grace acknowledged as she walked slowly to her personal parking space, except this was the second one in two days — and it wasn't the same tire.

David Reinhart was her first suspect, especially when she saw the jagged scratch on the door of her sporty SUV.

One giant letter. *B.*

For *bitch,* of course. Very creative.

He'd picked up his last check that morning.

She was coldly furious. But her car was just an object. Maybe her time as a police officer had made her too aware that people were capable of some truly terrible things, so her first reaction was to pull up Slater's number from her contact list. To her relief he answered promptly. "Hi, Grace."

"Is Ryder there, safe and sound?"

"As far as I know, yes. Want me to go out

to the barn and check?"

"Yes, please." She found it unsettling that her panic was so apparent, but he seemed to be tuned in to how she felt without her having to spell it out. "I'd appreciate that."

"Call you right back."

She phoned Meg as she started to walk to the house, asking her to get in touch with a tow company because the spare was already on, and the scratched paint would need to be fixed. It was convenient that she could walk back to the condo. If the weather held, she'd be fine for the next few days.

Just give her the good news that Ryder was safe, and then she could go ahead and get fighting mad, from the tips of her toes to the top of her head. Perhaps it was the result of working with some very brave men and women in law enforcement, and — although he had faults — being married to a man who considered risking his life for his country part of his daily routine, but she thoroughly despised cowards.

Destruction like this was the act of someone who didn't have the courage to face his victim. His *target*. Sounded way too much like David. Adding to her fear, he knew Ryder . . . All the staff did.

Her phone rang and she answered immediately, without even looking at the call display. "Slater?"

"He's here and he's fine. Mind telling me what's going on?"

She walked past the resort entrance, awash in relief, wondering how much to say. It was normal operating procedure to keep her problems to herself, but Slater had taken on responsibility for her stepson every afternoon. "Someone vandalized my car and I've had two flat tires this week. It's quite a leap from that to harming anyone, but people are unpredictable. Until I have a chance to talk to him, do me a favor and tell him not to go *anywhere* with *anyone* besides you or me."

"You talking about the guy you fired?"

He was quick, wasn't he? She said flatly, "I have absolutely no proof, but that would be my guess."

"I'll come and pick you up. You and Ryder can stay here at the ranch. We have plenty of guest rooms."

"That's jumping the gun," she said in exasperation. "And speaking of guns, I'm not only licensed to carry one, but I know how to use it. I can defend myself."

"My mother's issued the decree that I should invite you to dinner, and tonight is as good a time as any. Besides, we can go for that relaxing evening ride I promised you. Ryder is really a natural. I bet he'd love to show off for you by saddling your horse."

It sounded more tempting than spending the evening doing laundry and paying bills. She had the next day off, too, and for once, she might just take it. She could have balked at spending the night at the ranch, but that would mean Slater had to drive her home in addition to picking her up, and he was already being generous.

"It's last-minute. Are you sure?"

He said with conviction, "Positive. I'll be there in less than thirty minutes."

If she'd wanted to object, there would've been no opportunity, because he pulled a Slater Carson and just ended the call. Grace looked at her phone and said out loud, "Seriously?"

But suddenly, she was looking forward to her evening.

After a quick survey, she walked briskly to her front door, went inside and swiftly locked it behind her. She was more nervous than she'd realized. She changed into jeans, a light ivory blouse with feminine ruffles at the elbow-length sleeves, then ran a comb through her hair. She thought about putting it up, but the minute she was dressed, her phone rang. It was someone from the tow company with a few questions, and by the time she was done, she heard the engine of an approaching vehicle.

Slater.

She was annoyed to find her pulse had suddenly picked up, but the physical reaction was undeniable. She'd shoved a few things into a bag during the call, so when he knocked she was ready and opened the door — only to be barreled backward as he stepped in and pushed her against the wall.

She looked into intense blue eyes and demanded, "What are you *doing*?"

Slater's hands were firm on her shoulders. "Checking to see how on guard you are. Come on, Grace. I could've been anyone. Don't just open the damn door."

What she might have said was cut short because he kissed her just before she could knee him where it counted. He had maybe two seconds, tops.

The man moved like lightning.

It wasn't a gentle kiss, but she'd already come to the conclusion that he could read her easily and knew that she'd respond to his urgency. Grace kissed him right back — the attraction between them was spiraling out of control — and when they came up for air, he tantalizingly nuzzled the juncture between her neck and shoulder, murmuring, "I thought we needed to finish what we

176

started the other night."

She almost made the mistake of pointing out she didn't think they were finished at all, but she decided he didn't need the encouragement. With some effort Grace found her voice. "Uh, you just took care of that. Let me grab my bag."

He, of course, immediately removed it from her hand. If nothing else, he was unfailingly courteous. As they walked out to the truck, Slater told her, "The chief of police is a friend of mine. I hope you don't mind that I gave Spence a call and told him I thought you were being harassed."

Did she mind? She wasn't sure. It was presumptuous, but Slater didn't seem to be lacking in that department. However, it could be helpful if David — and she couldn't guarantee he was the culprit — took further action and she had to lodge a formal complaint. "I can't point a finger at anyone at this stage."

"Hop in and let's forget about it for now." He opened the door and deposited her bag on the backseat. "Worrying isn't on the agenda tonight. There's our horseback ride and a great dinner, including Harry's famous baked pork chops and her tomato tart. Also a dessert of some kind. I don't know what but it'll be fantastic." He grinned. "A lifetime of experience goes into that statement."

Grace got in and thought with a twinge of dismay that she'd be meeting two mothers this evening — Mrs. Slater and the famous Harry — and that would intimidate anyone.

Mustang Creek wasn't proving to be as peaceful as she'd anticipated.

Grace Emery sure could fill out a pair of faded jeans.

Slater had a feeling that "ladies first" was a selfish male ritual for a reason that had nothing to do with being polite. He didn't mind following her into the barn. Not at all.

Ryder was sweeping industriously, with enough straw stuck to his clothes that it looked as if he'd been digging into the job, exactly as required.

Slater had to admit he was impressed so far. Ryder did a good job of cleaning the stalls, but what impressed Slater was that the boy was still enthusiastic about it. It had been *his* first real job growing up, too, Red being a demanding boss to say the least, and he was cut no slack simply because he was a Carson. He and Drake and Mace had all quickly learned to do a superior job or else they either had a repeat performance in their future — or worse, had to take on someone else's chores and see his smug smile all afternoon. It had been a clever kind of motivation; the sense of competition among the three of them meant they tried to outdo each other, just like they did with anything else. The stable had damn tidy stalls during those years.

It wasn't looking too bad now, either. Ryder was already feeling relaxed with the horses, for someone just getting the hang of handling them. He was fourteen, and therefore ten feet tall and bulletproof. Horses were big animals; if you were skittish around them, they were the same way around you.

"Hey, Grace." Ryder looked up with an uneasy expression on his face. "What's going on? Why'd you want to know if I was here? Why am I not supposed to go anywhere with anyone? I'm smarter than that, anyway!"

In the kid's voice, Slater could hear the underlying question. *Don't you trust me?* He hadn't explained because he wasn't sure how Grace wanted to handle it.

Grace was Grace, though, and that meant straightforward. "Someone vandalized my car. I have an idea who it might be, and I don't *think* he'd hurt you to get back at me. That doesn't mean I know for sure, so I want you to be careful."

Her posture was perfect — spine straight, shoulders slightly back, eyes direct. But Slater could feel her tension, and he didn't blame her. She might've been a police officer. However, she was a woman on her own, responsible for a child. Unfortunately, if someone wanted to get at you badly enough, he or she could probably manage it. Her background no doubt made her very aware of how true that was.

He was absurdly proud of Ryder when he didn't scoff at Grace, but nodded and said, "I will," his voice mature.

"You want to saddle up Jupiter for Grace?" he asked casually, trying to ease the mood. "I'll take care of Heck. You can ride out with Drake to check fences after dinner, since you're staying over. We could pick up your clothes or whatever later."

"Yeah! Real cowboy stuff." Ryder grinned. "That's what I'm talkin' about."

The kid had been spending way too much time around Red, since that was one of his favorite expressions. Slater stifled a laugh and went to get his saddle. Heck was still far and gone too hard for a novice to handle, and he doubted the horse would calm down until he got a few more years on him.

They had the usual battle of wills, mostly because the horse was impatient to get moving. But having a saddle tossed on his back meant a good run, so Heck and Slater were getting used to each other and he wasn't nearly as fractious.

He did hand the reins to Ryder while he checked the girth on Grace's horse, and gave her a leg up. She settled into the saddle on the placid Jupiter — a mare his mother had always favored because of her good disposition and easy gait — and seemed to know what she was doing when she gathered up the reins.

He swung into the saddle, too, and they rode out into one of those evenings he loved, clear with a light cooling breeze, the air just ruffling Grace's bright hair. They didn't talk at first, but that was okay with him. The air smelled fresh and sweet as the horses walked along, side by side. Grace seemed comfortable, even composed. Finally, she said, "He likes it here. Thank you."

"Thank the horses and cows." Slater smiled lazily, trying to hide with a tight rein how much Heck wanted to run, testing his rider with every slow step. "I didn't do anything. Kids seem to find them really exciting."

That did draw a smile. "I have a feeling

it's a mistake to say this, but I think it's you. We've got some hero worship going on here."

"I'm glad if he likes it on the ranch. Even when my parents completely ticked me off, I always did. At one time I thought I was the single most beleaguered teenage boy in the great American West. You have to keep in mind that I had Drake and Mace on my hands, so I was usually dealing with a small war in progress. They're only eleven months apart in age."

"They don't get along?" She looked curious, and he was happy to see Jupiter moseying along in her usual calm manner.

"No." He had to take a moment to reflect. "They're actually best friends. They just don't know it. They're grown men, and they haven't figured it out."

"Too much alike?"

"You nailed it. They're both hardworking, intelligent, and would lay down their lives for someone they cared about, but let's not leave out pigheaded — and often about exactly the same things. We all fondly refer to it as the Carson way."

Grace laughed. She looked particularly beautiful in the setting he liked most — the mountains in the background, a lowering sun spreading indigo light, their horses

182

moving through the long grass, the breeze molding her light blouse to the curves of her breasts . . .

She caught the direction of his gaze and said tartly, "Carson, you are so obvious."

"Just admiring the view. Pretty night, isn't it?" Nope, he wasn't going to apologize, and if she knew what he was thinking . . . Well, it wasn't hard to guess.

He could fall in love with her.

His conversation with Mace had made him think about a subject he tended to avoid. He wasn't opposed to permanence; it was just that he hadn't met anyone who inspired that kind of thought. Casual relationships were about enjoying the moment, about charming company and transient pleasure. He wanted to see this woman first thing in the morning *every* morning.

Or maybe he had. It was startling. Two kisses and a little heat lightning and he was considering the possibility? Couldn't be! Even with Raine, he'd never felt that kind of . . . intensity. That kind of certainty. "You were right." Grace said the words quietly. "This is a perfect break from doing something every single minute of the day. I have a tendency to make myself as busy as possible."

Heck tossed his head restlessly despite the

tight reins. "I have the same flaw," Slater admitted, suddenly restless himself. "You up for a slightly faster pace? I think Heck here needs to work off some steam."

Grace said with a straight face, "I think maybe you do, too."

That was one intuitive woman.

"Maybe," he muttered and loosened the reins. "Hold on, we're going for a ride."

CHAPTER TEN

When Heck bolted, Slater was prepared and pulled him up immediately, making him settle into a reasonable pace, not a flat-out run. Grace saw that her companion handled the impatient bay so easily it seemed effortless, but she was well aware that there was skill involved. They made a striking pair silhouetted against the slanted light of the setting sun.

Her horse, Jupiter, followed; fortunately, he'd warned her and she was prepared, so she just decided to hang on because the last thing she wanted was to go sprawling in the dirt right before meeting his family, much less in front of him. She'd already cottoned on that Jupiter was going to obey Slater much more than she'd pay attention to Grace's tentative commands. That was confirmed when he barked out, "Slow up."

The mare immediately checked her gait.

When both horses obeyed, she reflected

wryly that it must feel good to have that kind of authority. She was impressed. Or maybe the horses were smarter than most human beings. That was entirely possible. Grace was just glad she didn't fall off and Jupiter was no longer like a torpedo being launched from a submarine.

They galloped across flat pasture, and she had to admit it was exhilarating, with the wind in her hair and the fluid motion of the horse, the air scented with pine and the perfume of crushed grass. Slater pulled up by a small stream so clear every pebble was visible, and her mount slowed to a reasonable walk. Slater gave her a grin of approval. "You did fine, Ms. Emery."

"I'll have sore muscles tomorrow," she predicted breathlessly. "Wow, look at that view. You can see the whole valley." The place was picturesque, dotted with grazing cattle, the ranch itself far in the distance, the shadows lengthening.

Slater's eyes were shaded by his hat. "I used to come up here as a kid all the time just to be alone. The ranch is always busy, three hundred and sixty-five days a year. Livestock don't believe in holidays. First thing I did when my father died was come up here to sit and try and make sense of it all. I don't know that it makes any more sense to me now than it did then, but it gave me some peace, anyway."

"I'm sorry," Grace said quietly.

"Me, too." His voice was somber. "You get used to it but you don't get over it. I still miss him every single day. Tell me, what's the story with Ryder's mother?"

Grace sighed, their horses walking along the stream. "She'd already decided to divorce Hank, even though she was six months pregnant. He was out of the country, of course, and not available for deep, personal discussions, but his parents persuaded her not to put the baby up for adoption, which was what she wanted to do. They took Ryder home from the hospital, and his mother has never seen him since that day. When Hank and I got married, he came to live with us — which really means he came to live with me. To Hank's credit, since there were a lot of decisions being made for him, he accepted the situation. That said, I figured out pretty early that one of the reasons he married me was so Ryder would have a built-in parent."

"I can think of quite a few other reasons he married you," Slater said with flattering emphasis. "Don't sell yourself short."

Ryder had been the hardest part of her decision to end a marriage she'd realized was going nowhere. Hank was very focused, just not on her or his son. She smiled briefly. "Thanks. Leaving Ryder with his grandparents again was really difficult for me. He's like a chessboard piece, being moved here and there, but not actually in the game. It really affects his sense of self-worth, and I'm doing my best to give him the emotional support he needs. Even though his grandparents adore him, they can't deal with a boy his age right now."

"He's a good kid, but all teens need a gatekeeper. Daisy's turning eleven next week . . . Time sure is flying by. Next thing you know, I'll be buying her a car and we'll be picking out colleges. But I'm lucky. Raine is there for her."

"No residual feelings? For Raine?" She asked it cautiously. He'd already said he and Raine had agreed they weren't right for each other, but that didn't mean he wasn't still involved emotionally.

"Raine is a friend. And friendship is worth a lot. I'm glad for Daisy's sake that it's worked out this way. I'll always have feelings for Raine, since she's the mother of my child. However, if I'm interpreting the nuances of your question correctly, I should explain they're not *those* types of feelings. My turn now. How about you and your ex?

Any residual feelings there?"

The conversation sounded suspiciously as though they were testing the waters of romantic availability. Grace's impression was that when Slater Carson made up his mind about something, he moved forward as fast as possible and damn the torpedoes.

He wanted to sleep with her, and she'd entertained a fantasy or two involving him and a bed, with clothing tossed haphazardly all over the floor, but she wasn't at a stage in her life for anything serious in the way of relationships. And she'd never indulged in one-night stands or the emotional equivalent.

Inherent honesty made her say, "Hank and I aren't particularly friends, but we're not enemies, either. It wasn't an acrimonious divorce. I'd just come to the conclusion that the life I was living was how it was always going to be, which fell into the category of only on his terms. He's an attractive, intelligent, driven man, but regardless of whether it was his fault, or mine, I wasn't happy."

Slater didn't immediately comment, sitting relaxed in the saddle, hands loose. Then he asked, "Did he even *try* to make you happy?"

Unfortunately, she was able to answer the

189

question. "I doubt that he thought about it one way or the other."

"Well, I can promise you this. I would definitely think about it."

What the hell did that mean?

He was moving too fast.

Making her problems his problem, thinking about her too much for his peace of mind, enjoying the sight of Grace at the dinner table with his family . . .

Promising — he'd used the word *promise* for heaven's sake — that he'd think about her happiness.

Maybe he should be annoyed with himself for saying that, but at the moment he was a lot more annoyed with Drake and Mace.

Shameless flirtation was a mild description of their behavior. Oh, they were needling him, but that wasn't unexpected.

What *was* unexpected was that it seemed to be working.

Drake wasn't a guy who tended to be gregarious and chat during dinner. Mace, though, was in rare form, flashing his smile, and while they usually butted heads like bighorn rams on a mountainside, his two brothers played off each other seamlessly. In fact, you'd think they'd rehearsed their little performance. Grace knew exactly what was going on, too, and damned if she didn't go right along with it.

The whole thing was designed to get under his skin. Although he wasn't entirely sure what *her* motivations were. The entertainment value? Or because . . .

He put up with it until just before dessert. When Mace, wearing his most innocent expression, suggested that the vineyard was particularly beautiful in the moonlight if she'd like to take a walk after dinner, Slater gave an audible snort of disgust. Ryder, who'd demolished his meal as if he hadn't eaten in ten years or so, looked up from his plate with a grin.

Grace said sweetly that she'd love to see it.

Drake went into a coughing fit, he was laughing so hard, and even their mother, the traitor, hid her smile, not very successfully, behind her napkin.

"*I'll* be happy to show her," Slater informed his younger brother with a scowl that was only partially feigned. He was both amused by their antics and irritated that they bothered him when he knew full well they were only kidding around. "You two idiots can stop spoiling everyone's appetite by monopolizing the conversation."

"Just trying to be pleasant," Mace said,

pretending to be affronted. "Jeez, Slate. We have a guest and you've barely said two words to her."

"Because you've been babbling in her ear nonstop ever since we sat down."

"You have," Drake chimed in helpfully from across the table, as if he wasn't equally guilty.

"I was doing my best to spare you the embarrassment of saying something stupid," Mace snapped at his brother.

"I think you might want to focus on your own conversational skills. There's definite room for improvement."

Their mother murmured, looking at Grace, "Oh, here we go. I've been dealing with this for over thirty years. To think I encouraged them to learn how to talk."

It became the usual Carson circus after that. Slater thought with resignation that dinner at the ranch was a trial by fire experience. Survive it once, and there should be a medal awarded.

At least dessert was delicious as usual, some concoction of baked apples with a light flaky crust topped by homemade vanilla ice cream with a hint of cinnamon. As predicted, Harry gave Ryder a double helping, beaming with approval as he scarfed it down so fast that Grace said to the table at large, "I swear I feed him. I really do."

When she lifted her hand to brush a red-gold curl from her neck, he experienced a pang of hunger that had nothing to do with the meal.

He'd been trying all evening to keep his eyes off her but not succeeding. Everyone was aware of it, he was aware of it and she probably was, too.

Actually, a walk in the vineyard wasn't a bad idea. He was, as Tripp Galloway had once put it, a ranch kid, so strolling hand in hand through rows of grapevines wasn't his first thought when he entertained a pretty girl. He usually took her for a horseback ride instead. But it was a lovely evening, so why not take advantage of that? Slater certainly realized that Harry had outdone herself to impress Grace. His whole family seemed to be meddling, not that he was surprised. They all tended to weigh in on his life, although to be fair, that wasn't a one-sided arrangement. If he had advice for Drake or Mace, he spelled it out right then and there. They all worked that way. Up front and direct.

He was getting the signal that they approved of Grace.

Now, if she approved of *him* . . .

When they rose from the table, he automatically moved to clear the plates, as did Drake and Mace, a long-ingrained habit, and his mother and Ryder went off to the den to review his homework. Grace insisted on washing up whatever didn't go in the dishwasher, and he offered to dry, just so he could stand next to her.

Harry, supervising her domain with a sharp eye, gave Grace a knowing look. "Now, that's what I like to see. A big strong cowboy with a dishtowel in his hand. Slater Carson has never volunteered to dry dishes in his life."

"Hey, I've done my share right here at this very sink," he argued, but he kept his voice polite. Sassing Harry wasn't a mistake he'd made since he was about six years old.

Harry put her hands on her hips. "Yes, you have. Because I've always insisted you boys help out as a favor to your future wives. No man should ever think he's above scrubbing a pot when it needs doing. That isn't a woman's chore, it's a chore anyone with a pair of hands can do. I was pointing out that you never *volunteered* before now."

That was no doubt true. Usually he and Drake and Mace vamoosed quickly after dinner, not to go sit around or goof off, but because the livestock needed to be checked, and one or another of them rode down to secure the main gate for the night.

Grace listened to the exchange with a faint smile, finishing up the last pan and handing it over. He took it, his return smile rather sheepish. "It's possible she could be right."

"Hmph. *Possible?*" Harry went back into the dining room, no doubt to check everything was cleaned and tidied to her exacting standards.

Grace raised her brows. "I'm flattered you were trying to impress me."

"Did it work?" He tried for an air of boyish hopefulness but had no idea if he'd achieved it.

"Maybe." She dried her hands and frowned. "Are you sure I shouldn't sit in on Ryder's homework discussion?"

"Positive." He could say that with conviction, and it had nothing to do with looking forward to their moonlight stroll. "My mother said he's doing better already, but she can tell he's worried he'll disappoint you. With her, he can simply listen to what she has to say and fix the problem, ask questions and so on, because he isn't nearly as concerned about what she thinks of him. With you, when he makes a mistake, he sees it as a failure."

"I have *never* tried to make him feel like a

failure." Her expression reflected her dismay.

"Nope, I'm sure you've done just the opposite." Slater was positive of that. "But think about it, Grace. You're the most important person in his life right now. In fact, you're the *only* important person in his life right now. You can drop in on Ryder and my mom if you want, but I'd leave it be. If there's one thing I can say for her, it's that she understands how the minds of young boys work."

"She seems wonderful."

"I'm not exactly impartial, but she is mighty special to all of us." He took Grace's hand. "Unless you'd prefer either of my annoying brothers, I'd be happy to show you the vineyard by moonlight. Or the barn, a field full of cattle, the rusty skeleton of an old tractor my father insisted we keep because his grandfather gave it to him . . ."

She was laughing now, shaking her head. "As romantic as it sounds, I think I'll skip the scenic tractor tour. The vineyard will be lovely."

Maybe he owed Mace one, for letting him do the honors by conducting the tour. Slater guided her toward the doorway. "I'm an excellent tour guide. You won't be disappointed."

"I'm afraid you're right."

CHAPTER ELEVEN

Once they reached the vineyard, Slater held Grace's hand again.

His fingers entwined with hers, his grasp light but firm, and the effect was decidedly romantic. When he'd reached over, she had to admit to being surprised because it was such a simple gesture from a man she suspected was more passionate than sentimental. However, having seen him with his gregarious family, she was getting a better sense of him as a person. Slater might be able to scorch a woman right down to the tips of her toes with a kiss, but his talents didn't end there.

She wasn't sure if he was good or bad for her at this time in her life, but she *liked* him.

The night sky was speckled with stars, and the moon had risen above the mountains, spreading a soft glow over the landscape. A low wail came from a distance, far enough away that it merely gave her goose bumps.

"Wolf," Slater confirmed, sounding pragmatic. "Drake is having some problems with our stock, and we're wondering if they're the issue."

They'd driven to the vineyard in his truck, since it was a few miles from the house, and he'd parked by the building she'd seen online. It was even more striking, even more attractive, than the photographs had suggested. Grace murmured admiringly, impressed by its rustic elegance. She wasn't immune, either, when Slater continued to hold her hand as he led her toward a shaded path between the vines.

"Mace actually should probably be here to explain what's what, but excuse me if I wasn't in the mood for a third wheel who can be a smart-ass now and then. I exaggerated my tour guide skills. I can't tell a merlot vine from a weed. It's a vineyard. Now you know as much as I do." He paused. "Considering your job, you probably know more."

Grace appreciated his sense of humor. "You and your brothers all seem very close." It was beyond obvious that he loved his family.

His fingers tightened on hers. "Despite their various quirks, I guess we are. And I'm just as guilty as they are on that count, having my share of quirks, I mean. If you're looking for a nine-to-five guy who wants meat loaf every Monday night, his last name isn't Carson. At least not around here, it isn't."

She wasn't looking for *any* sort of man, period. On the other hand, there he was, walking next to her, tall in the moonlight, his features shadowed, gazing down at her as if waiting for a response.

"You do all seem very different, but similar in certain ways, too." A neutral remark seemed the safest. Grace felt some conflicting emotions at the moment. She wanted to run as far and fast as possible, but at the same time, she was drawn to him. He was an artist and yet a cowboy, a history scholar who could handle a spirited horse effortlessly, and he might just have the world's sexiest smile . . .

"I agree. Let's set aside the Carson bunch for a bit, shall we? I like how we are now, just you and me. Between their nosiness and Ryder being your responsibility, moments like this will be hard to come by."

Moments like this? He spoke as if there were plans for future involvement.

And he also had a point. Privacy was virtually impossible unless, as he'd suggested, they went somewhere together. "Is that a presumption on your part — that I want time alone with you?"

The breeze ruffled his dark hair and he stopped walking and pulled her into his arms. "Yes, ma'am. Don't you?"

It wasn't as if she didn't know a romantic walk was going to lead to a passionate kiss. His hunger came through clearly, and yet the embrace was gentle, appropriate to the setting, and Grace might have acted more urgent, threading her fingers through his hair and responding in a way he couldn't fail to interpret.

This was one dangerous man.

"I don't really want this." She didn't mean to just say it like that.

"Me, neither." His smile was rueful.

"If neither of us wants it, why are we doing this?"

His arms tightened. "Can't help it?" he suggested.

"Don't say that." She pushed away from him and he let her go. She walked over to the edge of the vines and took a huge breath. "I don't *want* to fall in love with you."

She could not believe she'd just used the word *love*.

Slater had obviously followed her, because when he spoke again, his breath was warm against the nape of her neck as he lifted her hair and kissed that sensitive spot, making her shiver. "Mace and I recently had a discussion on this topic. Our consensus was that some things are beyond our control."

That could be true, she thought as she turned in his arms and rested her forehead against his chest, letting out an exasperated sigh. "It's too complicated."

"You've got that right."

"Stop laughing about it." She smacked his shoulder with her fist, but she was laughing, too.

"You're cute when you're mad, which is a good thing."

"Are you saying I'm ill-tempered?" She wished she had a *reason* to get mad. Now if he insulted her . . .

Predictably, he didn't cooperate.

"I'm saying the fire isn't all in your hair, Ms. Emery." His eyes were amused as they met hers. "But you know what? I find that irresistible, although I haven't quite figured out why."

"I haven't figured it out, either."

"In other words, you find me irresistible, too."

The man was way too full of himself. The worst part was that he was right. She contemplated smacking his shoulder again, but he homed in on that impulse and caught her wrist. His drawl was low and exaggerated. "No, you don't, sweetheart. Not unless you want me to retaliate like this."

The kiss was devastating. A thrill spiraled in the pit of her stomach, and Grace came to the conclusion that he could retaliate like *this* all he wanted.

"The office," he whispered against her mouth, holding her so close she could feel the tension in his body.

"What?" she asked, her heart racing. She had no idea what he was talking about.

"I think it's appropriate, since you and I have some *very* unfinished business."

No permission asked, he simply picked her up and started walking toward the old bunkhouse, ignoring her mutter of protest at his assumption that he could just carry her off.

Did it matter that she probably would've said, *Yes, please do, and hurry.*

She wasn't sure, but the dramatic gesture worked for two reasons, one of them being the *hurry* part. Slater Carson seemed like a man on a mission. Soft leaves brushed her arms as they went past the neat rows of vines, and she should've demanded he set her down, since there was nothing wrong with her own two feet.

Maybe she'd always been more of a sucker for romance novels than she'd realized because she was so susceptible to the grand gesture. If it even was. She suspected he was just being efficient in that cowboy way, ready to go for what he wanted as quickly as possible.

Whether or not she agreed with that approach, she wasn't being given a chance to argue.

Not that she would have, anyway.

Instead, she slid her arm around his neck and kissed the patch of skin exposed by the open collar of his shirt, feeling rewarded when he groaned. He muttered, "If you think I need encouragement like that, you'd be dead wrong, sweetheart. Hang on, I might break into a run at any moment."

On a scale of one to ten, his level of desire for the woman in his arms was about a thousand.

Slater had to set her down so he could fumble with the handle to open the old bunkhouse door. He felt like a teenager, refusing to let her go completely. Since the very first time he'd laid eyes on Grace, he'd had this moment in the back of his mind.

On the negative side, he was fairly sure he was going to skip foreplay. On the positive end, it seemed she might be just fine with that scenario. He doubted she needed to be coaxed and tenderly urged to respond, but could match him easily when it came to passion. She was confident in an unassuming way, and he found that characteristic almost as tantalizing as her physical beauty.

The old bunkhouse had once been a playground for him and his brothers, a place to pretend they were old-style cowhands, riding the range, herding cattle . . . until they got old enough to actually herd cattle and discovered that it was damned hard work.

Still, he remembered with nostalgic fondness how the place used to look. His mother had done a great job of preserving its Old West charm and yet making it an inviting venue for people to sit and sample Mountain Vineyard wines. Small wooden tables and high stools were arranged around the room. Racks of different bottles stood behind the counter, decorative barrels were placed here and there and soft lighting complemented the whole effect. The wooden floor had been polished to a high sheen, and the walls were rough, but that was intentional. A painting she'd done herself, a view of the Tetons, hung on one wall. Blythe Carson had an artistic soul, no doubt about it.

Grace looked around approvingly when he flipped on the lights. "Our guests will love this."

He appreciated her enthusiasm, but the only thing on his mind was that they were alone, and Mace's office had a very convenient daybed his brother used now and then when he worked a long day and decided to spend the night. He hovered over his precious vines as if they were his children, and any turn in the weather sent him into a tailspin.

Thank goodness, no frost in the forecast. He loved his brother despite his sometimes annoying sense of humor, but Mace was unwelcome at the moment. This was a party of two.

"Back here." He urged Grace toward the office. It wasn't much more than a few filing cabinets, a desk with a computer, a big beautiful window and that simple daybed. Mace and Drake had a lot more in common than they'd care to admit. Nature, no frills, a single-minded focus on their jobs . . . Okay, maybe all *three* of them had more in common than they realized. He was like that, too.

Right now his goal was to have Grace's clothes on the floor by the plain Craftsman-style bed, his piled next to hers. He wanted her warm and naked against him, wanted to touch all that long, luscious vibrant hair and every other inch of her. And if she preferred to call the shots, Slater doubted she'd disappoint him.

"I see now," she murmured as she caught sight of the bed. "Good idea. We really need to do this, you and I. Get it off the table — if you'll forgive the corporate cliché. Then we can figure out the rest of it."

Maybe he could've thought of some clever reply but she started to unfasten her blouse.

One slow button at a time. She knew he was riveted, and *he* knew *she* wanted him, too, and he could swear there was no place on earth he'd rather be than this little vineyard office.

"I don't even need to see your body," he said, his voice hoarse. "I've dreamt about it enough times, it's like a reel of film running in my head."

That was filed under *Way Too Honest.* Grace unsnapped the front closure on her bra. "Then let's test the limits of your imagination."

Her bra tumbled to the floor.

His imagination was good, he decided, but obviously not *that* good. It didn't nearly do her justice. Her breasts were full and firm, and his mouth went dry as her fingers moved to the top button on her jeans. The odd thing was that she was shy; he could sense it, and it didn't surprise him. She was unafraid, of course; she had no cause to be afraid of him — he'd never given her one and never would. And yet, despite her self-confidence, there was an uncertainty in her eyes that spoke volumes. If he had to guess, he'd say the problem had to do with her physical appearance, but not for the usual reasons. Any woman who looked like Grace would wonder if she was being pursued only because of her appearance.

Slater stepped toward her, meeting her eyes. "I'm not going to deny that I've got some serious lust going on. I think you saw that the night we met. But I want you to know that I think you're beautiful, and not just in this way —" he ran a finger lightly over the curve of one bared breast and then rested his palm between them, over her heart "— but here, too. You like to help people, not because it's your duty, but because you genuinely want to. That's rare and special. So are you."

Her eyes were luminous but her voice was tart with admonishment. "I thought I made myself clear earlier, so don't do that to me, Carson. I was counting on you just wanting to get me naked."

That was true; she'd stated with emphasis that she didn't want to fall in love with him. Well, too bad. If they were both on a sinking ship, it was every man — or woman — for himself. Or herself.

He said softly, "Take out the *just* and you've got it right."

"Hmm, you're one smooth-talking cowboy who also happens to be wearing way too many clothes." She tugged his shirt free of his jeans and tackled the buttons with vigor.

Their discussion was clearly over. He doubted he could put two words together, anyway, when she ran an exploratory hand over his bare chest. All the blood in his brain migrated south.

Slater touched her hair, marveling at its softness and silky texture. "I believe you mentioned naked?"

A heart-stopping moment later, he discovered that she wore some sort of wispy lace that was supposed to pass for underwear, and — not that he'd had any doubts — she was a true redhead. He shucked off his jeans and boots so fast he could probably win a prize and tumbled her to the bed. They fell together, and then he was exploring her body with purpose, learning every plane and curve, taking in each sigh and gasp, urgent but not in a hurry. This was something he wanted to remember with vivid clarity. Their first time together. He wasn't eighteen anymore, not by a long shot, but he felt the same sense of wonder he'd experienced back then. He'd have to sort that out later, much later, when Grace wasn't murmuring his name and touching him, testing the length of him with curious fingers in a way that took his self-control and dumped it right out the window.

He found the condoms he'd shoved in his pocket almost as an afterthought. More children would be fine with him — eventually — because his daughter enriched his life. But that was a discussion he and Grace needed to have well ahead of time.

Maybe before he asked her to marry him.

That wayward concept almost gave him pause, but her hands were pressed to the small of his back, and those gorgeous breasts were taut against his chest . . . He couldn't have stopped if he'd wanted to, and he sure as hell *didn't* want to.

Somehow he managed to roll on the condom, and then he sank into her, their breath mingling in a mutual exhalation of pleasure. She lifted her hips in unspoken acceptance, her lashes drifting down as she closed her eyes.

Not him. He watched her as he began to move, fascinated by how her expression changed as he made love to her, going from dreamy to intense as her climax began to build, her inner muscles tightening around him, her foot rubbing his calf, the slight rasp of her nails arousing.

Beautiful. It was a word that always seemed to apply to Grace, but never so much as now. She arched and clung to him, her entire body trembling, and her cry of release was like a lit match to dry tinder, and he went up in the same inferno.

The aftermath was silent except for their rapid breathing until Slater finally raised his head. "I think it's off the table now."

Grace laughed and that was interesting, considering their intimate position. "I'd say that and then some."

He nuzzled her neck. "Hmm, can we put it back on the table again sometime soon?"

She stretched luxuriantly beneath him, deliberately teasing. "Depends on you, doesn't it?"

"Oh, there's a challenge if I ever heard one." Slater grinned, but then he sobered and traced the contours of her shoulder. "We really started something here, didn't we?"

She didn't evade the question. "I'm afraid that's true."

CHAPTER TWELVE

When Grace opened her eyes she was disoriented for only a few seconds. All her law enforcement training might be responsible, but she realized quickly that while the surroundings weren't familiar, she knew where she was. Knew that was Slater with his arm draped over her, and that the moonlight slanting through the window when she dozed off had given way to a faint hint of dawn.

The bed was too small to share with Slater, whose rangy body took up almost the entire space. He lay sprawled in a relaxed pose next to her, breathing evenly. Grace rose up on one elbow and watched him, resigned to the fact that their early-morning return to the ranch house would be duly noted and the correct conclusions reached. A walk of shame would ensue when she went back wearing the same clothes as she had the night before. Facing his family — and Ryder — with some semblance of dignity would be a challenge, to put it mildly.

Why did she have the feeling Slater would just shrug it off, tell her to not worry about it?

She started to move away, but to her surprise the arm around her waist instantly tightened. He mumbled into the pillow, "No you don't. We haven't even said good morning."

It was impossible not to object. "You were asleep. I didn't want to wake you."

"I wasn't asleep."

"I believe I heard a snore."

"I don't snore." He turned over and sent her a mock glare that she somehow found irresistible — despite having slept on the edge of a bed all night . . .

"People never admit they snore," she pointed out, and if they'd been under the sheets, she would have pulled the top one up in maidenly modesty. He'd kept her warm through the night, and it appeared he wasn't letting her go quite yet.

That lazy smile surfaced. "Say it after me. *Good morning.* It's a great way to start your day."

No one should wake up looking so sexy with that shadow of a beard and disheveled hair. But he did, damn him. "Good morning." To her relief she sounded composed when she was anything but.

The night before had definitely rattled her.

He kissed her shoulder. "See? Not so difficult, is it? I take it you're having some morning-after regrets."

"No." That was honest. No regrets, but she was testing her level of comfort with the idea — the possibility — of emotional involvement. Her divorce had been a less than pleasant decision. Hank hadn't left her brokenhearted, but the experience did shake her faith in her own judgment, especially about men.

Yet, here she was.

"It's still early," she said, pulling free and searching for her clothes. "I'd prefer that Ryder didn't find out we never went back to the ranch house. This is the wrong time in his life to give him the impression that casual sex is acceptable."

"Casual?" Slater repeated. He sat up to swing his legs over the edge of the bed. The smile had disappeared. "Thanks. But I would've described it differently."

She slipped on her underwear and stepped into her jeans. "I said *impression.* I'm sure he's noticed we're attracted to each other — well, I know he has — but I don't want him to think that's all it takes."

Oh man, she'd bungled that one, judging by Slater's expression. Hastily, she tried to rectify her mistake, but it was hard to be quick-thinking when her fingers were shaking and she was having trouble with the clasp on her bra. "I meant neither of us really knows where this is going."

His scowl told her that the attempt hadn't helped. He said softly, "Because you don't want to fall in love with me."

It wasn't as if she didn't have failings, but a lack of honesty wasn't one of them. She bent down to pick up her blouse. "That's one hundred percent correct. The only time in my life I was seriously involved with someone, I didn't see the warning signs posted along the road I was traveling. Actually, it isn't you I don't trust, it's me."

"Oh, great. Now I'm getting the old 'it isn't you, it's me' speech?"

At least there was a hint of humor in his voice, so maybe he *was* getting the picture. She ran her fingers through her hair, trying to tame it a little, which was no doubt a futile endeavor. She gave a theatrical sigh, trying to lighten the moment. "Don't worry, we're still going steady. For now. As long as you behave."

"*Going steady?* What? Are we in high

school?"

She decided to ignore that as he pulled on his jeans and then his boots, his actions efficient and unhurried. "You heard me. It's all about good behavior."

"Hmm. Why am I getting the impression that you're the one making all the rules? Last I checked, you and I were both consenting, responsible adults. Ryder is bright enough to realize that. As for me behaving, depends on your definition. I think mine might not be the same as yours. So I wouldn't count on that if you're talking about last night because I'm expecting more of the same behavior, whether you call it good or bad — from both of us."

That promise, made with a searing look in those oh-so-blue eyes that went right through her, was effective. Grace couldn't even find a reply.

They drove back to the house without speaking. The silence wasn't uncomfortable, more like the quiet after a storm had blown through. Grace glanced at him once or twice, but Slater was preoccupied and distant. That wasn't what she wanted, but she wasn't sure just *what* she wanted in the first place.

To spend another night locked in his arms, skin to skin?

Yes.

To have to decide what she should do next?

No.

One of the problems with life, she thought morosely, was that it was full of decisions. You made some smart choices and some that weren't but it seemed to be the bad ones that stood out.

Maybe she shouldn't even worry about this relationship getting serious. Slater, after all, was in his midthirties and he'd never married, so he might not be interested in anything serious, anyway.

Problem solved.

Slater parked in what seemed to be his designated spot by the garage as the first rays of the rising sun swept over the mountains, bathing the peaks with gold. Any illusions she might have entertained about slipping into the house unnoticed were banished when they met Drake coming through the front door onto the veranda, a cup of coffee in his hand. His grin was quick, but all he said was a polite "Nice morning, isn't it?"

"Supposed to be a sunny day," Slater replied just as pleasantly, although there was a warning in his tone that shouted, *Don't say one word about us being gone all night.*

Drake was wise enough to heed it. Grace knew she was blushing, her hair more than a little mussed, but he pretended to not notice. He said blandly, "Harry's in there cooking up a storm as usual. We're moving cattle today, so I'm headed back out. I just needed some real coffee, not that black poison Red makes that could make grown men cry. If you feel like helping out later, Showbiz, we could use an extra hand. Oh, by the way, thanks. Mace owes me another twenty bucks. See you later, Grace."

He went down the steps, the two German shepherds that seemed to follow him everywhere directly behind. Grace sent Slater a perplexed frown, but all he did was hold the door for her and mutter, "Individually they border on irritating at times. Together my brothers can be downright insufferable. Just ignore them. It's always worked for me."

Pursuing whatever had prompted that observation didn't seem like a good idea. Grace could make an educated guess, anyway. "Men in general can be insufferable," she said loftily as she walked past him.

"You didn't think so last night."

That she couldn't deny.

She threw a look over her shoulder. "Don't get smug, Carson."

He said serenely, "I wouldn't dream of it.

219

Damn, it smells good in here, but then it generally does. Harry makes some sort of fruit bread that's so delicious it should be against the law. I swear I don't even know what kind of fruit she puts in it, and I don't care. I've never asked because it's impolite to talk with your mouth full."

It did smell good, she had to admit. She was hungry, but she needed a shower and change of clothes first, so she could at least pretend her life wasn't topsy-turvy. "Can you please point me toward my room?" He'd shown it to her, deposited her overnight bag there, but last night had apparently affected her memory.

"Of course. I believe when we met I told you this place is like a maze." He escorted her down a hall, turned right and — just her luck — they met his mother. Her hair was neatly pulled back, and she wore crisp white Capri pants and a light blue smocked top, a gold bracelet on her wrist. Tactfully, Blythe Carson said, "Hello, you two. Harry's making your favorite bread, Slater. I'm off to grab a slice before you get your hands on it. See you later."

She breezed down the hall, not looking back.

Slater was laughing when he indicated a door. "Here's some advice. Never play

220

poker for money. I think you might have the most expressive face I've ever seen. Grace, once again, and you've pointed this out, you and I *aren't* high school kids. My mother isn't going to faint from shock if she draws the conclusion that we spent the night together."

"We aren't married."

Horror swept over her. The man had a habit of making her blurt out ridiculous things. Things she'd never, ever say if she'd thought about them first. Earlier she'd mentioned love and he hadn't forgotten it, either, and now she'd mentioned marriage.

What was wrong with her? Getting married again was the last-place item on her to-do list. Right down there vying with root canals or getting frostbite.

Slater rubbed his lean jaw and although she was, according to him, an open book, she couldn't tell anything from his expression. He just said, "No, we aren't. I didn't realize you were an old-fashioned girl."

"Hardly a girl."

"I'd swear to that in a court of law. Definitely a woman."

Maybe it could be termed beating a hasty retreat — or more likely the coward's way out — but she yanked open the door of the room. "I'll see you at breakfast."

■ ■ ■ ■

When you were dealing with a skittish horse, you calmed it down with a soft tone and a gentle touch.

Same technique for a skittish woman. At least that had always been old Red's advice. And he'd certainly had a happy marriage . . .

Except, good advice or not, Slater had the feeling now was not the time to do anything except give Grace some breathing room. He refused to acknowledge one speck of regret about their night together, because she was right; they'd both needed to get past the physical part to find out if there was more.

There was. Ironically, that made it even more complicated. In his experience, women were always ready to get serious faster than a man, although Grace was an exception to that rule.

As he drove back to the condo, he chatted with Ryder instead of talking to her, which might be a good plan or might not. He wasn't sure how else to handle it. He asked Ryder how the job was going.

"Red's really cool," the boy informed him from the backseat. "At first I thought he was kind of mean, but that ain't the way the cow ate the cabbage."

Despite his personal dilemma, Slater started laughing so hard he almost went off the road. "What?"

"It means that ain't the truth."

Slater saw Grace was laughing now, too, her hand held against her mouth. He said, "I know what it means because he's been using that expression my entire life. I'm just surprised to hear *you* say it, that's all. Plus, maybe you shouldn't be picking up words like *ain't*. Red does old cowboy speak with the best of 'em. I got into trouble at school once when I repeated something he said — I won't tell you what — without knowing what it meant. My mother lectured me, and then she lit into him. Almost thirty years later, he hasn't said it in front of me again."

In the rearview mirror, Ryder looked sheepish. "I didn't think of that. He does say some funny things."

"I'm sure most of what he says is perfectly okay," Grace inserted into the conversation, "but maybe you should listen to Slater. I'd just as soon skip more calls from the school. How's the homework going?"

As someone who was once a fourteen-year-old boy, Slater winced. She could still do cop well enough. Question or interrogation?

Ryder's pose went from relaxed to tense,

223

and his reply was surly. "Fine."

"I want you to keep me in the loop."

"There is no loop, Grace. I get homework and I'm doing it."

Luckily, she was smart enough to understand she'd pushed the limit. After a moment she said lightly, "If that's the way the cow ate the cabbage, I'm very proud of you."

Good save. "My mother, she's a tough boss, eh?" Slater said. "Makes Red look like a fairy godmother in comparison. He'll just call you a no-account, wet-behind-the-ears kid with straw for brains. She'll give you that *look.* If you haven't seen it yet, I can't describe it, but I still get it now and then."

Actually, he'd gotten a similar one that morning, when he and Grace weren't talking at breakfast and she'd leveled it in his direction. *What have you done to upset her?*

Words weren't necessary after the *look.*

The answer to her unspoken question was . . . No idea. No clue. He'd shrugged and at least known he was telling the truth with his body language.

"Grace can do it, too," Ryder informed him, resting an elbow on his knee and his chin on a fist. "So I'm familiar with it."

"Like nagging without words."

Grace bristled. "As if guys don't nag —

224

you just do it in a different way."

She had a point. He said to Ryder, "I figure the Seahawks and maybe Green Bay. Wisconsin is looking good so far."

The kid was quick. "I don't know. Denver could do it."

Grace surprised them both. "Oh, please! What about the Colts?" Then, defensively, when they were both quiet, she added, "Come on. I worked with men for years."

It broke the tension.

But that tension returned tenfold when they pulled into the driveway. On the front doorstep sat a vase of dead flowers. Slater didn't get it until Grace said calmly, "Those came from the desk in my office. I wondered when they went missing a few days ago. Thought it could be housekeeping. I'm glad he didn't break the vase. It belonged to my aunt. Ryder, let's go check on Bonaparte."

The kid about knocked the door off the truck trying to get out, but Slater had already spotted a pair of unwinking green eyes in the bushes. "Whoa, he's okay. He's right there beneath the window under the hedge."

Grace looked immeasurably relieved and briefly rested her head against the back of the seat, watching as Ryder dashed up and knelt by the concealing bush, the cat coming out cautiously to greet him. Her voice quavered. "I value the vase, but if it came to cat or vase, the vase would lose. Ryder adores him."

"This guy is trying to spook you," Slater said between clenched teeth. "My buddy Spence and I can go have a little chat with him. What's his address?"

"I can't give it to you, Slater. I was his boss. That's disclosing personal information without a court order. There's no solid evidence he's committed a crime."

She was right, but of course she'd know what she was talking about. When it came to the legal aspects of the situation, he had to bow to her expertise. But when it came to wanting to protect her, he didn't bow to anything except his own instincts. He wasn't unworldly, and quite frankly, studying the Old West provided him with a good source of information about how the world worked. Back when there was no law west of the Pecos, this wasn't a safe place to be. Women were vulnerable, and there were men who protected them, and men who tried to take advantage.

Fact of life. One that hadn't changed as much as it should have . . .

Second fact. Grace didn't need him rushing in on a white charger — Heck didn't qualify, anyway — but he was really bothered by the pettiness of this guy's actions. She wasn't quite as unconcerned as she seemed. "But you do feel threatened."

"Uneasy."

"Let me cut to the chase here, to use an old film expression. I'm not letting you stay here alone. There's safety in numbers."

When she'd come to breakfast she'd resembled a college co-ed in her tan skirt and a yellow sweater that emphasized what he knew firsthand to be the world's shapeliest breasts. Mace had sure as hell noticed, and Slater had to suppress the urge to punch his brother in the nose over that appreciative stare. He didn't know when he'd developed this possessive streak a mile wide, but at the moment it was jostling for position with a protective streak about the same size. Grace was looking at him as if he'd lost his mind. "Did you just hear yourself? I don't think you have the power or the right to *let* me or *not let* me do anything."

Maybe this was a good time to get out of the truck. He opened his door. "That came off as undiplomatic. What I meant was now I'll be worried 24/7, and I think you should be sensitive to my tender feelings. Stress is proven to be detrimental to a person's health."

"Very funny, Carson." He started to walk around to open her door, but she beat him to it, probably to prove a point. Her expression softened as she slid out of the truck and straightened her skirt. "But the sentiment is appreciated. Look how worried I was about Ryder. That's not going to go away until this is over. The vase is theft, but I suppose he could claim he returned it *if* I could ever prove he took it in the first place."

"Don't you have security cameras?"

"Yes, and he knows where every single one is. There's a reason he's not in jail. He's a thief, but a pretty smart one."

"Can you get a restraining order?" He watched Ryder and the cat with somber eyes. He didn't care what Grace had to say about it, if someone hurt that cat to hurt her and consequently Ryder, he wouldn't sit still for one second. Obviously, it had occurred to her that the possibility was there. Besides, cruelty to animals in any guise, for any screwed-up reason, was intolerable.

"The problem with restraining orders is that until they're violated, they mean nothing more than telling the person to stay away from you. I'd still have to catch him, anyway. Yes, the scratch on my car and the flat tires are destruction of personal property, but as I've said more than once, I can't prove anything, and he hasn't overtly threatened me in any way." She was right — about that and about the fact that he couldn't tell her what to do. He picked up the vase. "I can't believe I'm saying this, but I'll be glad when your ex-husband gets here. Let's go toss these flowers in the trash and I'll look around, just in case."

Chapter Thirteen

He insisted on sleeping on her couch.

Men.

Slater had gone back to the ranch and then appeared out of the blue just before dinner, carrying burgers from Bad Billy's, along with thigh-fattening onion rings, coleslaw and some brownies that practically made her faint with pleasure. He refused to take no for an answer about spending the night — knew without a word being said that her bedroom was out of the question because Ryder's room was directly across the hall. After a lingering kiss good-night, he settled on the sofa.

When Grace got up in the morning to tiptoe to the coffeemaker, Slater was in what seemed like a cramped position, his body too long for the sofa, one arm behind his head. And he was wrong, he did snore. It wasn't loud or obnoxious, just a gentle but audible respiration.

She found it cute. Go figure.

Oddly, she found it comforting as she brewed a cup of coffee with a hint of caramel flavoring and stirred in some milk. That was when her uninvited guest flopped over, made an inarticulate sound, then opened his eyes. "Is that coffee I smell?"

"Plain?" She suspected he was a just-black-coffee sort of man.

"Yes. Put something in it and I'll get downright cranky." He ran his fingers through his hair and sat up.

"We can't have that," Grace said drily, deliberately selecting the pink mug Ryder had given her for Mother's Day. It had little red hearts all over it and when she brewed Slater a cup — she loved her fancy coffee-maker — and went to hand it to him, she got her morning laugh from the look on his face. She said sweetly, "Black, just the way you like it."

He eyed the cup dubiously. "I'm not sure a real man can drink out of this. I may have to go ride a bull later today or lasso a mountain lion or something like that to renew my masculinity card."

He didn't have to worry about that. The delicate cup emphasized the sinewy strength of his hand, and although she'd been trying to tease him, the joke had backfired. At the

231

moment she wanted nothing more than to yank that cup out of his hand, lead him into her bedroom and have a repeat performance of the other night at the vineyard. She murmured, "If you need someone to vouch for you about the male thing, I certainly can. That aside, since I assume all was quiet, you aren't planning to sleep on an uncomfortable couch every night until Hank gets here, are you? He's in Washington and he didn't give me a time frame, which isn't unusual for him. He could walk through that door two minutes from now, or he could arrive in a few weeks. Or not at all, which is always a possibility. If there's a new crisis of some kind and he's needed, he goes, whether he's on leave or not."

"For Ryder's sake, I hope *that* doesn't happen. Do you mind, since I'm already here, if I take a look at the basement at the resort today? I'm getting positive feedback on the project. Once a proposal flies, things happen fast, so I might as well start and see what we have to work with from that angle."

He'd just dodged her question.

She had to privately acknowledge that she liked him there, in her comfortable living room, sipping coffee from that very feminine pink mug. "Go ahead. I didn't investigate too far but —"

"Due to the scary spider," he interjected, his mouth twitching. He seemed to be holding back a smile.

She ignored the interruption. "There are a lot of boxes down there, and they aren't properly labeled, unless you consider *miscellaneous* to be a helpful category. I opened a few of them here and there —"

"Until the scary spider scurried by." He couldn't seem to resist. He grinned openly this time, looking rumpled and delicious in a white T-shirt and his faded jeans, bare feet on the floor.

"Hey, I know some self-defense moves that can drop a grown man in about two seconds, Carson. Just a word of warning." Grace glanced at the clock and set down her cup. "Stop by my office and you can get the keys. Right now I have to go to work. I'd normally leave Ryder a note, but please remind him not to miss the bus, since I don't have a car to drive him to school if he does."

"You aren't walking alone, Grace. Let me take you to work, and then I'll drive Ryder to school." He shuddered in mock fear. "Don't make me face the wrath of Blythe Carson for not taking care of you."

She wanted to protest that she didn't *need* anyone to take care of her. Hank certainly hadn't — when they'd gotten married she'd taken care of *his* life, not the other way around. Considering her words, she responded carefully. "I'm having a hard time figuring out how to react to your approach. You're high-handed, no doubt about that, cowboy. Let's put it this way — if I need your help, I promise to ask for it. Do we have a deal? In the meantime, I'm walking to work. I'm not scared of David Reinhart. But I'd appreciate it if you'd drive Ryder to school and make sure Bonaparte's inside before you head over to the resort."

He nodded. "A compromise. Okay, done. Can we have lunch? Since I'll be there and all."

"I'm only going to have a salad after that huge dinner last night," she replied, reaching for her purse with a smile. "But there's a balcony off my office, so if I'm free, we can sit out there. At least it's private. Say hi to the spiders for me."

She walked to the resort in a good mood, but that was tossed out the window as soon as she saw Meg with an anxious look on her face, waiting in her office.

"What?" she asked, feeling her shoulders sag, instantly regretting that she hadn't given her assistant a friendlier greeting. "I meant hello, hi, how are you? But I'm guessing you have something to tell me that I don't want to hear, so forgive me for not being more cordial. What's going on?"

"Someone hacked into our system and compromised your email. I changed the password a few minutes ago."

Grace wanted to scream, but that would be counterproductive, so she smiled grimly instead. "What did he do?" She was one hundred percent convinced that the damage had been done by one person with a vendetta. One person named David Reinhart.

Meg handed her a sheaf of printouts, her expression very somber although she was usually so upbeat. "Sent out a load of emails canceling reservations, saying the resort was in financial trouble and being closed."

Grace swore, and just managed not to slam the door as anger surged through her. "I'm getting ticked off," she muttered. "Fat lot of good Slater did sleeping on my couch last night, even though his heart was in the right place."

"Slater Carson slept on your couch last night?" Meg looked girlishly intrigued despite her unhappiness. "Are you *kidding*?"

Oops, shouldn't have said that. Oh, well.

Grace went around to her desk, knowing that she needed to involve the owner. This was getting more serious. "He was worried about me. It was nice of him. He and Ryder have hit it off in a father/son sort of way. Oh, he'll be here later to look at some of the old hotel memorabilia in the basement. If anyone asks, he has my permission. Now, let me see if I can unravel this mess."

Most of her morning later, she'd waded through the worst of it, spent time on the phone with their technical support team and talked briefly with George Landers about the problem. He blithely thanked her for letting him know and said he was sure she could take care of the situation. Unfortunately, the IT people couldn't work out who'd hacked into the resort computer system. This guy was good, they told her — which, of course, she already knew — but they planned to keep on trying.

Meanwhile, Slater had arrived and waved at her from the office door. Meg, looking dreamy-eyed, had handed over the basement keys.

Grace was in the middle of contacting the guests whose reservations had been canceled when someone said, "I hope shrimp salad is okay. The chef said it's what you usually order."

At the sound of that smooth drawl, Grace looked up, still preoccupied, still inwardly

236

fuming, to see Slater stroll into her office, holding two of the fancy bags from the spa restaurant. A glance at the computer screen told her it was well past noon.

She definitely needed a break. She clicked off the screen. "That's great. Thanks."

"You're still not going to talk to Spence Hogan about this?"

Meg evidently had a big mouth, or maybe it was just that she was obviously starstruck by the handsome Mr. Carson, aka Showbiz.

Grace didn't blame her. Even with a smudge on his cheek from all those dusty boxes, he was male cover-model material. "I might," she admitted. "But he's going to tell me what I've told you already. That without proof there's nothing he can do except talk to David, warn him that he's a suspect in a series of minor incidents. Although this morning didn't feel all that minor to me. I had other things to do besides putting out his malicious fires."

He walked away from her, out toward the little balcony. His stride was deceptively leisurely, but his shoulders were tense. "I wish you'd let me handle it, Grace. I know you won't, so why don't we just have a civil lunch."

He was burning up, he was so furious, but

she didn't want him to intervene. So the overwhelming need to rescue Grace had to be tucked away into a file labeled *Never Going to Happen.*

It was possible that her fresh-faced, sweet young assistant could be persuaded to give up the man's address, but that might get Meg in trouble with her fiery boss. He'd looked David Reinhart up online; all he'd been able to dig up was a postal box. That wasn't surprising for a thief and a coward, and as far as Slater was concerned, provided further proof that Reinhart might just quit playing his games and do something truly harmful. In any case, the man *wanted* to make it difficult to track him down.

The weather had grown cooler and Grace slipped on a dark blue cardigan, the light breeze teasing her hair. The balcony was only big enough to hold a café table and two chairs, a single potted plant in the corner. Small though it was, the mountain view couldn't be any more beautiful. He could tell that she appreciated this private corner, a place to escape, to refresh and recharge, since she worked such long hours. He did, too, whenever a project got rolling, so a life together would be challenging from a logistical standpoint.

Whoa, there! Slow down.

"This looks delicious," she said as she opened the fancy box and unwrapped her silverware. "I think half the time I forget to eat lunch at all. So, tell me about the basement. Any skeletons in those crates? Bags of gold nuggets? How about a Hemingway manuscript in his own handwriting? He stayed at the hotel once, you know."

Slater had opted for a Creole concoction with spicy chicken sausage and some sort of exotic rice, which tasted spectacular. He swallowed another bite and shook his head. "Didn't know that, but it'll be a good detail for the film. Makes sense given his Idaho connection. No, nothing like that in those boxes, but there's a wealth of history down there. I'm going to need my team to start sorting through, decide what we're going to use and catalog it. I tend to work out how the film's going to flow before I involve the director and the writers."

She'd given him access to a windfall of historical facts and artifacts. That was going to make all the difference, bring even more authenticity to his film.

She nodded, taking a sip of iced tea, her eyes reflective. "I suspect that when you're finished, the Bliss County Historical Society is going to faint dead away when we hand over those pictures and they realize you're making this film. My advice is to keep the project to yourself as long as possible. I haven't met her, but I'm told there's quite a formidable force on their board, a woman whose name is Lettie Arbuckle Calder."

Slater held his napkin to his mouth, choking back a laugh. "Oh, *I've* met her. I've known her since I was a kid. She and my mother are good friends. She's a force of nature, all right. The way a tsunami is."

Across the table, Grace speared a shrimp. "I always forget how far your family goes back in this area."

"We've been around for a while."

She pointed her fork at him, remembered there was a shrimp dangling from the tines, and set it back down. "Your family history is so tied to this county and to Mustang Creek. The hotel has a fascinating history, I agree, but the Carson legacy is equally compelling . . . Showbiz."

It was impossible not to laugh. "I knew better than to introduce you to my brothers. First they flirt with you, and then share stupid family nicknames. Documentaries are hardly the blockbusters of the film world. I do them because they showcase an era I value, an era I don't want to be lost."

"You're a dreamer."

That set him aback. "No, I'm a realist. I

don't romanticize guns and dust and horses pounding off into the sunset. I *am* guilty of supporting people who choose to defend themselves and stand on their own two feet, epic heroes and ordinary people alike. So what the heck are you going to do about Reinhart?"

"Are you calling me ordinary?"

He rested his arms on the little table. "Anything but, so don't make that mistake again. Extraordinary would be my assessment. Just answer my question, okay?"

She studied her plate. "I need to decide how to handle David. If you don't mind, I'll take your friend's number and talk to him personally. In confidence. If Spence Hogan can help me make a decision, that would be good. If it was just me, that would be one thing, but this could affect a lot of other people, too. Ryder, Bonaparte, the hotel staff, not to mention the owner . . . The list goes on."

"Bonaparte is a person?" He was immensely relieved that she was willing to be reasonable. He had every faith Spence could fix the problem.

"Essentially. He has a distinct personality and, like I said, he's important to Ryder."

"I need to snap you up before Drake figures out how you feel about animals. Will

241

you marry me?"

Her eyes went wide. Maybe he had the same shocked expression. As if he'd departed reality and flown off into an alternate dimension, flapping wings and all.

He'd just proposed?

Maybe he'd done exactly that. He was stunned, but then again he wasn't. This had been coming since the moment she'd dragged Ryder into his office.

"You don't mean it." Grace lost interest in her salad. She didn't look at him, but turned and stared over the balcony railing. "Slater, please tell me you aren't serious."

He studied the fall of her red-gold hair. Her profile. The enticing silhouette of her body. "I *could* be serious," he admitted hoarsely. "I'm not going to say I planned this, but you've been in love before and I haven't. Not really. How does it work? Have I done everything wrong? I need a crash course right now."

Her throat moved as she swallowed. "You *aren't* in love with me."

"To be honest, I wish that was true, because my life would be simpler that way, but I'm starting to worry you're wrong."

She made a moaning sound and rested her forehead on her clenched hands. "No."

"That's bad?" He was unwillingly amused.

"Very bad."

"Should I apologize for falling in love with you?"

She raised her head. "Slater, shut up, please. I had a terrible morning. Now you're telling me you think you're proposing? We *can't* get married."

He could hear the panic in her voice. "Why not?" he asked calmly.

The idea was growing on him. It was like hitting a ball off the first tee. As he'd told her, he really hadn't planned it, and he had no idea how high and far the ball would fly, but he'd made the swing. This wasn't the first time it had occurred to him, although he probably should've had a spray of roses in his hand and a ring in his pocket. However, he'd done it now — even if he hadn't done it well. "Because . . . because you have a daughter."

"So? She's wonderful. You have a son. We'd make an unusual blended family, since I was never married to Daisy's mother and you aren't Ryder's biological parent, but those are two really nice kids. I wouldn't mind having a few more."

That left her staring at him. "You don't do anything halfway, do you? Marriage and babies in the same conversation?"

"I think we both agree that making babies

wouldn't exactly be a chore. We're already lovers."

"One night does not make us lovers. And for the record, *lovers* is an archaic term only used in historical romance novels, along with smelling salts and perfectly tied cravats."

"Tell me you didn't wish I was in your bed last night, making passionate love to you, instead of on the couch."

That scored a hit. A flush rose to her face. "Of all the arrogant, conceited —"

"Tell me."

If there was one thing he'd discovered quickly, it was that Grace didn't lie. She just avoided the question.

"I have a good relationship with your son. I bet he'd be pretty supportive," he said persuasively.

"I don't have a —" She stopped, then said quietly, "All right, I do. I have a son. He's certainly more mine than Hank's. And speaking of Hank, you do remember my little speech the other morning, right?"

Slater took another bite of chicken, because it was delicious and he was hungry, and he needed to think before he spoke again. Finally, he nodded. "I understand you don't want to make another mistake," he said. "Do you really feel it would be?"

CHAPTER FOURTEEN

There were some moments that were going to be embedded in her memory forever, and this was one of them.

Shrimp salad, her little balcony and Slater Carson proposing out of the blue with dust on his shirt, while munching on his Chicken Creole. They might have a chemistry she couldn't deny, but they didn't know each other very well.

Okay, maybe that wasn't entirely accurate. They knew each other's bodies intimately, she'd met his family, she'd stayed at his home, he'd stayed at hers and Ryder had accepted him in their lives with atypical teenage enthusiasm. He was an intelligent man whose actions revealed decency toward others and staunch loyalty.

Only a fool would refuse him.

On the other hand, he was used to running the show — literally — and so was she. She felt almost certain that his self-assurance and hers were going to clash, and this particular moment was an example of that. Yes, it was memorable — but not for the usual reasons. He'd proposed to her, or so it seemed. Impulsively. On a whim.

No bended knee.

No glittering diamond.

No flowery words.

She didn't care about any of that, since she'd had it once and hadn't exactly ended up with starry-eyed happiness, but still . . . Slater had just *assumed* she'd say yes. She doubted he'd given it a minute's thought until now. He was simply so used to getting what he wanted. "You didn't *mean* to ask. Did you?"

He settled his elbows on the glass table. "Grace, you keep telling me what I meant to do and not do. I'd prefer if you just considered the question."

This time, he didn't interrupt her. He sat there calmly, watching whatever emotions were flitting across her face — elation and dismay, confidence and uncertainty, reckless joy counteracted by the knowledge that she needed to stay steady, to bear in mind that rash decisions were the enemy of happiness.

When she still hadn't spoken, he finally said, "We don't have to rush the engagement." His voice was mild. "My mother will want time to plan the wedding, anyway."

Grace threw her napkin at him. "She's *not* planning our wedding."

His eyes were alive as he caught it in a swift reflexive movement. "Is that a yes? You just said *our wedding.*"

She had. No one was more surprised than she was, and Slater had an unfortunate way of doing that to her — getting her to blurt out things she hadn't intended to say. "The sentiment I wanted to convey was that although I think your mother is delightful, if we *were* to plan a wedding, I doubt I'd ask her to do it for me."

He looked at her, the laughter still sparking in his eyes. "If this was the olden days, I'd give you twenty-four hours to meet me in the middle of the street, come hell or high water, with your answer."

"That's for gunslingers, not men and women."

"Feels like the same kind of decision to me."

True. Sort of. They weren't talking life or death — like a gunslingers' battle in one of those old Westerns. They were talking life or . . . a better life.

And yet, there were more reasons *not* to marry him than to go ahead and do it.

The worst of it, she thought in despair, was that she was in love with him, too. She felt as if she was tumbling down a mountain slope unchecked, a canyon yawning at the bottom. "If you want someone who could gun you down, Carson, you're looking at her. And really? *The olden days?* I hate to break it to you, but you aren't in grade school anymore."

His smile was engaging. "True enough, but I hang out with someone who is, and that's one of her favorite expressions. Of course, Daisy's usually referring to *my* youth. I once mentioned riding the school bus, and she looked at me as if she didn't quite believe there were gas-powered vehicles back then. In light of my extreme age, I can't wait around forever. Unless you want some sort of elaborate event, we could just elope and have a reception at the ranch later."

"Slater!"

"Just thinking out loud." He looked absolutely unrepentant, lounging in his chair with masculine grace, that faint grin telling her that now he'd made up his mind, he wasn't giving up easily. With an almost desperate firmness, she said, "I don't *want* to get married again."

The grin faded as he searched her face.

"Wouldn't it be more accurate to say you don't want to get divorced again? I'm not asking you to change your life, Grace. I just want to share it."

Unfortunately for her, that was exactly the right thing to say. She pushed her salad away. Then she massaged her temples. "This is turning into a very complicated day."

A minute later she discovered that was one heck of an understatement.

"Grace?" Meg stepped into her office and spotted them on the balcony. "Oh, sorry, but . . . well . . . you have a visitor. He said you're expecting him."

What now?

When her ex-husband walked through the door and onto her balcony, she had to stifle a bubble of hysterical laughter. Somewhere, Fate was chortling, probably hooting it up, as the infamous Red would say. Slater took in her expression, the military uniform on the man coming toward them and came to the correct conclusion in a split second. He rose to his feet, and she noticed that they were almost precisely the same height. Evidently, she liked tall men. Hank spoke first, eyeing her companion. "Hello, Grace. I tried your cell, but just got your voice mail. Then I went to the condo. When no one answered the door, I came here."

"Hi, Hank. Sorry, I had a busy morning. This is Slater Carson. Slater, Hank Emery."

"I gathered that," Slater said, getting up to extend his hand. "Very nice to meet Ryder's dad. He's a good kid."

She could see that Hank, too, was drawing the correct conclusion and not liking it, but he was cordial enough as they shook hands. "Mr. Carson. Ryder mentioned you on the phone. Said he has a job on your family ranch. That was kind of you. He seems to like it."

"I doubt he likes it when he has to shovel out horse stalls, but he's doing a fine job." Slater turned to Grace with a meaningful look. "I'm headed back to the basement and my new treasure trove. I'll give Meg the keys when I'm done. Talk to you later?"

Great. He didn't seem any happier than Hank did. *What bad thing have I done in a former life to bring me this particular day?*

She'd agree to just about anything to escape this awkwardness. "I'll call you."

He left, and then she was stuck there, alone with her ex-husband, who sent her a glance that should have been conciliatory, but wasn't. "It's good to see you, Grace. You look beautiful, but then you always do."

He looked well, fit as ever, sporting a tan that wasn't from a beach somewhere. It

250

enhanced his chiseled features, and the uniform didn't hurt. The problem was that living with him had been an adventure in frustration, so *older and wiser* definitely applied. "Thanks. Let me give you the entry code to the condo. Just make yourself at home. Ryder has to work, but I'll pick him up early."

"It's good to see you, too," he said with unmistakable sarcasm.

He was right; she should be civil, but her world was completely out of alignment. She took a steadying breath and walked past him to her desk. "I had a stressful morning, so my apologies if I sounded brusque. Ryder might not act like it, but he's very excited to see you." She jotted down the numbers. "This will open the garage, and the door to the inside is unlocked. Like I said, make yourself at home."

"You don't mind me staying there?"

She needed to answer that question carefully. Meeting his eyes, she said, "Ryder wants you there. So I don't mind for his sake. I guess it's kind of unusual, but then our whole situation is unusual. How's your mother doing, anyway? I haven't talked to your dad in a couple of days."

"The chemo is a bear, of course. She's pretty sick." He hesitated. "Thanks for taking on Ryder."

Here was the part where he should apologize for never being around. Surely at his rank, he could request different duty. The government wasn't insensitive to the fact that military personnel had families. He just wouldn't think of doing it.

No, worse, it wouldn't even occur to him.

She said simply, "I love Ryder. We're figuring a few things out, but Slater's right. He's a good kid. I hope the two of you spend a lot of time together."

Hank might be insensitive, although he was hardly stupid. "I'd consider that unsolicited advice, but I get it, Officer Emery. I assume I'm going to be seeing Carson fairly often during this visit."

She wasn't interested in an argument, plus a single glance at the cell phone she'd ignored all morning showed a long list of missed messages, two of which she actually welcomed. "See you at the condo later. I have an errand to run. Please excuse me."

She practically sprinted out of the resort, wondering if she should leave Hank and Slater in the same building, but decided it was their problem, not hers.

Her car, delivered as promised, was sitting in the resort parking lot, all the tires inflated and the scratch repaired. She grabbed the extra set of keys from her purse, unlocked it and jumped in, eager to get the hell out of Dodge.

A discarded husband and a potential husband in the same building — that state of affairs was probably about as stable as two hand grenades with the pins pulled. At the moment Grace didn't care. The new quilt she'd ordered on one of her shopping trips was ready to be picked up. When she'd stopped by the shop in Mustang Creek, she'd loved the designs but had specific colors in mind, so she'd ordered a custom quilt.

On a day like today, she needed to do something nice for herself.

A bell sounded when she opened the door to the quilt shop. She saw two toddlers sitting on a blanket, arguing over toys, babbling in baby talk with the occasional recognizable word tossed in. *Mine* seemed to win the day. A pretty blonde leaned on the counter; the owner was chatting with her, but smiled in recognition when Grace came in. Grace knew that her husband, Tripp, was the friend of Slater's who'd flown Ryder to the football game. Hadleigh Galloway said graciously, "Hi, Grace. Glad you got my message. That was quick. This is Melody Hogan, by the way."

That was a familiar name. "Is Spencer Hogan your husband, by any chance?"

The blonde nodded, her gaze curious. "He sure is."

"I need to talk to him."

Both women looked at her and their brows rose a fraction.

"Not right now. Sorry, but I'm tired of the male of our species," she explained. "For today, anyway. Even if I occasionally need their help."

The other two women exchanged a grin. "Oh, we get that," Hadleigh said. "Want a cup of tea? We can sit down and talk about your man problems."

Slater just plain didn't want to discuss it.

That was a hope born to be dashed.

The second he walked through the door late that afternoon, he ran into his mother in the hallway, which made him suspect she'd been hovering there, waiting for him.

Blythe Carson only hovered for one reason. She wanted answers. "Is Grace okay?"

Slater figured there were probably cobwebs in his hair, so maybe his spider joke wasn't so funny anymore. He put down the box of pictures he wanted to start with and sighed in exhaustion, picturing Grace with her ex-husband, who didn't have cobwebs in his hair but instead looked like the classically dashing war hero, with insignias and whatever all across his uniform jacket. Then his heart froze when he thought about her vindictive ex-employee. "She's fine last I knew, and I saw her a few hours ago. Why? Has something happened?"

His mother instantly shook her head. "No, not that I know of, so wipe that alarmed expression off your face. But Ryder looked a little wound up when he came to the house."

Slater consciously relaxed his shoulders. His mother didn't need to know about David Reinhart. "His father just arrived in Mustang Creek," he said. "I met him. He seems okay, but Ryder's going to have to adjust to his presence here, and of course, Grace isn't all that comfortable with it, either. There are some complicated emotions involved."

His mother propped her hip on the table in the hallway and folded her arms. "Hmm, and how many of those emotions involve Slater Carson? And since we're on the subject of emotions — how are *his* emotions moseying along when it comes to the lovely Ms. Emery?"

"My emotions are just fine." Not exactly true. Her handsome ex-husband had clearly identified him as competition, and the man was going to be living with her for a month.

"You wouldn't tell me if they weren't, anyway." His mother's voice was resigned.

Well, that *was* true. "I'd be reluctant to," he acquiesced. "You'd try to fix every little thing. I'm afraid to ask, but can you tell me why we're having this conversation?"

"Mace and Drake have a bet going about when you're going to propose to Grace, and I got in on the action."

If she hadn't winked at him, he might have stomped off and throttled his brothers in front of witnesses. "You all think you're so hilarious. For the record, I have no intention of proposing in the future."

Not a lie. He already had.

"What did she say?"

He forgot his mother was the most insightful person he'd ever known. Slater gave up. "She's thinking it over. Mom, she's divorced, I didn't plan it properly and her ex-husband walked in on the big moment. I'm not sure of anything right now, but I *am* sure that if Drake and Mace don't stop these bets, the three of us are going to tangle."

She sent him a purely Carson triumphant smile. "I just won that round."

"You have to be kidding me."

Her eyes twinkled with mischievous laughter. "I see no reason why Drake and Mace shouldn't water my flowers for a week. I deserve a vacation. I suppose it's a teeny bit much that they have to wear my gardening hat while they do the watering, but I couldn't resist."

Slater found that quite funny. He slid an arm around his mother's waist and squeezed gently. "If that doesn't cure them of gambling on my love life, nothing will. I'm going to take pictures of them in that big floppy hat."

She hugged him back. "I'm so glad for you, darling. As soon as I saw the two of you together, I knew Grace was the one."

"Yeah, well, let's see if she feels that way, too." He said it with a touch of grimness. "She told me flat out she doesn't want to get married again. She meant it, too. And I see her point in a way. Her ex-husband was — and still is — away from home a lot, he's dedicated almost exclusively to his work and she's had to shoulder almost sole responsibility for his child, other than what he provides financially. Let's face it, she isn't going to get a much better deal with me. I even made the mistake of saying I want more kids. Grace is a bright woman, and I'm sure she instantly reminded herself that

I'd be gone for months at a time, leaving her as the one and only parent all over again."

He wanted to kick himself for mentioning more children, but he was just being honest with her. Better now than springing it on her once they were married. Yes, they'd have Daisy and Ryder, but to share a child . . .

Maybe Mace was right and he did have a romantic soul, whatever the hell that meant.

"Wanting a child is never wrong." His mother supported him instantly, her tone full of conviction. "You're a wonderful father. Daisy adores you. For that matter, I think she and Ryder have formed the Slater Carson fan club. And may I point out that on this ranch, no one parents alone."

With a rueful smile, he said, "I have no idea if Grace would even want to live on this ranch. We haven't talked about it. There's a lot to discuss, because I didn't think through the proposal. Talk about acting spontaneously."

Jeez, that was true.

"Regrets?" His mother's gaze was assessing.

"No." Crazy as it was, he didn't. It felt as if the minute he'd first seen Grace, something had snapped loose inside him. A taut wire had broken free. One he didn't know was there, holding him back from an important part of life he didn't realize he was missing.

He repeated, "No."

His mother linked her arm with his. "I think Harry, who was positive I'd win this bet, made you some lemon bars. Let's go have some to celebrate."

CHAPTER FIFTEEN

Slater was nowhere in sight.

Just as well.

Only trouble was, Grace didn't *want* to see him and yet, perversely, she did. She wanted to find him waiting for her on the elegant veranda of the ranch house in eager anticipation of her arrival. She'd texted that she'd pick up Ryder at seven, so he knew she was coming.

They hadn't talked in three days.

Since he'd proposed, he'd been remarkably absent from her life. It was hard to say whether he was running scared, or if it was because of Hank's presence. Or maybe he was just busy, since he seemed to be jumping feet first into this new project. Boxes were being carted from the basement daily, and she was given receipts signed with his sprawling signature. But she hadn't actually seen the man himself . . .

She parked and got out, hoping she

wouldn't have to go to the door of the house, in case he'd told his family about his off-the-cuff proposal. She knew this much about the Carson clan, though — Blythe would support his decision, his brothers would be amused and Harry might poison Grace's food if she didn't accept.

Grace, on the other hand, didn't have nearly as much of a support network. Oh, Slater was right that Ryder would be pleased, to the extent that a teen could be excited about anything. But her brother was a busy man with a young family, and her parents hadn't approved of her divorcing Hank. Her Seattle friends all had busy careers and complicated lives; their contact was rather perfunctory these days. So she was on her own.

Except for an unexpected gift in the form of Hadleigh Galloway and Melody Hogan.

Those two women had been a source of boundless information, not to mention that she'd made two good friends. The three of them had connected instantly, and had already made plans to get together again. Other than Meg — and she wasn't going to confide in someone who not only worked for her, but was also quite young and obviously had a crush on Slater — she hadn't been in Mustang Creek long enough to make friends.

Especially ones who were lifelong residents and had the real scoop. Like Hadleigh and Mel.

Slater Carson, they'd let her know over a cup of Earl Grey, was considered a player. Not that it meant he wasn't known as an all-around terrific guy, but his reputation was love 'em and leave 'em. Now, when he'd gotten Raine pregnant, he'd stepped right up, so no one could fault him for not being a great dad. When he was in town, he attended Daisy's ball games and went to parent/teacher conferences, and when he was off on location, his family pitched in to fill the void.

That was the good side.

Bad side existed, too. He'd shown no desire to commit to one woman and settle down. He was too focused on his job, and as they sipped tea, neither Hadleigh nor Melody had given her any lace-edged promises that this was likely to change. Based on her experience with Hank and her knowledge of Slater, she had to agree. She admired Slater's talent and vision, but would that be outweighed by the fact that she'd be on her own most of the time?

Back to square one.

Driven man equaled uncertain future

spent mostly alone. Yup, she was all too familiar with that equation.

Both Hadleigh and Melody had just about toppled off their chairs when she confessed that he'd asked her to marry him. If she wasn't so conflicted and confused, she would've loved to take out her phone and snap a quick picture of their comical expressions.

Hadleigh Galloway had plopped down her cup so hard tea sloshed over the side. "Slater Carson asked you to *marry* him?"

Gloomily, Grace had nodded. "And he made it clear he hoped the deal would include more children."

"He did?" Melody Hogan had sounded positively astonished. "Was he drinking? I mean, he doesn't overindulge, but I suppose if he had one beer too many —"

Before Grace could explain, Hadleigh broke in. "Mel," she'd said, narrowing her eyes. "That's not it. Look at her!"

Grace couldn't decide if she should burst into laughter at the sudden female assessment or dash to the nearest mirror and fix her hair. Melody had studied her for a moment, then nodded slowly. "Yeah, I see your point. She's exactly his type, right? Slater likes them pretty and smart."

That had been flattering, but it didn't

solve her dilemma. "He wasn't drinking unless you count iced tea. We were having lunch." Grace had sighed. "I couldn't even tell if he was serious at first. He asked and then went on eating. Just munching away."

Hadleigh snorted. "Men."

Melody said, "Par for the course. If they can mess anything up, it's a romantic moment. Will you marry me and please pass the ketchup."

Grace did start laughing then, and was grateful for the shared amusement.

They'd all agreed no man was perfect, but their consensus was that she'd be a fool to pass up his offer. Why she'd confided in strangers was a mystery to her, but she supposed she'd just needed some advice.

If it was any consolation, they'd both agreed he was one very good-looking man, with both brains and charm. An ideal groom in some ways, or as ideal as you were going to get. But they weren't going to lay down any promises. His father had been a notorious womanizer until he'd met Blythe.

Clean as a whistle once he'd spoken his vows, though. Devoted to his wife and his family.

She hoped Slater followed in the family footsteps.

Grace hurried to the barn, determined to

get Ryder and go home, which would involve another dinner with Hank. Those dinners were proving to be difficult. Slater was actually there, stripped to the waist and hefting Heck's saddle, turning as she came in.

She stopped dead in her tracks and to her horror, her eyes filled with tears. It wasn't like her, damn it! She didn't normally cry. He set down the saddle, and his voice was low as he walked over and placed his arms around her. "Grace? Hey. Take it easy. Everything all right?"

No, this *really* wasn't like her. She didn't need a man to reassure her that everything was going to be fine. Grace hiccupped against his neck and said, "You haven't even called."

He touched her cheek, his fingers gentle. "I thought you didn't want me to call."

"Think again, Carson."

His bare shoulder was salty, and she gave it a shove, but not before she'd kissed it.

He ran his hand through his hair after he let her go, his eyes intense, inquiring. "I was trying to give you some space."

There was no reason to be mad at him. She knew it, and he knew it, but somehow that didn't make it better. She wiped the tears from her cheeks. "I'm not like this."

"Understood. Is this about Hank?"

"No. It's about you."

He rocked back on his heels, his chest gleaming with a faint sheen of perspiration, and she wondered if he'd been working so hard for the same reason she was acting out of character. "I don't even want to ask how. Just because I didn't call for three days? I didn't notice you calling me, either."

"You asked me to marry you."

"I remember," he said, smiling. "And don't make it sound like a crime. If I recall, the idea wasn't met with handsprings and loud cheers, was it? I was hoping you've been thinking about changing your mind." Luckily, Ryder came out of a stall just then with a bucket in his hand, straw stuck to him from head to toe. Straw that would end up all over her car. At least his timing was good. She didn't want to answer Slater's question, but she had one of her own.

She took the plunge. "What weekend did you have in mind? For . . . for our trip."

Slater's expression lightened immediately. "To scope out sites for the shoot? You name it. I'm there."

"How about this coming one? Seems to me we should talk about . . . a few things."

He leaned over and picked up the saddle he'd put down. "We're on. What time should

266

I pick you up on Friday?"

"I'm driving." She needed to take control of *something.* Everything seemed to be slipping away. She had no control over having Hank back in her life. No control over David Reinhart's little stunts — because Spence Hogan had regretfully agreed with her that the lack of any concrete evidence tied his hands. And no control over her volatile love life.

"Hi, Grace." Ryder had obviously sensed the edginess, suddenly swiping at his clothes. "I didn't have any homework today, so if Slate says it okay, we're done."

"*Slate* says it's fine. He's also looking forward to Friday night."

So was she. Of course, she still had to get through *this* night, and that wasn't going to be easy. She turned to Ryder. "Let's go. I'm picking up some hamburger and buns. Your dad claims he'll grill them. I don't know that I've ever had anything he's cooked, so we'll cross our fingers."

Wasn't that the unhappy truth? She'd give him credit for eating whatever was set in front of him, but Hank didn't even pour milk on his own cereal. His desire to insinuate himself back into cozy cohabitation was so transparent that she was worried Ryder might've been right when he'd said her ex was more interested in her than in his son. No wonder her nerves were shot.

It didn't help that Slater caught her hand and pulled her in for a brief, hard kiss before he promised, "I'll call you."

Fortunately, Ryder had left the building.

He'd been showing some hard-won restraint, in his opinion, but this afternoon had lifted his spirits.

Slater tipped back a beer, took a swallow and admired the sunset.

Grace had cried because he hadn't called her.

He had the feeling that was simplifying it, since women seemed so damned complicated. He didn't think he'd ever get an angle on it, but she'd come into his arms willingly . . . and she'd asked for a weekend with him.

He'd smelled the sweet scent of her hair, and for once, hadn't said the wrong thing.

He felt like he was in heaven, or at least close. Especially when Drake stepped outside with the watering can, cautiously looking around, that hilarious hat perched on his head.

"Oh, shit," his brother grumbled, seeing him in the tilted-back chair, booted feet on the railing. "I knew I wasn't going to catch

268

a break. Good, you can be my witness. I wore the damned hat. I'm a man of my word. All of this is your fault, you know."

Slater was laughing so hard he was sure he'd be crying soon. "How so?" he managed to gasp out.

"That impromptu proposal ruined my timeline." Drake glowered at him and dumped half a can of water on a poor inoffensive plant. "Any reasonable adult male would talk to his next of kin, meaning his closest brother, before proposing marriage. Hint, hint, me. I thought I had this in the bag. Instead, here I am." He gestured at the rows of potted plants around him.

Slater held up a hand, still shaking with mirth. "I'll attest you wore the hat, so you can take it off now. If you don't, I might bust a gut. I beg you, have mercy on a fairly innocent man . . ."

Drake whipped it off and tossed it on the table, but by then he was laughing, too. "Innocent? Even fairly? Yeah, right. Dream on. So tell me, when's the wedding? After this, you'd better ask me to be best man."

Slater shrugged but couldn't resist saying, "Only if you wear the hat."

Drake looked as if he might pour the contents of the watering can over his head, so Slater added sardonically, "Problem is,

Grace hasn't answered me. And I can't help it if our mother has miraculous deductive powers."

"Hasn't answered? Where's the reputed Slater Carson charm?"

"I think that's the problem — it might be reputed but it's unproven. Apparently, a skill I don't really have."

"Yeah, right." Drake came over and perched on the railing. Like favorite ghosts, Harold and Violet trailed along and dropped down on the porch with a thump. "You haven't had a problem that I've ever seen. Raine fell for you pretty hard."

It wasn't the first time he'd sensed that maybe his younger brother was in love with Raine. But Drake didn't disclose that sort of thing; he was a true cowboy, sentimental but intensely private. Keeping his tone neutral, Slater said, "I always wondered why you didn't do anything about your feelings for her when she and I split."

There was a pause, and Slater thought Drake was going to tell him to go jump off a cliff, that it was none of his business, but to his surprise he hoisted himself up on the railing of the veranda and looked him in the eye. "I did ask her out. By then, she already knew she was pregnant. She's Raine . . . so she was honest about it. I even took her to one of her doctor's appointments when her car was in the shop and she needed a ride."

Slater wasn't going to deny that this information was a shock. "You knew about Daisy before *I* knew?"

"Listen, Showbiz, you were off on location, remember?" Drake wasn't defensive; that wasn't his style. "She was having a Carson baby, so she turned, logically enough, to one of us when she needed a favor. Mace or Mom would've insisted she tell you. I'm sure not a saint or anything but I can keep my mouth shut. She hadn't decided when she was going to tell you."

He couldn't decide whether to be outraged or just shake his head at Drake's revelation. He settled for saying, "Guess if I ever have a life-changing secret I want to keep from someone, I can tell you."

"Yep." Drake's grin was crooked. "I figured she'd tell you when she was ready, and she did. Besides, you weren't here, anyway, so she had a point that it would just make you crazy not to be involved. We both agreed on that."

That could have been true, but it was all over and done with, anyway. Raine had eventually told him, and he had Daisy in his life.

Now if he could persuade Grace to become a permanent part of his life, as well . . .

"Maybe this weekend will settle things between Grace and me," he said, idly setting aside his now-empty beer bottle. "One of the perks of having her ex-husband visiting — well, the only perk I can think of — is that he can keep an eye on Ryder while we take a short trip. Next week we're having the production meeting at the resort, so I'd like to suggest locations, take some pictures. Grace is going along."

Drake scratched his chin, approval in his eyes. "That ought to do it. Though I was pretty sure the night you spent in Mace's office would've sealed the deal for you."

Slater stared at him suspiciously. "There wasn't any betting on that night, was there? I swear —"

Drake did his best to look innocent, but failed. "Of course not! What do you take us for? This isn't Las Vegas, it's a working ranch."

"Says the cowboy in the floppy old-lady hat watering flowers."

That observation was ignored. "Hey, I need to ride out and do my usual gate check. Want to come with?"

He did. It was a fine night, and he still was in high spirits after seeing Grace. A relaxed evening ride sounded like the perfect ending to a day that had started with him rolling out of bed, a sinking feeling in the pit of his stomach. He'd been afraid she'd never agree to marry him, and he was an idiot for asking so early in their relationship.

The real problem, he mused as they walked over to the stable, was that he'd felt so *sure.* He thought maybe Grace was sure, too, but she was also scared. For some reason, he wasn't. Certain things made him nervous — like letting go of Daisy's bike that first time without training wheels. Or when his mother had called after a biopsy that turned out benign, but had him more upset than he'd even realized until the flood of relief left him weak-kneed. And yet, in the wake of his impromptu proposal, his attitude was that it had been the right decision.

Love was like fire, he decided. You could try to control it, but it wasn't always possible. Sometimes the flames burned you and sometimes they just warmed you from the inside out. Like now.

Good analogy, he thought with some satisfaction. But when he was tightening the cinch on his saddle his phone beeped and he frowned, taking it out of his pocket.

The text said:

Sorry, probably canceling this weekend. Something has happened.

He went from warm to ice-cold in a second.

CHAPTER SIXTEEN

Hank said irritably, "You might've pointed out that there's a problem. At the very least, Carson should've told me."

Grace could take being blamed for the incident, but she didn't think Hank had any right to point a finger at Slater. What was *he* supposed to do? "You met him for less than two minutes. Besides, I'm not going to say he wouldn't consider it his concern, because he's been good to both Ryder and me, but I *can* say it would be presumptuous of him to mention one word to you. I'm sorry about what happened, but . . ."

He held the cloth to his head, looking a little gray. "Someone knocked me out cold, Grace. I can tell you aren't exactly surprised, and Ryder said there've been other incidents."

The answer was yes to both. Did she have a suspicion that David Reinhart was starting to feel that his options were narrowing?

Maybe even that his past was catching up to him? She did. He was smart enough to know it, too. For one thing, references were probably hard to come by.

She really hadn't expected physical violence, though, and she felt terrible about that. Bonaparte was nowhere to be found, either, which worried her, although by now she had a fair amount of confidence in his street smarts. That cat knew something was up.

"I think you were an unexpected complication," Grace said, keeping her voice low so Ryder wouldn't hear their conversation. "No, I'm not surprised. *You* surprised *him.*"

"You know who it is?"

"I have a good idea but no proof."

"Elaborate."

She could do without the reprimand in that military tone. However, she wasn't the one who'd been clonked on the head. "Someone I fired didn't take it well, and he seems to be conducting a vendetta against me. Up until now, it's been relatively petty stuff. Assault is different from deflating tires and scratching some paint and even hacking into our email. So, like I said, my guess is that he didn't expect you to be here. He was going to pull another one of his stunts and you walked out and he panicked. So far, I can't prove anything. Are you *sure* you don't want to go to the hospital?"

"Positive. I've been shot at in five countries," he said matter-of-factly, "but I come to a sleepy little town like Mustang Creek, Wyoming, and some idiot takes me down. The boys in my command would find it funny as hell."

She didn't find it funny at all. Okay, no doctor. But what about a drink? He did approve of that plan. Somehow, somewhere, in *sleepy* Wyoming, Hank had managed to buy a bottle of his favorite whiskey, and since he truly did seem to be okay and obviously wasn't going to cooperate with her suggestion that he get checked out, the least she could do was pour him a drink. She went into her tidy kitchen and got out one of the crystal tumblers she owned but had never used. She put in a couple of ice cubes and was in the act of dashing the amber liquid into the glass when the police knocked.

Hank was obviously annoyed that she'd called them, but too bad. The deputy who showed up — one Ryan Grant — was professional and businesslike. However, she could tell that he wasn't used to what would be a serious crime in any city, big or small. Still, he asked the right questions, looked around and was taking notes when Slater arrived.

Enter the cavalry. The man practically fishtailed his truck into the driveway.

The last thing she needed was him walking through the front door, and she deduced immediately that his close friendship with the chief of police was probably part of the equation.

The deputy didn't help by addressing him with the ease of old acquaintance. "Hey, Slater. Thought you might show up."

No secrets in Mustang Creek. Hadleigh and Melody had told her that flat out. *Just consider the mountains and the scenery as compensation for the lack of privacy* was their advice. People were nice, but it was a small town. Her romance with Slater Carson was already a topic of discussion, Melody had said. Once people got wind of the engagement . . .

Hold on, she'd told them both. *There is no engagement. Not yet, anyway.*

Now she threw Slater a quelling look. "I didn't call you."

"Yeah, let's talk about that sometime. Why *didn't* you call me? Ryder did. What happened?"

"Ryder did?" Hank tossed aside the cold compress. "That a fact?"

She shoved the drink in his hand, since she could sense he was going to say something testy, which wouldn't help a thing. She had no time for male drama. "Please excuse us for a second, Hank and Deputy Grant."

She grabbed Slater by the arm and tugged him outside onto the patio, leaving the deputy and Hank to hash out the details.

"You don't have to rush to my rescue," she informed him, but truthfully, she was happy to see him. He looked tall and capable, and seeing Hank down and out had been a revelation about how vulnerable she and Ryder could be — despite her police training. The attack on her ex-husband had also revealed how easy it was to take someone unawares. If he'd known about the danger, Hank could have held his own and then some, so she felt a little guilty for not warning him that there was a problem.

No, a lot guilty.

"I'm not rushing to your rescue. Hell, Grace, I just saw you a short time ago, and then I got your message. *Something has happened?* What was I supposed to think? I know what's been going on. I wondered if you needed me, if I could help. *Something has happened* is hardly an adequate message. Then you cancel on me. It was all rather vague. At least Ryder thought I should know."

He had a point. She said contritely, "Sorry. Finding my ex-husband unconscious on the patio blew my communication skills right out the window."

"Understandable." He nodded. "I forgive you, if you'll forgive me for rushing over. Let me make an educated guess. Hank isn't interested in the hospital, and if he'd seen anything, you'd be on the phone with Spence instead of having a deputy poking around. So we really haven't made much progress."

"No." She wished she could disagree. "Hank was taken completely off guard. That's my fault."

"We'll figure this out." He sounded very sure of himself.

"Oh, yes, Mr. Producer, how is it that you think you can do it better than a former police officer?"

"My network is a little larger."

The Carson connections. He could even be right. In Mustang Creek the Carson name had influence — and they knew everyone in the area. "This has taken a different, more dangerous turn," he said, his face grim. "Your ex-husband isn't a small guy. So if Reinhart is willing to go after Hank, no more fooling around. Ryder is still a kid, and former police officer or not, you're a woman. Let's just assume the worst could happen. I have a plan."

That declaration made her pause. "Like?"

"I can move in here or you and Ryder can move to the ranch."

If he moved in here . . . that would mean Hank and him in the same space. *That* was hardly going to work. "No."

Slater's gaze was unflinching. "That was not a yes or no question."

If it wasn't for the fact that she wanted to fling herself into his arms again, she'd be more irritated. Actually, she was irritated that she *wanted* to throw herself into his arms. "I don't want to leave either one of them here alone."

"Then I move in."

"Oh, more males," she said sarcastically. "That works out well for me. Let's see, you, Ryder, Bonaparte and Hank? Where would you even sleep? The floor? Hank's got Ryder's room and Ryder's on the couch. And don't you dare say my bed."

He did grin, but it held an edge of exasperation. "I'm suggesting a solution to keep us both sane. If you think for one minute that I'm not worried sick about you, get real. I'd happily camp out on the floor to keep you safe."

She hadn't been particularly worried before this incident, but felt a whole new level of concern over what might happen next. Slater was right about that. David had taken a step that could land him some major jail time if he was caught. "If I were David Reinhart," she said, her voice calmer than she felt, "I'd be headed straight out of town. I suspect he's long gone."

Slater glanced in through the glass doors. "I doubt he realizes he attacked a high-ranking military officer. Hank's wearing civilian clothes right now, so he looks like an ordinary guy."

David probably assumed Hank was you, Grace realized with a start, *and that you'd gotten your hair cut.* David and Slater had seen each other briefly and only in passing. Slater's height and coloring were similar to Hank's.

Wonderful. Now she was going to worry about Slater, too.

Luckily, one of her worries evaporated when she heard a faint meow and saw Bonaparte sitting on top of the fence. He licked his paw and then jumped down to saunter over. If only cats could talk, she thought as she bent to stroke his fur. She'd bet he'd been a witness.

Despite her faith in his sense of feline self-preservation, it was a relief to see him alive and well.

Slater went to the door. "Hey, Ryder. Someone here to see you."

Boy meets cat was a happy reunion. One cloud banished from her horizon, anyway, but the sun wasn't exactly shining.

Slater wasn't sure how to handle the Hank Emery situation. He hoped Grace might agree to stay at the ranch and bring Ryder along.

Well, maybe. Although it didn't seem quite fair to leave Emery here on his own, military training or not.

Besides, Grace would never go along with either scenario — staying at the ranch or him moving in here. She had an independent spirit, and he probably wouldn't be as interested in her if she didn't, so that part of the problem was his own damn fault. He couldn't dislike Emery, because he seemed decent enough, and for Ryder's sake alone, he wanted to believe Emery was a good guy. Maybe not husband material, maybe not a stellar father, but as a man, not so bad or Grace wouldn't have married him in the first place. Neither could he forget Emery's dedication to the armed services. That was something he had to respect.

So they now sat looking at each other, and ironically they probably had exactly the same thing in mind. Protecting Grace and Ryder — the number-one priority for both of them.

While Grace answered her phone — a call from the resort — he and the major took each other's measure. They watched Grace take her cell into the kitchen. Calls from work seemed to be a recurring theme. She worked long hours, but Slater did, too, so he could hardly fault her for that. The deputy had departed, and Ryder was still out on the patio with his cat, giving him his evening meal, apparently unwilling to let the animal out of his sight. That meant Slater was on his own with Grace's ex-husband.

He'd chosen a patterned chair and considered the man seated on the couch across from him. "You're a strategist. Tell me, what do we do now, Major Emery? I don't want Grace or Ryder alone. I assume that, considering the bruise I can see on your temple, you agree."

Emery's eyes were such a pale blue they were almost gray, and he leveled a stern look at Slater. "They won't be alone," he said. "I'm right here. I didn't know there was anything going on. Now that I do . . . well, that changes things."

"But you won't be here indefinitely. If I could, I'd like to relocate them to the ranch, where there are always people coming and going, and most of them are hefty ranch hands. Convincing Grace is my main problem. I was kind of hoping you'd help me out."

What a gamble. He didn't have any illusions. They wanted the same woman, and they both knew it. Hands-down rivals and members of the same I-Want-Her club.

Despite that, Emery responded reasonably. "When I get new orders, I'll suggest it. If we'd had this conversation yesterday, I doubt it would've gone this way. It doesn't hurt that your background check came out clean."

Slater wasn't surprised. He probably would've done that, too. "How about my degenerate brothers?"

Emery actually laughed, but then winced and put the compress back against his face. "They're also upstanding citizens. The worst I could find was that the younger one, Mason, got a speeding ticket when he was eighteen, but I think we'll just let that one slide since he went on to graduate with honors from UCLA. Ryder spends a lot of

285

time with the Carson family, according to Grace. I suspect she does, as well. Don't blame me for being careful."

"I don't." Slater meant it. He added with a hint of humor, "And I knew about the speeding ticket because I lent him the money to pay it, but don't mention that ticket in front of my mother. All these years later, she still doesn't know."

"My lips are sealed."

At least they weren't antagonistic. There was no way for two men — two people — to go after the same thing and be best friends. Respectful, yes, even cordial. To a point. But what Slater really wanted was someone watching out for Grace and Ryder. "I can't tell Grace what to do."

Emery gave him a male look of brotherhood, a look that wasn't confrontational. "No, you can't. Take it from me. I tell people what to do all day, but she just won't go along with the program."

"Up until now, all this guy was trying to do was get under her skin. The attack on you changes the whole game."

"I can't disagree with that. At least with his job at the ranch, Ryder isn't coming home to an empty house anymore."

That was true. This evening had proven that Reinhart was willing to do anything to avoid getting caught.

Grace came back into the room, unable to conceal the surprise on her face at seeing the two of them talking like civilized individuals. "Something's wrong with one of the ovens, and apparently that means the spa chef has to use the hotel kitchen for tomorrow's breakfast. That'll be World War Three. I'll brace myself, bring earplugs to drown out the temperamental shouting. I can picture those two chefs facing off with spatulas like fencing masters."

Her forced levity didn't fool him at all. She was upset under her cool facade, and that was both good and bad. He hoped the emotion wasn't because of a resurgence of feelings for Emery. She'd never said she didn't love the man, just admitted she couldn't live with him.

Well, hell.

Time to go.

Slater got up. "I guess you don't need me. Tell Ryder I'll see him tomorrow."

That was hard to say out loud. *I guess you don't need me.*

Grace nodded and he could tell she wanted to say something else as she walked him to the door. But maybe not. All she offered him was a simple thank-you. His smile was ironic. "But you don't need me rushing to your rescue, I know. You were very clear about that."

"I love having you rush to my rescue." Grace followed him out the front door, and suddenly her hands were warm on his shoulders as she rose up to kiss him. "*Need* is different."

He pulled her close and savored the contact, murmuring against her mouth, "Feels good to hear the word *love.*"

She finally pushed him away with a soft laugh. "I'll see you tomorrow night."

For his production company event. He climbed into his truck mollified, but not sure if all signals were registering on his channels — or registering correctly. A very satisfactory goodbye kiss, though.

With the ex-husband right there.

It was an iffy situation and he couldn't decide what to make of it, but he did know that driving off wasn't the easiest thing he'd ever done. His entire adult life, he'd shied away from clinging women, but Grace took it a little too far in the other direction. He wanted to protect her; instead, Emery got assigned that duty.

His phone pinged and he pulled into the parking lot at the local bakery, which had been closed for hours now, to read the message. It was from Spence.

We have a description from a neighbor of a man hopping Grace's fence. It fits Reinhart.

He typed back:

Enough to bring him in?

For questioning, yes. Have to find him first. Got kicked out of the apartment he was sharing with a friend for being in arrears with the rent. I was able to uncover that he has a major gambling problem.

He suspected that wouldn't surprise Grace and typed back:

Keep me posted.

Will do.

Slater sat there for a moment. Maybe Grace was right and the man had left town, but if money was enough of an issue that he was skimming from the bar at the resort and not paying his rent, he was probably desperate.

And had a lot of time on his hands to plot revenge.

With that disquieting thought, Slater put

289

the vehicle in gear and drove back toward
the ranch.

CHAPTER SEVENTEEN

Grace did another lap, flipped around, pushed off the side and finished her swim at full speed.

It felt good and there was nothing like exercise to relieve stress, she reminded herself. She climbed out of the pool and reached for her towel. Lately she'd become an expert on the subject of stress, but she wanted to relinquish that particular honor.

Slater's production company event was only hours away. She'd considered letting Meg handle it, but for big bookings like this one, she always oversaw the details and it was important to the resort that it go well. She didn't think Slater would be concerned about whether or not his napkin was folded in a certain shape, but his investors would be there, and they were all wealthy and connected and would have very specific expectations. A good impression was her goal, not to mention her responsibility.

To her job, and to him.

She was beginning to understand how much trust was involved in their relationship. She'd compiled a short mental list. She trusted him with Ryder's well-being, and that was no small thing. He trusted her with Hank, who was staying at her home, but he didn't go all male ego on her. Equally, she trusted that he was telling the truth about his relationship with Raine. He trusted she might someday respond to his proposal.

She was a little hung up on that one.

"Hey, Grace, we have a problem." Meg came through the glass doors to the pool area, waving a piece of paper. "No salmon."

"No salmon?" Grace finished drying her hair with the towel. "What does that mean?"

Her assistant was clearly flustered. "Full service menu for the Carson Production meeting tonight and we didn't get in the fresh wild salmon."

On the scorecard of disasters, this was about a two at most. "All right. What about the other fish we offer?"

"We have those."

"Then relax. I keep waiting for a perfect day. You know, when not one thing goes wrong? It hasn't happened in my lifetime. So we can't serve salmon. Okay, that's too bad, but we'll soldier on and none of the guests will starve to death. Everything else good?"

"I think so."

"I appreciate your attention to detail."

"Are you really going to marry him?"

Grace almost dropped her towel. "What?"

"Slater Carson." Her assistant smiled apologetically, hair curling in the humidity of the pool enclosure. "This is Bliss County. Word has it he proposed."

She was going to kill him. Then she reconsidered. "He'd never tell anyone he proposed." She knew in her heart that Melody and Hadleigh wouldn't, either.

Meg looked slightly superior. "Were you alone?"

"Yes, we were."

"Hmm. Balconies below your office. Balconies above. One on each side. Still think you were alone?"

The housekeeping staff *was* around at that time of day . . . Oh, this got better and better. That was when they cleaned the rooms *and* the offices. Checkout at eleven, check-in at three. She and Slater had that lunch around one . . .

"I guess not." She wanted to grind her teeth, but that wouldn't change anything. "I just *thought* we were. Silly me. As for the question, I'm sure the entire world also knows I haven't answered him yet."

"You can't blame everyone for being curious." Meg flashed her impish smile. "It's *Slater Carson.* He's probably the closest thing to a celebrity we have in Mustang Creek, and, well . . . you've *seen* him."

Maybe if she wasn't sleep deprived because of current events, she wouldn't have said it. "Yeah, I've seen him. All of him," she went on recklessly. If there were no secrets here, why try to keep them? "Feel free to let everyone know he's definitely worth looking at. Now, please tell me the waitstaff understands that this really isn't about impressing Slater. It has more to do with making a positive impression on his guests. He already likes the resort and gives us his business. Let's make sure his trust in us is well placed, shall we? I'm going home to shower and change."

"The black lace dress. Since you're his date."

Her wet feet on the tiles, Grace swung around so fast she almost lost her balance. "I'm what?"

Meg looked sheepish. "That dress is fantastic on you, and he called today and specifically asked for you to be added to the guest list. He said he'd pick you up at six-thirty."

It was *such* a Slater move. "He might've called me himself," she muttered.

"He said he knew you were busy."

She was, but what he really wanted to do was not give her a chance to refuse. Meg was obviously part of the conspiracy and she didn't seem to feel guilty about it at all. Instead, she smiled brilliantly. "So, the black lace. I mean . . . you always look great, but that dress could've been made just for you."

Grace had worn it only once, to a board meeting that included dinner, right after she was hired. Her lucky dress . . . Maybe this *was* the time. "Great suggestion. Thanks."

Meg's eyes were warm. "I'm happy for you."

She was still waffling over whether or not she was happy for herself. "Slater's a good man," she said slowly. "But a match made in heaven? That's a myth. I'm so gun-shy it isn't funny. One minute I want to say yes, but the next I tell myself I never want to go through a breakup again. It's so heart-wrenching when it happens, I can't sleep or eat."

"He's really in love with you."

Her innocence was touching, but still . . .

"What makes you say that?"

"I've seen him look at you." She seemed so sincere.

It must be nice to be that young and naive, Grace thought, feeling slightly jaded, but then her assistant turned the moment on her by adding, "*And* I've seen you look at *him*. I'll make sure the dinner goes smoothly, I promise. If you trust me, this will be my first executive party going solo. You just sit there and be a guest. Let me handle everything. I'd love to take a shot at it."

Great to know she wore her heart on her sleeve. Grace was used to being the one advising people, not the other way around. However, she'd be grateful to hand over the reins now and then, and Meg was certainly capable. Besides, worst-case scenario, she'd be right there. "Okay, take the shot."

"Go get ready." Meg pointed at the door. "There's nothing like having the boss there watching your every move. Excuse me, I need to run now. I have a thousand things to do."

She ran. She booked it out of the room so fast, her feet barely hit the floor. When she'd left, Grace changed into sweats, bunched her hair into a swift twist, and tossed her bathing suit in a bag. To her relief, her car sat there unscathed, tires inflated, paint immaculate. She'd taken to parking by the main entrance, while she used to park near the back to leave the better spots for guests, but she still subscribed to the theory that David Reinhart had left the area.

That was a cheerful thought. Even more appealing was the prospect of the coming evening. Despite his methods — how did Slater know she'd find it harder to deflate Meg than to say no to him — she was looking forward to seeing him in action as the boss, to meeting his colleagues and investors, to sitting next to him . . .

To knocking his socks off. Black lace dress, check. High heels, check . . . the ones with the small ruffle on top and the open toe. Light makeup, and she might even tame her hair into an elegant style.

Be careful what you wish for, Mr. Carson.

"What do you think?" he asked.

Daisy cocked her head and considered the question. She was spending the night at the ranch, much to his mother's delight, because Raine had some out-of-town business. She'd knocked on his door just as Slater was shrugging into his suit coat and she was now perched on the edge of the bed, studying his evening attire with a critical eye.

With the frankness of a ten-year-old going on eleven (although he often felt she must be going on thirty), she said succinctly, "Lose the tie, Dad. I don't like it."

Definitely going on thirty.

Slater glanced in the mirror. He wasn't fond of ties to begin with but it seemed fine to him. "What's wrong with it?"

"You don't look like you."

What the heck did that mean?

She went on earnestly, "My dad doesn't wear ties. He wears cowboy boots and jeans and a hat."

When had she gotten so gangly? He could swear she'd sprouted up about half a foot in the past month. "It's all about you, huh? Okay, I'll lose the tie. But this isn't a dinner for jeans and a hat." He might as well be honest. "I'd rather dress that way and be more comfortable, though."

"Then why don't you do it? Grown-ups get to do what they want."

He loosened the tie and then tossed it aside. Her endless questions never ceased to amaze him, and the most remarkable part was that he actually got stumped now and then. "Not quite true, honey. I wish I could promise you that you'll never have to do anything you don't want once you hit a certain age, but then I wouldn't be telling you the truth. Grown-ups have to do things they don't like, but that's life. However, I think you're right about the tie. Good call. I'll wear the suit, skip the tie."

She nodded. "Is Grace going to be there?"

It wasn't as if he hadn't expected this to come up. "I hope so. I invited her."

"Because you like her." Her eyes were solemn.

"Because I like her, yes." He unbuttoned his collar and really *was* a lot more comfortable. Not with the conversation, though it had to be addressed. "Is that okay with you?" He didn't need her permission; however, it was important to know how she felt.

She did think it over for a moment, then nodded. "She seems cool."

He could agree with that. "She *is* cool."

"Her hair's pretty." Daisy swung her legs and creased her forehead.

He agreed with that, too. "Very."

"I asked Uncle Mace if you were going to marry her."

At least it was Mace and not Drake. Drake was so painfully honest that a direct question, even from a ten-year-old, would be answered frankly. Mace had the ability to evade if necessary. Cautiously, Slater asked his daughter, "And what did he say?"

"He said it's possible." Her dimples flashed as she smiled. "Then he gave me some ice cream. Whenever I ask him something he doesn't want to talk about, he gives me ice cream."

Slater burst out laughing. "In other words, you played him."

"A little."

Still smiling, he went over and sat down beside her, hands clasped between his knees. "Why didn't you just ask me?"

The answer was significant to him. He wanted to be accessible if she ever had a question.

"Mom told me if I wanted the truth I should ask Uncle Drake, but if I wanted ice cream, I should ask Uncle Mace. I wanted ice cream."

That was so Raine.

It was impossible not to laugh again, but he gave Daisy a brief hug. "Your mom was right there. I do want to marry Grace, and I hope that won't upset you, because it doesn't change anything between me and you, or me and your mom. Got it?"

"Got it." She had a child's pragmatic attitude. "I want chocolate cake for my birthday party with that whipped cream frosting."

Moment passed, moment saved. He nodded. "I'll tell Harry."

She stood up and waved her hand airily. "I already have, Dad. Just wanted to make sure you didn't want yucky strawberry or anything."

He thought the real point of the conversation was Grace but didn't argue. His inquisitive daughter had asked her mother about the subject, and he wasn't surprised by the response, which sounded exactly like Raine. Then she'd let him handle it however he wanted, and that was exactly like her, too.

He hoped he'd done a good job. He remembered the day he'd heard about his father's death. His mother had dealt with it in a straightforward manner. In retrospect, she'd obviously been devastated, but she was calm when she spoke to her boys, pointing out that life was unpredictable and looking at what you had instead of what you don't have was the only way to cope. She'd told them their dad would always be part of their lives. He admired her and wanted to offer that same rock-solid guidance to his own child.

"I won't do any cake interference," he promised, and Daisy's sunny smile told him she'd been teasing; she knew Harry wouldn't dream of baking anything except the cake she wanted on her birthday.

"Mom said if she was going to pick someone for you, she'd pick Grace."

With that declaration Daisy went out the door at her usual hundred miles an hour, signaling that their discussion was over. He went back to the large mirror his mother had hung on the wall and reconsidered his image, something he almost never did. Shaving when he realized it had been a couple of days — that was about the only time he paid attention to his appearance. Daisy, he decided, was absolutely right. Losing the tie made him look more relaxed . . . even if he wasn't.

Tonight was important in a way that had nothing to do with the upcoming project.

He and Grace would be out in public as a couple for the first time. He wished she'd answer his question, but he wasn't going to push it, because he sensed that patience was the best strategy. It didn't help his ego that half of Wyoming seemed to know he'd asked her to marry him and that she hadn't given him a resounding *yes.* At least he hadn't gotten a firm *no,* either.

With that in mind, he went off to find Ryder, drop him off at home and pick up his date.

CHAPTER EIGHTEEN

Just her luck. When she dashed to the door to answer the knock before Hank could get there, it was the Chinese take-out delivery man. Hank came to the door, anyway, paid for the food and took the bag. Her ex-husband informed her, "Carson and I are not going to decide on pistols at dawn just because you're going to dinner with him. Do I wish it was with me instead? Hell, yes, I do, but the minute I walked into your office I figured you weren't going to change your mind about us. You look fantastic, by the way. He's a lucky bastard."

At that moment the lucky bastard pulled in. Ryder jumped out of his truck and waved with delighted familiarity at the delivery man, then came inside to head straight for the shower. In passing, he said casually, "Hey, Dad. Hi, Grace. Hey, you look nice."

The job at the ranch had certainly improved his attitude. She wondered if Hank had any idea what his parents had tried to handle, and the difficult child she'd ended up with when they couldn't do it anymore. She doubted it. Already she could sense that Hank was bored with the visit, unhappy she was involved with someone else. Ryder was probably right; he wasn't going to stick around. If she had to predict, she'd give him about three more days. Luckily, Ryder had Slater, Drake and Mace, not to mention the old cowboy, Red, who seemed to be something of a hero to him. So when Hank came up with an excuse to leave early, he wouldn't be without a father figure.

"Thanks," she murmured to his retreating back as she reached for her black clutch.

The look on Slater's face was worth the hour she'd spent getting ready. His oh-so-blue eyes widened and he stopped abruptly as he walked up to the door. "I am officially," he said in a husky tone, "speechless."

"You just said something, so that isn't true," she pointed out as she swept past him. "Don't expect salmon tonight, by the way. File all complaints with the management."

"I'm sure I won't have any complaints at all." Hurrying to his truck, he made a beeline for her door and got there in time to open it for her. She was nervous for some reason she couldn't fathom. Part of it might be that he looked incredible in his dark suit, and she was simply too susceptible.

She needed to get a grip and remind herself that her life was complicated, but the chaos would pass, and she'd find a steady pace again. For the moment, though, Slater Carson made her feel *unsteady*.

She climbed into his truck, which was a little complicated in her dress. "Keep in mind that Meg's in charge and she's kind of nervous."

"Gotcha." His smile was charming as he clasped her elbow and helped her in. "I think my guests will be suitably kind to her, so stop worrying. If anything goes wrong, besides the very minor salmon issue, I'm sure you'll leap up and save the day. Relax."

Easy for him to say. She wanted to ask if she looked okay, but that was a stupid idea on several levels, one of them being that he would inevitably answer *yes*. The other was that she didn't require his reassurance every five seconds. If he didn't like how she looked, acted or anything else, he was free to move on.

But she was coming to the conclusion that she didn't want him moving anywhere . . .

However . . . That meant she had to accept his proposal. Marry him, move to the ranch and hope for happy-ever-after.

He climbed into the driver's side and started the truck. She, in turn, stared out the front window. "I love you."

He accidentally put the vehicle in neutral and they coasted backward until he found the brake and jerked to a stop. "Mind repeating that?"

Grace still didn't want to look at him so she continued to stare straight ahead. "I think you heard me. And . . . I've already told you I didn't want to fall in love with you."

"I remember," he said in a thick voice. "Quite clearly."

"You have the right to expect me to jump up and down over your proposal. You have the right to expect tears of joy at the idea of becoming your wife. You have the right to —"

"Remain silent?" he interrupted, and when she glanced at him, she was smiling.

He had a unique way of turning a situation to his favor.

"No," she said with a sigh. "You can say whatever you want and it won't be held against you."

"I'm going to respond to that by saying

the evening's started out well. Couldn't be better, in fact. You love me, and I love you. When it's time for us to sit down and really talk, let me know."

"What? We'll have a meeting?"

He laughed, and she said, "The meeting to worry about is the one tonight."

"Oh, I'm not worried. All the men in that room will look at you, and they won't be able to think about anything else, so everything should go my way. They'll just put up the money and they won't be able to string two words together."

He was a charmer, and she needed to remember that. "Slater, can we come to an agreement? First, let me make sure David Reinhart is going to either leave me alone or do jail time. Let me get my ex-husband out of my hair. Let me make sure Ryder's adjusted to his new life before I have to decide if a white dress and a change of last name is a good idea."

He didn't skip a beat. "Take all the time you need, Grace, but maybe you should look at it from my perspective. Let me help you with David Reinhart. Hank Emery won't be around long, as we both know. Ryder's adjusting well, according to my mother. And the white dress is totally optional. I like the black number you're

307

wearing now — a lot. Did I mention that?"

"You did, and thank you for the compliment."

"I meant a *real* lot."

"That's not even good English." She was laughing.

He drove out of the condo complex. "I suspect you're right. So Meg and Mace? Thoughts?"

Now he was a matchmaker, not just a filmmaker? She did think it over. Mace Carson was good-looking but that applied to all three brothers. "Maybe. She has a crush on you, by the way."

"She's a very nice girl, but I'm kind of taken. I hope."

How, exactly, was she supposed to survive this evening without falling into his arms? And his bed. She knew full well that he'd booked a room in the resort. "You did hear me a few minutes ago, didn't you? I need more time."

"Oh, absolutely. That's why we're not talking about us, but about my brother and your assistant possibly hooking up."

"You should've invited him to the dinner, then."

"I did. I also invited Drake, since he's a fourth-generation rancher and represents part of what the film's going to be about.

Also some of my guests fund animal rights groups, and I think he belongs to most of them, especially the ones that concentrate on endangered species in this area." He sent her a sidelong look. "Lettie Arbuckle-Calder will be there, too."

Grace raised her eyebrows. "Should I be afraid?"

He grinned. "No, *afraid* is the wrong word. I actually like the woman, but your problem is going to be that she happens to be fond of me, as well. Since privacy around these parts is pretty much nonexistent, she'll probably pounce on you like a starving chicken on a stray kernel of corn. Uh, this won't surprise you, but she's heard about my proposal."

He said it in his best cowboy drawl, and she was afraid she'd ruin her mascara, with tears of mirth. "Let me guess. Red?"

"Of course. As I said, Lettie knows *everyone* around here, and she's as impressed with him as the rest of us. That man makes a powerful impact on a person's psyche." He paused. "Especially a young person's. Who knows what Ryder will pick up next."

What Ryder seemed to be picking up was a solid work ethic, and she was grateful for that. When his report card arrived, she'd find out more, but there'd been no calls from the school lately — a welcome change. "He's a good influence," she added with a smile.

"He is that. Shall we?"

The room was elegantly decorated, with white tablecloths and crystal, the music as understated as he'd requested. He hated dinners that had so much background noise, you couldn't hear what anyone was saying, even the people seated beside you. The point of the meeting was to talk about the upcoming film, and his assistant, Nathan, had done an outstanding job with the slideshow that was flashing during the cocktail hour. There were views not only of the Tetons, groves of aspens, meadows with grazing elk, but also old photographs of mining camps, towns founded in the late 1800s, the former hotel and even his family's ranch.

He — or rather, he and Grace — hadn't been able to take their site-scouting trip, due to the attack on Hank Emery. However, Nate had pulled the visuals together, using what they had available from a variety of sources. Everyone was clearly impressed, and the evocative images stirred that needed excitement.

Great start to the evening. Except that

Grace was distracting every male in the room. He'd be the first to admit she was stunning, and he also had the feeling she'd dressed like this on purpose to get back at him because of the way he'd arranged for her to be a guest instead of the efficient resort manager. Okay, he'd been a little manipulative, but . . .

Call it even.

He wasn't trying to be high-handed; he was feeling his way around their relationship. And he really just wanted to spend the evening with her.

The rest of his *life* with her.

One thing he would say, Grace stuck by his side as he moved around the room. She wasn't technically at work, so she did accept a glass of Mountain Vineyards wine Mace insisted she try, since she appeared to be his new favorite critic. She took a sip of the pinot noir, proclaimed it the best yet. Meg bustled in now and again, very competent and unfailingly sweet. At one point Grace murmured, "She's *so* going to replace me one day."

It was said with affection, and he didn't blame her. Too public a place for his own show of affection? He risked the PDA and put his arm around her waist. "No one can replace you."

"Carson, you are so transparent it isn't funny." She leaned toward him and whispered in his ear. "Might be why I'm being won over."

Now, *that* was the best news he'd had in a long while.

"I'm listening."

Mrs. Arbuckle-Calder (still generally known as Mrs. A) walked up at that very moment in a waft of some expensive perfume, and dressed as usual in a suit that probably had a Parisian label. She held a crystal glass in her hand. By way of greeting, she said succinctly, "Melody Hogan."

Slater was used to her imperious manner, so he didn't bat an eye. "Good evening, Mrs. A. Have you met Grace Emery?"

"No." There was a nod of approval after a sweeping assessment of Grace's person. "You know how to pick them, young man. But back to my original point. Melody Hogan."

He didn't dare look over at Grace, afraid he'd shout with laughter at her expression. People not used to the Arbuckle approach were often flummoxed by her, confused about how to respond. Just being called a *young man* at his age was funny enough. He said mildly, "I know Melody. What about her?"

"For the ring." Mrs. A scowled at him as if he was an idiot for not discerning exactly what she meant.

The light dawned. Melody designed custom jewelry. It was actually a very good idea, much better than walking into some generic jewelry store, squinting at a case of diamonds and randomly selecting one. He could make films and had plenty of other skills, too, but jewelry was not in his area of expertise. However, since Grace didn't want to be pushed, he hadn't taken that step yet.

"That's an excellent suggestion."

"I'll take care of it. I'm thinking a sapphire the color of her eyes. Yes, that's the ticket. I need more wine."

Grace was still speechless when the woman walked away. Slater spoke first. "Conversations with Lettie Arbuckle-Calder are never dull. I believe I warned you. They always end the same way, too. When she's finished saying whatever she has to say, she either hangs up or leaves. She isn't being rude, or not to her mind, anyway. The discussion is over, and that's that."

Grace finally found her voice. "*She'll* take care of it?"

"Look at it like this. You'll have a much prettier ring than if it was me doing the shopping. I might've asked Red to go along

313

with me, and you'd end up with a forty-pound nugget of gold to lug around on your finger."

"I haven't agreed to anything." Her eyes flashed, but her mouth twitched.

He looked straight back at her. "Not yet. I'm hopeful, though. The slideshow's over and Meg's having the staff clear off the appetizer table right on cue. She's doing a great job. Let me make my brief speech and then we can relax and have dinner. I'm thinking of ordering salmon, just to see how Meg handles it."

Grace gulped down a mouthful of wine, no doubt sorely needed after Mrs. Arbuckle-Calder's drive-by visit. "You're impossible."

He took her elbow. "Get used to it."

CHAPTER NINETEEN

She was seated next to Drake, which was welcome, since she'd describe him as the quiet brother, and Grace didn't need a lot of questions at the moment. He ordered sea scallops, risotto with a sweet potato puree and an endive and hearts of palm salad.

That would never have been the menu choice she figured a six-foot-plus cowboy with a nonchalant demeanor would select. He'd chosen to wear boots and a denim shirt even to a gathering like this one, but all the pomp didn't bother him, even if he'd picked beer instead of wine, and there was no crystal glass involved, just a cold bottle.

The Carson brothers were an interesting trio.

In an attempt at humor, she remarked, "You do realize I'll have to tell Red about the salad. Hearts of palm does not seem like standard cowboy fare."

"He won't blink an eye. You'd never guess

it but he's kind of an amateur chef," Drake informed her, his amiable smile surfacing. "I know, he's a wizened old cowhand — and I swear I'm not making this up — but he made paella last week. Borrowed Harry's special pan and everything for the occasion. He scoured the shops in town for the ingredients and drove sixty miles to buy saffron. I was just riding in while it was cooking, and let me tell you, it smelled great. So I stopped and had a plate."

"And?"

"It was good stuff. Not joking. It would make his day if you asked him to whip some up for you." Drake brightened. "I'm serious here. Hey, at your reception, you should pit him and Harry against each other. I doubt you'd need fireworks then. Oh, man, toss in Bad Billy, and you could light up the night sky. Those three could be the caterers from heaven if you gave them the chance to compete with each other."

She was trying to decide how irritated to be at the assumption everyone seemed to have that she was going to marry Slater simply because he'd asked her. Time for a change of subject. Besides, she really did need his help. "I'll think about that, but in the meanwhile, I was wondering if you could do me a huge favor."

"Yes."

She looked at Slater's brother with wry amusement. "You don't know what it is yet."

"Doesn't matter. I'll do it."

This unswerving acceptance was getting to her. "Ryder's cat —"

"Bonaparte, right? The stray you took in. The kid talks about him constantly. What? Please tell me there's nothing wrong."

Well, what were connections worth if you didn't use them? Grace explained, "No, not wrong, but we do have a small problem. Slater said you're like a magician with animals. There's no getting that stubborn feline in his crate to go to the vet. The complex won't even let us keep him if he isn't up to date on his shots, and I doubt he's had a single one. I need to turn in the paperwork before someone reports him. Plus, he needs to be neutered. He seems to be able to read my mind whenever I've tried to grab him for an appointment, and then he does a disappearing act, so we've missed at least three."

"Done."

That type of confidence — with a finicky cat — made her blink. "You're sure?"

"Pretty much." He shrugged, and she believed him. "I reckon I can talk some sense into the critter. Do you love my brother?"

Back to that *and* — he was a straight shooter, too. Got right to the point; she hadn't distracted him one bit.

Grace fought the urge to slug back her wine, but took a deep breath instead. "Wish I didn't."

"You *should* love him. Not an easy proposition, maybe, and Slater isn't perfect, but he's . . . great." Drake smiled again. "Don't tell him I said that. He's loyal to a fault, so he'll never be unfaithful. He's fantastic with Daisy. Which means that when you have kids, you can be sure they'll have a wonderful father. He makes those artsy films, but he can rope a calf with the best of 'em. Family means a lot to him, so I'm afraid the Carson bunch is part of the package. Hope that doesn't bother you."

"You don't have to sell him to me." Grace was amused and also touched. Evidently, Slater wasn't the only loyal Carson.

When you have kids. Yet another assumption.

"Then just say yes."

That sounded so simple. "Is there a family debate going on?" *Or a bet?*

"No, but I think there might be in the future. Wear your nicest nightgown in case we decide to abduct you and haul you in

318

front of the preacher at midnight. This *is* the wild West, after all."

He looked like the classic romantic cowboy with his tousled curls and ingenuous blue eyes.

"I'll keep that in mind, but doesn't the bride's family usually do the 'at gunpoint' thing?"

"The Carson family can improvise."

She was sure that in this neck of the woods the Carson family could do just about anything they wanted. They were unquestionably the royalty of Bliss County. "I promise I'll find a white negligee somewhere," she said, "if they even make such a thing, but in case everyone has a faulty memory, I've been married before. It didn't work out. And . . . Slater and I haven't known each other very long."

"Not a good argument." Drake shook his head. "The right woman hasn't walked into my line of vision yet. I'll know it when she does."

"You believe in love at first sight?"

"Damn straight I do, pardon my language."

He really *was* that romantic cowboy. And she understood what he was saying. The minute she'd hauled Ryder into Slater's office and he'd gotten to his feet, she'd been

319

struck by something hard to define and unique in her experience. When she'd met Hank, she'd been attracted to him — his natural air of command had appealed to her — but there was no lightning bolt.

There was a thunderstorm raging on the Carson front. However, operating from logic rather than emotion was the wisest course in her opinion. She told Drake, "She'll be a lucky lady, whoever she is."

"I'll do my best to make her feel that way. If my brother loves you and wants to marry you, he'll do the same thing. I'll bring Ryder home tomorrow and take care of Bonaparte. Jax Locke, he's our vet, will see him after-hours. No one understands more than he does that animals don't believe in appointments. He's seen many a sick calf for me in the middle of the night."

Then he went back to polishing off his risotto.

She had the impression she'd just been given an ultimatum, Wyoming-style.

Even while chatting with the important people who'd help him make this project happen, Slater was acutely aware of Grace. And of course, he noticed his brother talking to her. A lot.

Drake was an action-is-better-than-words

sort of guy, so Slater felt a certain amount of trepidation about what their in-depth conversation might be about. Him. That was an obvious conclusion, but Drake was straightforward enough that he was worried she was going to get the full-court press and wondered if he should rescue her.

Oh, wait. She didn't want him to rescue her.

So he should just leave her to Drake's tender mercies?

"Terrific party, and everyone seems on board with the film." Mick Branson's sophisticated voice came through loud and clear as he walked up. "Great wine, too. I don't need another investment project, but your brother's doing a good job of convincing me without saying a word. Is he open to incorporation? I know a company in California that might be really interested."

It was Slater's absolute policy never to speak for anyone else. "I don't have any idea, but I can set up a meeting if you're serious."

Mick looked at him over the rim of his glass. "Slate, when am I not serious? About business, anyway. Your redhead looks gorgeous tonight. Progress?"

Slater didn't really know the answer to that one, either. "Maybe. I might be planning a wedding cake with her — though I have to admit I don't care, even if she wants neon pink — but she might just say no. I don't think we have a ruling yet."

"Hmm. Sorry to hear that. I can guess you're getting a bit anxious." What an understatement. Other than his insistence on being part of Daisy's life, he'd never wanted anything more than he wanted this. "I've asked. Like I said, I'm still waiting for an answer."

"You'll be the first to hear."

"One would hope," he said with true humor, "but this is a tough negotiation. How was your dinner? Grace will ask me."

"Very good."

Mick was conservative when it came to praise, and he'd eaten in high-profile restaurants on most continents. The *very* meant he was impressed. Slater could see that while Grace had to put up with some rivalry between her chefs, there was a reason she tolerated them. The food at both the resort and the spa was excellent. "She'll be glad to hear it. Let me know when I should talk to the writers." He thought regretfully about his lost trip. "I'm scouting location shots in the next few days, one of which will be right here. As you saw in Nathan's slide show, the old pictures of the hotel are fantastic."

"Can't wait to see what you do with this."

That was also high praise. "If I can top the last one, I'll be happy, too."

"You should be. *160* might make you a household name."

He wasn't sure about that, but he *was* sure the party was ending, and he was about to make a major play that might decide his future. "We'll see. Now, if you'll excuse me, I think Grace is finally free. Thanks for coming."

Mick grinned as he waved him on, and that was unusual. Mick did not grin. Slater caught up with Grace by the drinks table where she was doing inventory.

He thought about touching her, but decided to stay hands off. Instead, he said from directly behind her, "Meg gets five stars from me. Tell her thanks. Great party."

Grace turned. "We have a room, don't we?"

We sounded promising. "I'd complain to the management if that wasn't true. I reserved one. I'm probably okay to drive, but I'm not taking any chances."

"Let's go there now. To your room. Do you mind?" She tossed back that gorgeous hair and gave him a challenging look.

Mind? Had the chef put loco weed in her salad instead of lettuce? She didn't have to

323

ask him twice. "No, I sure don't."

"Don't do it, Carson." Grace correctly interpreted his urge to pick her up and cart her out the door. "I work here. I'm the boss, remember? You leave first, I'll talk to Meg and the staff and tell them they did a great job, and then I'll join you. Discreetly."

That was fair enough.

Maybe he was prone to theatrical demonstrations — for obvious reasons — but he understood discreet, too. "I'm in room —"

"You think I couldn't find out?"

Flattering to be informed that she'd paid attention. "Okay. I'll be waiting."

Then she sweetened the deal. "Not for long."

He could swear both Mace and Drake were laughing and money exchanged hands, but he'd just kill them later. He made last-minute thank-you rounds and took off his suit coat in the elevator; luckily, he was alone. He loosened another button on his shirt as he practically jumped off on his floor, ran to his room and fumbled with his key card to unlock the door. Dropped the card, laughed at himself and on his second try got it right.

Took a deep breath. Walked in . . . and waited.

Grace was excruciatingly late — if ten

minutes even qualified as *late.*

The light knock finally came and he walked to the door slowly, with dignified restraint. But when he opened it, his first thought was that sexy black dress had to go. He caught her by the waist, pulled her in for a hungry kiss and was happy — no, *thrilled* — when she said, "I guess we'll talk later."

Perfect. Yes. Later.

She didn't seem to object to the agenda.

A room with a view really meant something when she was part of it. He slipped off her dress and should probably have appreciated her lingerie, but he was in kind of a hurry. Her high heels were tossed aside. He'd planned to mention that she smelled like lilacs, but he was so desperate for her, he doubted he'd make any sense. As they fell onto the bed, he did manage to say, "I love you. I can't believe it."

"You need to work on that line."

He gazed into her eyes. "My problem is that it's not a line. I was starting to think this wasn't going to happen in my life." He kissed her shoulder. "Okay if I don't use a condom tonight? Say the word and I will."

She was so incredibly beautiful lying beneath him. "Slater, we both know I'm going to marry you."

He'd felt it, but *knowing* was different. It heightened the moment, and that wasn't what he needed. "You'll have to work on *that* line. I think how it usually works is the proposal's made and then accepted, but . . . I'll take what I can get." A flat-out yes seemed to be an elusive goal. "I hoped you'd eventually agree. But have mercy on me here. I want you now. Right now."

"The condom is optional." Her voice was soft.

Maybe that wasn't the resounding *yes* he wanted, either, but it was certainly a sign that Grace was looking toward a future that included both of them. Three of them maybe. Plus Daisy, plus Ryder . . . that was five . . . And he couldn't forget Bonaparte. Would he live on the ranch? Then his family would be in the mix, too.

This might get a little complicated, but he was ready to handle it.

He slid his hands beneath her and moved forward into her heat, her acceptance. Grace's receptive body told him more than any words that she wanted him as much as he wanted her.

Making love to a woman you loved, a woman who also loved you, was an unrivaled experience, he decided as pleasure flooded through him. He and Grace had a special communion that shook him, and when her hands tightened on his shoulders he got the message without a single word being said.

The aftermath involved more unspoken messages. He had a lot of things to say, but wasn't sure quite how to say them, so he followed his instincts and kept his mouth shut. Unless he was lightly tasting her nipple, or skimming the arch of her throat and holding her as intimately as possible, because he knew she wouldn't stay the night.

Correct on that count. Sometime later, she said, "You need to take me home."

"I will if that's what you want, but I think your ex is a big boy. If you spend the night with me, he'll just have to get over it."

"But Ryder isn't a big boy. I don't want to risk leaving him there alone, especially now. More than once, I've woken up in the morning to find a note from Hank that said 'deployed.' No warnings, no details, nothing."

He raised himself up on one elbow. "Do you really think he'd take off like that, leave him on his own?"

"I don't know. Even though Ryder's only fourteen, he's easily going to be as tall as you. He looks like an adult, but he isn't, and I'm not sure Hank understands that. He isn't used to taking care of him. My point is that since I'm the one Ryder counts on, I should be there. If Hank got orders, he'd just up and go. I'm speaking with the voice of experience here."

As he searched for his clothes, he reminded himself that this was why he was convinced she'd be his ideal life partner. Her sense of responsibility, caring, commitment. A woman Ryder could count on. A woman *he* could count on. Just like she could count on him . . .

Yes, he'd take her home, which was ironic since she currently lived with her ex, but that wasn't her choice. He was.

This had been one hell of a happy evening.

Bonaparte was sleeping on the front stoop when he drove up and even approached him to rub against his ankles. Grace told him in astonishment, "I buy his food and he barely lets me pet him."

"I have a romantic soul." He kissed her. "I've got that on good authority. Bonaparte senses it."

"Cats and romance? I don't quite see how they fit together."

"Think about it. He loves you and I love you, so we're kindred souls."

"Slater, I hope we aren't rushing this."

Her poignant expression tugged at his heart, but she'd agreed to marry him, so . . .

He kissed her again. "I get it. You don't *want* to love me. You don't want to get married. Mind setting a date for that wedding you'd rather not have? Once Mrs. A orders the ring, everyone will know, and my mother will start making her plans."

She pushed him away, laughing. "I'm being railroaded."

"No question there." He held up his hands. "We're definitely on a runaway train. Okay, the wedding. How about early November? Autumn's really beautiful here. And," he added, "we don't want to wait too long. You could be pregnant right now."

Her smile was tremulous. "You must be joking. About getting married so soon . . ."

"Would I joke about one of the most important things in my life?" Grace fell into the category labeled *Essential to Happiness*. He said simply, "I know this is very real for me. Very right for me. For us."

Grace took a deep, shaky breath. "I've told myself far too often that I didn't think it over long enough the first time, so I'm choosing to trust your instincts instead of mine. Yes to November, but *you* have to deal with Mrs. A."

He could handle that. Maybe. "I'll do my

best, but if you plan to bet on it like the rest of my family, I'd put my money on Lettie Arbuckle getting her way."

CHAPTER TWENTY

She was going to get married again.

Insane. Yes, that describes me.

Except there was every chance she'd be an idiot to say no. She didn't feel any obligation to tell Hank, but there was someone she did feel obliged to discuss it with.

Ryder was still awake. Grace had no doubt he would be. He was a night owl, and if he thought for a split second that she didn't know that once she was in bed, he went back to reading Sci-Fi novels and watching movies, he was sadly mistaken. In this case, since his dad was staying in his room and he was sleeping on the couch, he was easily found out, because when she walked through the door, he was in the kitchen making microwave popcorn, an action movie playing — quietly, at least — on the television.

"You're busted." She dropped her purse on the side table and kicked off a shoe. "It's well past your curfew."

He removed the popcorn bag. "*You're*
busted, Grace. Past curfew for you, too. I
could've pretended to be asleep when I
heard the truck pull up."

She *was* late.

"It wouldn't have fooled me."

"I know. That's why I didn't do it." He
dumped the contents of the bag into a glass
bowl. "Want some popcorn?"

She'd been nervous during dinner, so
while her meal had been delicious, she
hadn't eaten much. Plus, now that she'd
come to a crossroads and chosen a path,
she actually craved a snack because her tension had eased. "Sounds good."

"So you're going to marry Slater, huh?"

Evidently, she wasn't the one who'd have
to bring up the subject. The other shoe clattered to the floor. "How did —"

"You just seem really happy."

Did she? Happy enough that a fourteen-
year-old absorbed in his own life would
notice it? "I am happy, yes. And yes, I'm
going to marry Slater."

Job done painlessly. Although she needed
to find out how he felt about it. "I know
you like him. So, you're okay with it all
around?"

He divided the popcorn into two bowls. "Sure."

"Ryder?"

When he turned, his face was composed and for a moment the flippant fourteen-year-old wasn't there. "Grace, I think Slater is really great. My dad will never be here for me all the time. I know that. You will, and I know that, too. You're always there for me. So . . . I'm okay."

The best part was she believed him. He also didn't thank her, which was a relief.

Almost everyone accepted their parents' unconditional love; they expected it, actually. That was as it should be. Even though some people didn't receive it, and the damage that did could last a lifetime. The fact was, Ryder didn't owe her anything. She probably owed him for teaching her what it was like to assume responsibility for another person. She wished he was wrong about Hank. The upside was that he'd read her absolutely right.

Always there. That sensation of being alone had gone away for her, too. Now she had not only Slater but also Blythe, Drake, Mace, Red, Harry . . . even Mrs. A . . . and, of course, Ryder.

Her eyes filled with tears. "I'd hug you, but I assume you aren't interested. What are we watching?"

He dropped to the couch. "*True Grit.* Slater told me I should watch the original, and then the remake. He wants my opinion on which one I think is better. Kind of like homework."

"Homework?" She took her bowl and sat next to him. "Why?"

"I might want to try my hand at ranching. Or maybe film production. I told Slater that, and he suggested the movie."

Her response was careful. He was going to get to choose his own life. "Not the military?"

"I don't know yet."

"You have some years to decide."

"Red told me the time goes fast. I can't sit around waiting for the rabbit to hop over the damn crick."

Choking on popcorn was an interesting sensation. Grace recovered and took a swallow from her bottle of water. "He's a profound man but I wish he wouldn't swear in front of you."

Ryder grinned. "He didn't. I threw that in just to bug you."

Red's wisdom was a gift of a unique kind. She wasn't sure if she should be grateful for his quaint sayings or not, but he was a positive influence. "I suppose that's his way of saying you should start thinking about it now. You shouldn't rush into a decision, though. Slater was planning to run the ranch, and that's not what he ended up doing, and I was a police officer and that isn't what I'm doing now, either. To his credit, your dad's always known his path and been dedicated to it, but that isn't true of everyone."

He dropped his gaze. "Drake said I'm good with horses. A natural. Any chance I can do some amateur rodeo? Slater used to ride the circuit. He said he'd help if you agreed to it."

Instinct told her to say no. Rodeo was hardly the safest sport, and while she'd seen the trophies in Slater's office, he'd been riding his whole life, and Ryder was just learning. "I'll talk to your father about it."

Hank would, of course, say yes. Risk was a given to him and although he didn't disregard it, he thought of it as a way of life. His first duty had been working the deck of an aircraft carrier, landing fighter jets, for which he'd gotten danger pay. That word didn't scare him at all.

Ryder came to the same conclusion about his dad's likely reaction. He brightened. "Cool."

"In the meantime, cue up the movie. I

think I've seen the original about thirty times. John Wayne. You have my permission to stay up, but the minute it's over, hit the hay. You can watch the second one tomorrow night."

"Red said his favorite John Wayne movie is *Big Jake.* Hey, are we going to live on the ranch?"

She hadn't even gotten that far, nor had she and Slater discussed it yet. Since the day she'd met the man, everything had been moving so fast. Helplessly, she responded, "I don't know."

"I vote yes. That'd be great."

It would be for him, no doubt. But whatever happened, she wasn't giving up her job. Ryder was already staying at the ranch until early evening — so he was practically living there, anyway. Harry had jumped into full mothering mode, and Blythe had assisted immeasurably with his homework, thanks to her patience and her sense of humor.

But it was overwhelming to imagine inheriting a big, busy family, plus a second stepchild, and she'd agreed that they could try to get pregnant. Slater might take it all in stride, but this kind of life hadn't been hers. She'd grown up in a conventional family on a quiet residential street. Her parents had had children later than most couples did, so the ranch with its chaotic exuberance would be quite the new experience.

It was too much to think about at this late hour.

"I'll see you in the morning," she told Ryder, yawning and heading down the hall.

"Wait, hey, I almost forgot." Ryder leaped up from the couch. "The neighbor brought this over. It was accidentally put in his mailbox."

No, it wasn't. Sure, it was stamped and correctly addressed — to her — but it wasn't even postmarked and there was no return address.

Immediately, she knew who it was from. A sudden tension stiffened her shoulders. "Thanks. Go back to your movie. Sleep well."

She went into her bedroom then the bathroom, took a pair of gloves she used for cleaning from the drawer and slipped them on. She sank down on the side of the bed and opened the envelope. Inside was a set of pictures.

Of her.

Getting out of her car. In the frozen food section of the grocery store. Unlocking her front door. Walking into the resort, talking on her cell phone.

Oh, that wasn't a clear message, was it?

I'm watching.

The worst was a picture of Slater talking to a man she didn't recognize, but that didn't matter. She was so chilled she could hardly breathe. She grabbed her cell phone and hit speed dial. To her relief, he answered right away. "Grace?"

She was practically babbling. "Are you back at the resort? Are you in your room? Is the door locked?"

"Yes. Yes, and yes. What's up?"

"You need to be careful." She explained about the envelope, her heart still racing.

"I'll let Spence know first thing tomorrow. Doesn't sound as if the theory that he left the area is viable." His tone was grim. "I'm getting very tired of this guy."

So was she. But there was a positive slant to this latest development. "You want the good news?"

"Besides the fact that no one's been seriously hurt? Go for it."

"David Reinhart committed a federal offense when he put that envelope in my neighbor's mailbox."

"Can you prove it?"

"If we can lift prints off the envelope or the pictures, I can. I think he just made a big mistake."

Slater sat across from Spence Hogan's desk and rubbed his jaw. "I'm concerned about this whole situation. You know that. Now what do I do?"

Spence raised his eyebrows. "Slate, you're talking about someone who understands procedure. She brought us the pictures. She used latex gloves to open the envelope. We'll run the prints. I suggest you do nothing. I get that you want to protect her, but I hate to point out she might be better at that than you are. Go do your movie stuff. We're on this, I promise."

It wasn't bad advice, but it wasn't what he wanted to hear. "I'm going to marry her."

There was a glint of humor in his friend's eyes. "Oh, if you think I don't already know that, you've lost all sense of reality. You do remember where you live, right?"

"Yeah." He did. Slater hoped Grace would be given time to adjust to life in a small town and what that meant. "No secrets. I'm hoping Reinhart will figure out that it isn't just her and a teenage boy he's targeting."

Spence leaned back in his chair. "I wish I didn't know how these people think, but unfortunately, I have some insights. It's an occupational hazard. I did some research on Mr. David Reinhart, and long before this issue with Grace, he was on a downward spiral. She caught him stealing and fired him, but as far I can tell, he's had run-ins with the law his entire life. She represents authority, which for whatever reason, he hates. Luckily, she can handle herself, but unluckily he knows it, so he'll come at her in an oblique way if he keeps on threatening her."

Valid point. Slater had told her the same thing. "Surely in a place like Mustang Creek we should be able to find him easily."

"I suspect he's holed up with one of his gambling buddies or a girlfriend and lying low. The friend who kicked him out said he's a personable guy and that there were always people coming and going, mostly new friends who hadn't got the picture yet, quite a few of them women. There are enough gaps in his background check that it suggests he sometimes uses another identity. I also doubt we're the only ones looking for him. His credit cards are all maxed out and the payments are overdue."

As he drove back to the ranch he thought sardonically that if the man put as much effort into staying straight and getting help for his gambling habit as he did into harassing Grace, he'd be much better off.

Half an hour later he was saddling Heck, since he did his best thinking on horseback.

"Take a slicker. It's gonna rain."

He glanced up as Red ambled through the stable in his usual bowlegged way. Slater might have argued that there wasn't a cloud in the sky; instead he grabbed one off a peg and nodded his thanks. Life experience had taught him that every single time he'd ignored his human barometer, he'd suffered for it.

"So you're getting hitched to your pretty redhead, huh?" The older man scratched his head theatrically. "Not quite sure what she sees in you, but love can be a mysterious thing. Kind of like an owl that doesn't like the dark. Just don't make sense."

That didn't make sense. But never mind.

Slater checked the frayed strap on the bridle. He'd been meaning to replace it, but it looked as though it would hold for this afternoon, anyway. "Well, I bet you can tell me what I see in her."

"Yeah, that's obvious." He chuckled. "But to give you credit, you've brought around some pretty girls who just didn't ring your bell, so I say if she does, marry her quick before she changes her mind."

"November," Slater informed him.

Bushy eyebrows shot up. "*This* November? That's fast work, son. Harry is gonna win that damn bet. The pool's big, too."

It took some effort not to make an exasperated comment. By now, he knew everyone was just doing it to irritate him, and that was his fault for ever showing a reaction. He knew better.

Grace would have to get used to this bunch. Jokingly, he remarked, "I plan on keeping her away from the ranch as much as possible, in case you all cause her to change her mind." He swung into the saddle, slicker in hand. "Would you do me a favor? Drive down to the main road and meet the bus when Ryder's due to get off. Right now I don't want him walking up the drive alone."

Red gave him a quizzical look, but didn't pry. "Will do."

"I appreciate it." He touched Heck lightly with his heels.

The horse was as restive as always. They took off, and Heck clattered out at his usual reckless speed, which matched Slater's mood just fine.

He trusted Spence completely, knew he'd do everything possible as far as law enforcement was concerned. But Slater's instincts screamed that he needed to jump in for

Grace and Ryder . . . and damn it, he had a life and successful career based on instincts.

Good camera shot or bad? Should he match music to the mood or not? Did he have the perfect angle and location? Or could he find something else that might more effectively capture what he wanted to say? He made calls like that all the time, so it wasn't exactly new to him, but this was up to Grace.

He stopped Heck by a trio of sapling pines and thought it over, the reins hanging.

Just let her handle it?

He really wished Spence hadn't pointed out that damage could fly sideways instead, since that made him very nervous. No one could protect him or herself from all possibilities.

He felt it was time for a Carson-style intervention — but he could be wrong. He listened to what the mountains were telling him. *It wouldn't hurt if you were around in case of trouble.*

Was he just hearing what he wanted to hear?

Maybe you should stand back. You're already crowding her.

He tipped back his hat, listening not just to the river flowing past him, but to his heart, as well.

CHAPTER TWENTY-ONE

Blythe Carson had an air about her that showed an unmistakable personal confidence Grace admired. This particular afternoon she was dressed in a long ivory skirt and a dark blue silk blouse, and Grace would guess that the pearls in the clip holding back the elegant twist of hair weren't imitation.

An invitation to lunch by her future mother-in-law wasn't something she could easily refuse. Practically impossible to say no when she was given the choice of day and time. The restaurant was a new addition to Mustang Creek called Sara-Anne's — certainly more genteel than Bad Billy's Burger Palace — and only served tea and sandwiches with ingredients like watercress and smoked salmon. Grace chose the organic chicken salad on homemade wheat bread and wondered exactly what Blythe wanted to talk about.

There was a sinking feeling in the pit of her stomach that it was going to be the wedding.

Of course.

Newsflash: Oldest son is getting married. Finally. Yes, this was going to be a conversation about weddings. Blythe obviously knew the restaurant owner, who bustled over and seated them at a table overlooking a small water fountain and mums that were still blooming, and they greeted each other by name.

"I want to say," Blythe informed her after the fresh rolls were delivered, "that I'm delighted you and Slater have decided to get married."

"Well, he's a decent guy."

That was so lame. She cleared her throat and tried again. "Let me rephrase. He's way too interested in meddling in my life, and he's on the controlling side — but I suppose I am, too. And yet . . . I said yes. If you can explain it to me, go ahead."

Blythe took one of the rolls, quietly laughing. "That certainly describes my relationship with his father. Not love/hate but love/love. His assumption that he could take care of any problem better than I could infuriated me, but then I reminded myself that his motivation was to protect me. So I threw the anger out the window and fell in love with him instead." She paused. "Over time, we developed our compromises, the ones that worked for us, but the basis of everything was love."

There was obviously something this woman wanted to know. It wasn't about the wedding; Grace understood that now. "I *do* love him."

"So you should. He's a wonderful man."

They regarded each other over the table, and Grace finally caved, "You're deliberately testing me."

Blythe put down her roll and touched the linen napkin to her lips before she spoke. "Of course I am. He's waited for you. I know my son. Once he's decided, then he's decided. I need to know you've decided, too."

"If you had any idea how hard this was for me, you wouldn't even ask. I'm so frightened of risking his happiness, I can't begin to tell you."

Her future mother-in-law smiled and it was genuine, not merely polite. "His happiness is important, but so is yours. Let's talk about Ryder's, too. He's happier about the engagement than I think you realize. He doesn't really talk about it, but he wants a traditional family. He's been an only child

346

his entire life, and he's always struggled with his place in this world. He never mentions his birth mother."

Grace doubted his birth mother mentioned him, either. She certainly hoped the woman treated her other children better than she'd treated him.

It wasn't news, but she had to ask, "Did he say that? Out loud?"

Blythe laughed and shook her head. "Of course not. Boys don't admit they struggle. They pretend they don't. Their emotions go as deep as ours, but they're often not very good, very practiced, at expressing them." She studied the linen tablecloth for a moment. "You know, Slater isn't over the death of his father. But it's made him a very good father to Daisy, I promise you that, and I console myself with it every single day. I don't mean to get maudlin. Things happen. We all know that. You were a police officer so you're especially aware that the world isn't perfect. Anyway, let's move on. This discussion is about happiness. What color?"

Grace had been about to say the chicken salad was delicious and had no idea how to answer Blythe's question. She stopped with a forkful halfway to her mouth. "We're talking about . . ."

"Dresses. Bridal gown and bridesmaids'.

What color? Long skirts or short? Harry and I were thinking long because of the season."

Slater's prediction came through like a bright light shining down a tunnel. The wedding was being planned — just not by her. "Light blue," she said, at least prepared for that question. "Something very simple. I thought I'd ask Daisy if she'll be a bridesmaid. My assistant, Meg, has already said yes. Two of them to balance Drake and Mace. That's it."

"I understand you want simple, since you've been married before, but Slater hasn't. There hasn't been a Carson wedding since mine, and that was quite some time ago." Blythe's smile glimmered. "We won't go into how many years or I'll start to feel old. Also, I'm sure Ryder will be included, so you should have three bridesmaids. Who else?"

Slater came by his ability to get what he wanted honestly. Maybe they *should* elope, but . . . Blythe seemed to be enjoying this, and Grace knew he'd want his mother to be happy. "I could ask my sister-in-law in Texas, but she has a busy life and young family . . . What about Raine?"

Blythe's smile widened, and there was a hint of mischief there. "I was going to suggest it, but I was afraid you might find that awkward. It isn't. She's one of Slater's very good friends, and I know she's happy for him. I, uh, might already have mentioned it to her."

She clearly would not be planning her own wedding. Grace could feel it skidding out of her control. She said with a certain resignation, "I'll call her."

"She'll appreciate that. Now, shall we talk flowers?"

An hour later Grace got into her car and hit Slater's number on her cell phone. Skipping hello, he said, "Told you."

"Smug is not how you're going to win my affections."

"I thought I had that in the bag. So, how was lunch?"

"Delicious. And I love your mother, but how come I didn't agree to elope — somewhere tropical? Or maybe Las Vegas for a quickie wedding?"

"That's my question, too. Has Harry decided on the menu?"

"Oh, yes. And the table settings right down to the napkin rings. I was asked a few questions, but most of it was figured out quite a while ago, and they were just pretending I had a say."

"Welcome to Carsonville, USA. I might be the oldest male, by the way, but I am definitely not in charge."

"I think Red's the oldest male, and he has more clout than you."

His response held amusement. "Can't argue with that. His name might not be Carson, but Drake, Mace and I stand at attention when he comes into a room. That old coot could probably still wipe the floor with all three of us if we got out of line. What are we doing tonight?"

"I just had lunch with your mother, so you're having dinner with my ex-husband."

She felt no small sense of satisfaction when he said in audible dismay, *"What?"*

"Steaks on the grill, twice-baked potatoes, seven-layer salad. I figured since you're bringing Ryder home this evening, you could stay and eat with us." What she didn't add was that she wasn't interested in another tension-filled evening alone with Hank, especially now that he knew she was marrying another man. Ryder often ate dinner at the ranch, so she'd sat across the table from Hank one too many times, trying to defuse the silence with polite conversation. Slater would be good company, and it would help to have Ryder there, too. Hank would make an effort to converse with his son.

She needn't have worried. When she got

to the condo, his rental car was gone . . . and so was he. There was a sealed note on the counter with Ryder's name on it and for her, the usual. *New orders. Hank.*

No thank-you for her hospitality, but she didn't really expect one. He'd caught on immediately that she was involved with someone else, but he and Slater seemed to have if not a liking for each other, at least mutual respect and civility.

Part of her was overjoyed that his stay had been cut short because she hadn't been pleased about it in the first place, and part of her mourned for Ryder yet again. However, he was in a stable environment now, where a lot of people cared about him. She took one of the steaks she'd bought and stuck it in the freezer, went over to Bonaparte, who was napping on the couch, and stroked his back. "Plus," she informed the cat, "he has you."

Ryder's best friend managed to purr and yawn at the same time.

Her phone beeped and Grace got up to check, expecting it to be the resort since she was taking a day off, but it was Slater and he sounded tense. "Grace, Ryder didn't get off the bus. I can't find him and I've been looking. Can you call the school?"

Well, hell.

Slater drove his truck along the bus route one more time, his throat dry. Ryder, so far, anyway, hadn't missed the bus once since he'd started working at the ranch, and Slater felt a gnawing worry that grew worse with each passing minute.

It had been almost an hour. He wasn't the only one worrying, either. Next to him, Red asked, "You mind telling me exactly what's going on, cowboy? Because I'm getting the feeling that there's a dead mouse in the pantry."

He could tell Red anything; he knew that. "Grace fired someone who thinks he needs a bit of revenge, and Ryder would be just the way to do it. Maybe I'm panicking for nothing, but maybe I'm not. I have to go with my gut . . . and my gut says this isn't good."

"I kinda wondered why you were so jumpy earlier." Red took off his hat and ran his hand through his graying hair. "Nobody better hurt that kid."

"Got that right." Slater meant it, too. He took a fast turn that made his tires squeal, then slowed it down. The cops wouldn't appreciate it if he caused an accident. They had enough to do. No one seemed to know where Ryder Emery was. Spence Hogan had detailed several officers to search for him. The fact that Hank Emery had been knocked unconscious recently and Grace had reported the repeated vandalism of her car, as well as those photographs, meant Spence was taking this very seriously. When Slater passed a state trooper's car and then a second one, he knew just how seriously.

If Slater was in full panic mode, he could only imagine how Grace felt.

Grace's car was in the driveway of the condo and she was hovering in the doorway, talking on her cell phone. Her face, framed by her vivid hair, was extremely pale.

When he got out, she ended the call and came outside. But before he could take her in his arms to offer comfort, Red beat him to it. He hugged her and patted her back. "L'il darlin', we'll find him. That boy is a smart cookie."

She hugged him back, composed, and yet her voice held a distinct wobble. "I know he is. But he's only fourteen, and Reinhart is a coward. I had some experience with this sort of thing when I was a cop, and I can tell you cowards scare me a lot more than the big bad boys. He's a sociopath, and having a lack of conscience also means a lack of empathy. I am so damn mad right now I could —"

"Spit?" Red supplied helpfully.

That wrung out a weak laugh. "Okay, yeah, spit."

Slater asked, "Where's Hank? At the school? I have Drake and Mace out there looking, so we don't want to overlap. Raine's going to all the local teen hangouts, and my mother and Harry are going to call instantly if he shows up at the ranch."

"Hank left for who knows where." She raised her phone. "I can't get hold of him. I keep trying and leaving messages on his voice mail. He either can't or won't answer. Your guess is as good as mine as to which one it is. He's ticked off at me because of you."

It wasn't as if this was startling news.

"None of this is your fault." He kept his voice gentle.

His feisty bride-to-be shot right back. "Oh, I know that. Hank's misguided assumption that I'd ever be interested in a repeat performance of our failed relationship is his problem. And I'd fire David Reinhart's dishonest ass again tomorrow."

That was the Grace he knew. And loved. But he could see the distress in her eyes —

354

and was still in shock because as far as he knew Red had *never* hugged anyone (other than his long-ago wife). Maybe a handshake or a slap on the shoulder, but a real hug? Forget it.

"We'll find him," Slater repeated, but this was outside the scope of his experience.

"Where?" She was much more practical. "How? I'm open to all suggestions."

But his phone rang then, which meant he could avoid answering her. Just as well, since he was at a total loss. He saw Drake's number on call display. "Hello?"

His brother was as eloquent as usual. "Got 'im."

"Ryder?"

"Yeah, who else am I looking for? I'm not the FBI or anything. He's the only kid I was tracking down."

He reminded himself he loved Drake so he could overlook the sarcasm and gave Grace a thumbs-up and mouthed, *He's safe.* "Where was he?"

"Is. County fair. Told me his dad said it was okay. Another parent took him there. Seems one of the other kids broke his leg and has one heck of a cow pony. So all his friends agreed Ryder should enter the calf-roping in his place."

If Slater wasn't light-headed with relief,

he might've tried to hunt down Hank Emery and given him hell for not letting Grace know.

He could hear the reluctance in Drake's voice, but his brother admitted, "I feel responsible. That kid's really taken to roping and said he wanted to go watch the rodeo. Of course I thought he'd ask Grace, too, not just the old man. It finally occurred to me that might be where he was, since he'd asked for a day off. I'm sorry I didn't put two and two together faster."

Grace hugged Red again, but this time in relief and pure joy. Slater was beginning to feel a little neglected.

"I've been busy," Drake was saying. "Another missing calf, running a ranch, brother getting married . . . the usual stuff . . ." He rambled on, and he wasn't a rambler by any means. Then, to make the day even more interesting, he added in disgust, "Mace deserves the credit. He remembered the Bliss County fair was due to start today because Harry always wins with that pie he likes. Remember how he shamelessly hogged the whole damn thing when she made it the first time? He ate an *entire* pie. She's won, like, five years in a row. Finally his overactive pie-hole did someone a favor."

Slater started laughing and had to choke

356

out the words. "Bring Ryder here, please. Grace needs to see with her own eyes that he's safe."

"Hell, no," Drake said, his refusal firm. "They're about to start the qualifying in his age group. I'm telling you, he's got a shot if that horse is as good as it's supposed to be. Get over here and cheer him on."

From hell to heaven. Plus, everyone would love it if Ryder qualified. "We'll be there as quickly as we can make it."

"Well, we'll all be here."

He ended the call and pointed at Red. "County Fair Grounds. You've been coaching him, haven't you? The kid's there. If Ryder qualifies, maybe someday Grace will forgive you."

Red looked about as guilty as he ever did, which was not at all. He muttered, "I don't study the calendar and didn't remember the fair was this week. All that happened was he asked me if I thought he should try it someday. I said he should. For a beginner, he's pretty good. Got the hang of it right away. Besides, you know I always say if you don't try for something, you won't get it."

"I'll bump beers with you later, since he seems to be safe. You and Grace and I are headed out to make sure that's true, although I do trust Drake and Mace."

"You should." Red looked affronted. "Those two ruffians are like oil and vinegar, but they're protective enough of Ryder that they'd charge into a buffalo stampede to save him."

Grace stared at them as if they'd both lost their minds. But at least she had a faint smile on her lips. "Buffalo stampede? I assume that's a thing of the past, even around here."

"Red's watched too many old Westerns." Slater took her hand and laced his fingers through hers. "Come on, let's go — right after I call off the search."

CHAPTER TWENTY-TWO

She was trying not to be too elated, but the nightmare had lifted like a fog evaporating over a cold lake, and Grace couldn't believe the surly teenage boy who'd suddenly become her responsibility was whooping it up as the finalists were announced.

She'd seen Ryder in just about every mood possible, but joyous was rare.

She tapped Slater on the shoulder as they sat in the bleachers. "Isn't roping a calf hard to learn?"

His blue eyes flashed with humor. "I'm not sure. I think I was about five the first time I did it. In the Carson family it's sort of like potty-training. You do that at a certain age, you learn to ride next and then you learn to rope a calf. Daisy's quite good at it, too, but Ryder really caught on fast for someone who was raised in the city. He understands animals, so maybe you should nudge him toward a profession that involves a special talent like that. He's too big to be a jockey, but what about horse-training? You can make a decent living at it."

It wasn't on the usual list of professions, with doctor, lawyer and architect. But Ryder had warmed up to the environment at the ranch with more enthusiasm than anything in his life so far. "He's still so young," she murmured, "but it's a thought. He seems happy. Just don't suggest rodeo as a profession, okay?"

He slipped his arm around her waist. "You're in charge. I'm impressed that he pulled it off. Honestly, Grace, he just learned how to ride a horse!"

Slater was as elated as any proud father. No wonder she'd fallen in love with him.

For that matter, Drake, Mace and, of course, Red were all taking credit. Then the scores were announced — with Ryder getting an honorable mention, to tumultuous applause. But to Grace, his success was secondary to the fact that he was *there,* in her line of vision, safe and sound.

She could finally lose the tightness in her throat. Maybe her blood pressure would return to normal in the next few hours.

Hank was lucky he wasn't anywhere close by.

And the thing was, she knew he hadn't

done it on purpose. That was just typical Hank. It obviously hadn't occurred to him to mention it in his note. It wouldn't have occurred to him to come and watch his son participate in this event, either. She tried to picture him at a rodeo and found she didn't have enough imagination for that one.

However, she couldn't complain about the tight-knit Carson family. Everyone had been willing to bring their busy lives to a halt, willing to pitch in and help, and that moved her. "Dinner at the ranch, instead?" Slater's expression was sympathetic. "You still look pretty shaken, and everyone will want to celebrate with Ryder. Or would you prefer some peace and quiet? Either way is fine."

Slater was right; she wasn't very interested in cooking at the moment, even something fairly simple. "Harry won't mind?"

"We've been through this before. She won't, and trust me, if she did, she'd tell me flat out. Let me call and ask her. Cooking seems to be some sort of therapy for her. She probably roasted three chickens worrying over Ryder, and made a gallon of potato salad. Just a rough guess. Maybe two gallons. And we won't speculate on dessert."

This big, noisy family was fascinating to her. As he called, she leaned forward and kissed his jaw, and Slater turned to brush his mouth against hers. Ryder was pounding up the auditorium stairs just then, shouting for Red, Drake and Mace, and all hell broke loose with man-hand smacks and big grins.

She was, after all, going to marry one of the Carson sons. So Grace stood up and joined in the bedlam and figured she was a lucky girl indeed.

Harry was in rare form, as Slater had predicted, and that was really saying something. She'd made chicken, but of the fried variety, because she'd learned that was Ryder's favorite food, with milk gravy, her garlic mashed potatoes, the sweet corn she put up every season, homemade rolls . . . and for dessert that chocolate brownie pie thing that made Mace want to cry with happiness.

Needless to say, all conversation came to a halt when the food arrived. Even Daisy stopped chattering. In true Blythe Carson style, this had turned into a full family dinner. She, Harry and Raine bustled around in the kitchen, carrying dishes to the table, refusing to let Grace help. Slater noticed that as she relaxed, her smile resurfaced, and both Drake, with his dry sense of humor, and Mace, who served his latest wine for everyone to sample, seemed particularly conscious of her mood, both smiling when her strained expression finally eased.

They weren't bad for younger brothers, he thought.

No one had told Ryder yet that a full-on search, including law enforcement, had been launched. He was still on cloud number nine, and Slater had to admire that Grace hadn't said a word about it so he could enjoy the moment. Maybe she never would, because there'd be implied criticism of his father and, as far he could tell, she tended to avoid any censure of Hank.

Good for her. Especially since she was Ryder's mother in every way except the biological. He was lucky that he and Raine got along so well — she was right across the table from him at the moment, laughing at something Mace had just said — but he'd always thought it was unfair when quarreling parents involved their children.

Everyone pitched in on the cleanup, ordering Harry and his mother out on the porch to enjoy their cup of coffee. Chilly enough to need a light jacket, but still a beautiful night, and they'd done the cooking, so relaxation was in order. While Ryder and Daisy cleared the table, everyone else rinsed dishes, loaded the dishwasher and scrubbed pots.

As usual, Drake and Mace sparred verbally while the rest of them shook their heads.

"Pass me that gravy boat, will you?" Drake held out a soapy hand.

"What? Your arm broken or something?" Mace passed it over, anyway, grumbling. "Put an apron on you and you think you're Harry."

Drake replied, "I don't see *you* washing a damn gravy boat, Mr. Vineyard. I still have to ride fences tonight. Here's some info for you. You're coming along. I could use help looking for that missing calf."

"Fine. That means you'll whip off those boots and squash grapes with your toes the next time I need a hand."

Drake, who was rinsing a wineglass, looked at it in feigned alarm. "You don't really do that, right? I've smelled your feet and —"

Raine, wiping off the kitchen island, gestured at Slater and Grace. "I'll manage the rest of this if you want to go for a walk. Run while you can. When these two get going . . . well, you know what happens. And yes, everyone will keep an eye on Ryder."

Didn't have to ask him twice. Slater grabbed Grace's hand and practically dragged her to the door. They needed to talk. "Let's go."

They even brushed past his mother and Harry with just a wave, and then suddenly he had Grace all to himself on a perfect Wyoming night, with stars everywhere and just a hint of a cloud over the moon.

"You're good for Ryder," she said as she walked beside him on the path to the stable. "All of you. The two of us did okay together, but we were hurting in the 'circle the wagons' department. Only two of us. No wagons. In my former line of work, that translates to no backup."

Maybe Red's influence had rubbed off in the *Old Western Idioms* department. "As a family we do tend to stick our noses in. I wish I could promise you otherwise. We like Ryder. Enough said."

She continued to walk next to him, her expression pensive. "The thing is, I didn't come from a big family, and he's an only kid, so I can't give him advice about how to adapt to another change in his life. No mother, then his father and I split, and *then* he was bounced off to his grandparents, and sent back over the net like a tennis ball —"

"Grace, he's doing fine."

"I know. Thanks."

"I have a question." He needed to ask this carefully. Not everyone would be comfortable with it, and if she wasn't, fine. But he hoped she'd agree . . .

Grace glanced up at him. "What is it? With everything that went on today, I'm in a fairly mellow mood."

Might as well just ask. "In those pictures of the hotel you let me take, there's a woman who reminds me of you. She's gorgeous, with long hair like yours, and supposedly she was quite the legend around these parts. I'm definitely including her in the movie and . . . I wondered if you'd pose for some footage? The records say she was a redhead and married one of the owners. I want a reenactment and you'd be perfect."

"I'm gorgeous?" Grace shot him a killer look. "Way to try to flatter, Carson, to get me to do something I have no idea how to pull off. In a *movie*?"

"I want it in the beginning of the movie. I'm getting that sense of how I want to structure it. I emailed the director and he agrees, since he met you at the dinner. So . . . there we go."

"I've never acted in my life. Not a school play, not anything. I could arrest someone on camera, but otherwise you might just doom your movie."

"I was being honest." He really thought she was the right fit. The first time he'd seen the old photograph, he'd instantly thought of Grace.

"What, is she naked?"

He had to laugh at her suspicious tone. "Sweetheart, do you think I'd let anyone else see you naked? No, she's leaning over and giving her husband a kiss while sitting on her horse. It's quintessential Wyoming."

"Does he happen to look like you?"

"He?"

"The husband."

"No. I wouldn't say that. Why?"

"Tall, attractive rancher type? Dark hair and blue eyes?"

"It was in this area a hundred-plus years ago. Yes, I guess tall rancher type would work. You think I'm good-looking? Good to know."

"That's the only way I'll do it. If my co-star looks like you — exactly like you, in fact. Then I'll do it. Otherwise, no."

"You want *me* in the shot?" He stopped and turned her toward him.

"That's the deal."

She had him over a barrel. He wasn't an actor, either, but for a few minutes of footage without dialogue he could pull it off, and he already had the scene in mind.

"Are you saying yes?" he asked.

"If you are, Showbiz."

Everyone was going to love this, from his staff to his family. But he had to admit he didn't want anyone else kissing her, so . . . it might as well be him.

"All right, I'm game. On-screen kiss. Let's make it memorable."

He was actually looking forward to it. In fact, maybe they should rehearse right now. "Grace, I'm feeling my way with this, acting in a scene together, but I'm so in love with you, I can't think of a better reason to do it."

Her expression softened and she melted into his embrace. "If that's your pitch, I can see why you're successful in the movie business."

"Hmm." He led her toward the closest fence. When they got there, he lifted her up and set her on the top rail. "Now, kiss me. Let your hair fall down over your shoulder. Romantic?"

"You're too bossy. If you're like this on location, I'm not sure I can put up with it." Her mouth curved provocatively.

"The director is more in charge than I am when we're actually filming." His hands lingered at her waist, her long legs dangling. "I'm just trying to see that we get the right shot."

"We might have to practice it a few times."

368

She leaned down and teased him with a brief touch of her lips. "Is this what you were thinking of?"

Hardly. He wound his hand into her hair and tugged her closer. "You know damn well I have something else in mind."

"I'm new to this acting thing." She failed at looking innocent.

The second kiss was much better with him as director. Grace seemed to approve, too, her mouth soft and receptive, her arms around his neck.

He wanted nothing more than to lay her down and make love to her, but they had the rest of their lives for that and of course, Drake and Mace could come riding through at any moment, no doubt arguing all the way.

So he settled for one more electrifying kiss under a beautiful Western sky.

Not too much of a sacrifice.

CHAPTER TWENTY-THREE

Bad day/good day.

Grace couldn't bring herself to scold Ryder. On the one hand, she felt like pointing out that he knew what his father was like, knew he couldn't count on Hank to tell her. And *hello,* didn't he realize she'd be worried? But another, more pragmatic impulse won out. She acknowledged that he wasn't ultimately responsible — and she didn't want to spoil his elation at tonight's success.

So instead she listened as they drove home.

"He was brilliant." He was talking about the horse he'd ridden in the competition. "I wonder . . . I mean, you let me have Bonaparte, but if I worked hard, could you think about me getting a horse?"

That meant he was probably getting about five horses already. Let's see — Red, Slater, Drake, Mace, Blythe and Harry. Wait. That made six.

Raine might buy him one, too. She was as bad as the rest of them.

"You can have a horse if you take care of it." Grace turned onto Main. She didn't want to put too much emphasis on one accomplishment. He was exceptionally good at horse-related activities, apparently, but school was important, too. "I have a feeling the Carson ranch will let us board your horse there. Why don't we make a deal? You pass English and at the end of the school year, we'll ask Red to come with us and we'll go pick out a horse. Okay?"

"I got a C on my last assignment."

She was fine with that. C was a passing grade. "Ryder, I'm never going to ask you to be perfect at everything. None of us are. It's just impossible. This person can do one thing, and this other person can't. I want to know you're trying. That's all. You did really well today. You —"

"Could our place be on fire?"

Distracted by the sudden change in subject, she said, "What?"

He pointed through the windshield.

The plume of smoke was alarming. They said in unison, "Bonaparte!"

Grace cared about her personal belongings and even more about the things she'd inherited from her grandmother, but she cared a lot more about the cat. As she drove in, she saw that volunteer firefighters were already there and taking care of the problem, but it was definitely her condo with the plume of smoke billowing out.

"We'll find him," she told Ryder, thankful they hadn't been there when the blaze started. "That cat is so smart . . ."

She prayed it was true. The first thing she did was call Slater. There were fire trucks all over the place, and she usually was calm under pressure, but nothing like this had ever happened to her. "I need you here."

He didn't even ask. "On my way."

She had to park down the street, and she and Ryder ran to the closest truck. There was a firefighter standing next to it, and Grace had enough experience with this type of situation to figure out that he was the one in charge. She caught Ryder by the arm as he was about to charge past her. "Grace Emery," she told the firefighter. "That's my place. We have a pet. A small black cat. Can you please find out for me if anyone's seen him? We'll stay out of your way, I promise, but that would really help the situation."

He was thickset and had a goatee liberally streaked with silver, and he looked as if he'd be at home at Bad Billy's. He took one look at Ryder's anxious face and at her hand, clamped on the kid's arm, and nodded. "Yes, ma'am. Lots of smoke, but not much real damage. We got the alert from your security alarm when the back door was broken in. Hopefully, the critter left that way. We realized right away that it was arson, but things are under control now, and none of the other condos were affected. Whoever did this didn't know what he was doing. Thank God . . ." He looked around. "Let me ask about the cat."

"Grace, he'll come to me but not to them." Ryder tried to wriggle away as the man walked off.

"You'll interfere with them doing their job. You're staying right here. I mean it."

He muttered a word she usually disapproved of, but the situation did warrant cutting him some slack. He was having a rollercoaster kind of evening; they both were. Hers had started low, gone high and was now back to low.

The ranch was hardly right next door, so when Slater arrived twenty minutes later, she'd already filled out a police report and surveyed the damage, which, as the firefighter had told her, was mostly smoke and water. Whoever had done this — and that wasn't really a question in her mind — had set her new couch on fire.

She was going to miss that couch, but at least they'd found Bonaparte in his usual hiding place, and Ryder had coaxed him out from under the bushes.

Child safe, the child's beloved cat safe . . . So, not a bad outcome to a bad event.

But she was sick of it. Sick of the constant threat, the malicious and increasingly dangerous incidents.

"I'm done," she said when Slater and Drake walked up. "This is over."

Slater watched a fire truck pull away. "Can't say as I'm opposed to that. Let's board up the broken door and head back to the ranch. Drake will get the cat in the carrier. Mom loves cats. She's still in mourning over her last one, who finally passed away at the age of twenty-one. Bonaparte is more than welcome." He held her gaze steadily. "I want you there. Please agree that this is getting way too dangerous."

She did agree. "For David Reinhart it is."

She saw Drake walk over, point at the open pet crate, and the cat scooted right out of Ryder's arms through the open door.

"The sight of that crate usually sends that cat into deep hiding." She really was incredulous.

Slater shook his head. "Don't ask me how,

but it just happens. He's a wizard. I've told him he should grow a long beard, wear a robe and put a nest of baby birds on his head."

Drake looked pretty comfortable in a hat and worn jeans versus the wizard getup, but the cat had gotten his message without any trouble. Grace managed to find some solace in that.

"We'll go home and sort it out."

Home. That sounded comfortable. But . . . "I don't want to depend on you for every little thing."

"You don't want to depend on me for anything. Hey, look around, someone set your house on fire. That's not little. Besides, Grace, I'm the person you should count on for *everything.* Just like I should count on you."

No, it wasn't little. What had begun as a simple matter — firing a dishonest employee — had escalated way out of control. She couldn't look over her shoulder every minute of the day, nor could she send a bodyguard with Ryder, or for that matter, Slater. She had work, Ryder had school and Slater seemed invincible with his broad shoulders and male confidence, but she knew he wasn't. Her ex-husband came across that way, too, and he'd been knocked unconscious. She gestured at the ruined remains of her living room. "I wonder if this is why he was here when he hit Hank. He was getting ready to break in to start the fire and Hank walked out the door. Obviously he came prepared with something heavy enough to break some pretty solid glass."

"Tell Ryder to grab some clothes, go get some for yourself, and Drake and I will take care of the door." He grasped her by the shoulders then gently turned her toward the hallway and the bedrooms.

Everything, all her clothes, would smell like smoke, but knowing Harry, by the time she got up in the morning, it would all be washed and neatly folded. Drake was a wizard and Harry was a genie from a bottle. Slater had told her that when he went off to college he'd realized with dismay that he could run cattle, mend a saddle and do just about everything else on a working ranch, but he didn't know the first thing about washing a load of clothes. He'd sheepishly called Harry for a phone lesson in Laundry 101.

She should make Ryder do his own laundry, Grace decided as she stuffed clothes in a suitcase. It wasn't something she'd ever thought about, but now . . .

They were going to live at the ranch. She'd suspected all along that it would happen. Still, she was furious to have the chance to discuss it with Slater taken from her. She zipped up the case, told herself the tears in her eyes were from residual smoke and stomped out of her bedroom.

The woman had a serious mad on, and Slater couldn't blame her.

He certainly wasn't marrying a woman who dissolved in a puddle of tears when a crisis came along. She was justifiably angry and that wasn't a secret, but then again, he'd be angry, too. Since Drake was following with Ryder in her car, he ventured a conversation. "If you don't want to live at the ranch, we can buy a house."

"Would you stop reading my mind?" From the passenger seat of the truck, she sent him a lethal glare. "And, by the way, that's not what I was thinking."

It was tempting to point out the contradiction, but he preferred to believe he was smarter than that. "Okay, what *were* you thinking?"

"I was thinking you and I should both have a choice. I didn't want it to happen like this — Ryder and me having no other place to go. I wanted you to *ask* me, not feel obliged to take us in."

"I told you I wanted you there with me."

She shook her head and gave a humorless laugh. "I'm not making sense, I know. Maybe I'm more romantic than I thought. I suppose I pictured us sitting on your porch, holding hands, discussing it in the moonlight."

He understood. She was used to making her own decisions, and this situation had been thrust on her all at once. "Well, we can't hold hands while I'm driving, and I need to keep my eyes on the road, but let's talk about it. If you don't want to live at the ranch, let's rent a house while your condo's being fixed and then we can live there. Or somewhere else. We can build our own house. Whatever you want."

He wasn't destined to know how she might have responded because at that moment his phone vibrated and he picked it up to peer briefly at the screen.

Spence.

He punched a button on the dash so he could talk hands-free. "Hey."

"We got David Reinhart, who is also by the way David Lipman, according to the driver's license he showed the arresting officer. We took him into custody about fifteen minutes ago. He ran a stoplight. Luckily, everyone at the station knows the story. The officer recognized him from the pictures we'd passed around."

"That's great news! Let me pass you to Grace. She's here with me."

The cop speak was rapid-fire and he caught only about half of it, but he gathered that there was enough evidence in the vehicle to validate the arrest. She sounded relieved when they hung up. "He's off the street. The judge will go over all of it, and set bail, pending a hearing on assault and arson charges. The accelerant was in his car. Or rather, the car he was driving, which apparently belongs to his girlfriend. *His* car was repossessed."

He carefully navigated a turn. "I knew Spence would get him, just wasn't sure when."

"I didn't doubt him, but this is one of those elusive cases that don't usually show up very high on the urgent scale. Harassment that doesn't cause harm is considered more of a nuisance than a crime."

"He tried to burn down your house!"

"That's my point. He finally caused harm." She laid back her head and closed her eyes. "It isn't over by any means, but there's enough to charge him — between the eyewitness who saw him trespassing on my property and the fact that they now have his prints."

"This has certainly been an interesting day."

It became *more* interesting.

She said slowly, "I think we could try living at the ranch and see if it works for us. I like having my own space, but Ryder would love being there. And having your family around would help me, not just with him, but if we do have a baby. You'll be away a lot. I'm not talking built-in babysitters, although I'm sure they'd be all over that. I'm talking *family.*"

There were two deer standing in the driveway to the ranch, so he waited until they loped off. "I'm really willing to work on the baby thing."

"You," she said, "have turned my life upside down. I'd just gotten it all in order and then you come along."

He loved her sulky smile and how she completely failed to convince him she meant it. "Really?" he said as they went up the drive. "Life in order? Seems to me you moved, inherited your ex-husband's problem child, started a new career, had serious trust issues and acquired a stalker. You met me, and *now* your life's in order."

"Oh, right. I'm getting married for the

second time — something I swore I'd never do — I'm apparently going to live with my rambunctious in-laws, including a housekeeper who rules with an iron fist, your brother the wizard and the other one who plies me with wine. *And* we have to ride off into the sunset every evening since that's your favorite way to relax."

He glanced at her, eyebrows slightly raised. "Well, that point can be debated. There's another way to relax that I like even more. It involves a different kind of ride, but it's still you and me together."

That won him a genuine laugh despite the tense evening. "I'll give you the sweet-talking cowboy award, but you lose in the subtle category, Carson."

"Hey, I wasn't even aiming for *that* belt buckle." He parked the truck in his usual spot. The porch lights were on, and he knew both his mother and Harry would be up, waiting anxiously.

He leaned over and put his thumb on Grace's chin to tilt her face up to his. "I am planning to enter the best husband category, though."

Just before he kissed her, she whispered, "You go, cowboy."

CHAPTER TWENTY-FOUR

She was nervous, which made no sense. Or maybe it did.

It wasn't as if she hadn't done this before.

Well, that was the point, wasn't it? Grace had been a bride before, but — as she reminded herself emphatically — she'd never married Slater Carson. And she'd never had a birthday wedding. Daisy had very sweetly asked her father if they could have the wedding at her party. So she could wear her new dress in front of everyone, she said. That was what she wanted for her present.

Considering that he'd been stumped by what to give her, the look on Slater's face was priceless.

Since the wedding was so last-minute, Blythe and Harry had gone straight into high gear. Grace still had to work at the resort so she was grateful for the help. Not surprisingly, based on what she'd learned about those two formidable women, she hadn't been involved in the plans.

She adjusted the two combs holding her hair in a chignon of sorts and looked at it critically.

"I like it that way," Raine said. "Although . . . I'd tell you he loves you for your mind, but that's giving any man too much credit. I think he fell in love with your hair. Wear it loose," she advised.

Grace turned around. "He likes my sense of humor."

Raine, beautiful herself in her blue dress, a shade darker than Grace's, rolled her eyes. "Oh, yeah, that's it. He took one look at you and made up his mind. He *told* me so."

Melody Hogan and Hadleigh Galloway, who had volunteered to pitch in with wedding preparations the minute they heard about it, agreed with her. "Yes," they said in unison. "Do what she says."

Grace could hardly argue against such a united front. It actually felt better, more natural, more *her,* to have her hair free in long loose curls. She tossed the jeweled combs aside and just finger-combed it. In the giant living room, she could hear children shrieking with laughter as they played a party game. That wasn't exactly what she would've pictured for her wedding — but then, she hadn't planned on getting married again, so she really hadn't imagined anything at all.

She and her attendants walked into the living room to see Slater — handsome in his suit — talking to Ryder and his two brothers. Adding to the general mayhem, the two dogs that seemed to follow Drake everywhere were sitting at his feet. All the young girls started clapping at the sight of the bridal party, and a harpist began to play. (Who knew how Blythe had found a harpist in Mustang Creek?)

Most of the guests had birthday cake on their faces. Children's birthday party combined with wedding. Daisy strolled out first, and her friends cheered and she waved regally, smiling a wide smile, probably more the star of the day than Grace, which Grace didn't mind at all. Meg and Raine followed, holding bouquets of white roses provided by Mrs. A.

It made Slater happy to see his daughter happy, and Grace felt the same way.

Red walked her down the makeshift aisle. Her parents hadn't been able to come because of the short notice and the fact that her father had some minor surgery scheduled. Slater had arranged to fly out to Seattle with her next week so he could meet them, and that was met with approval, especially since her mother hated to travel. Although they hadn't been pleased about her divorce from Hank, they seemed much more accepting of her new marriage than she'd expected. And to her delight, her brother and his family would meet them in Seattle.

Red wore new boots, but that was his only concession to the solemnity of the occasion. The usual flannel shirt, old hat (removed for the moment) and jeans. Everything was neatly pressed, probably thanks to Harry.

He grinned as he offered his arm. "You're making a powerful mistake, young lady." He patted her hand, eyes twinkling. "I'm the better catch. Oh, sure, he has looks, talent and all his hair, but I'm like that old stallion who's proven he can run the course. We could still sashay off together. You positive about that young fella?"

Grace nodded, although she did her best to appear regretful. She knew just what he was asking. "I'm afraid that, tempting as your offer is, I'm positive. He's the one."

"That, honey, is exactly the answer I needed to hear. Slater's been waiting for you his whole life. That hooligan is like my own son. Good to see him so sweet on the right girl."

Grace could swear he was misty-eyed. Slater had already said that Red must be getting soft in the head because of that comforting hug he'd given her, but if he cried in front of the Carson boys and their guests, she had a feeling he'd never live it down. She whispered, "Don't worry, I'll keep him in line."

"Well, he's about to officially become the thorn under your saddle, not mine, young lady. The preacher seems to be ready so I'm handing over the reins. You ready, too?"

"I can't believe it, but I am."

That was the truth. And nothing but the truth.

Happiest day of his life, hands down. Took the trophy.

It even eclipsed the day Daisy was born, whole and perfect, because she was part of this celebration, as well, as junior bridesmaid. She wore a long blue dress to match the one Grace had chosen, enjoying her birthday with glowing joy and being quite the little princess. She looked like one to him, but he was her father, so objectivity could be in question.

The audience was an array of family and friends, not more than about thirty people, including Mrs. A and her husband, the

Galloways and Hogans and Calders — and
the vet, Jaxon Locke, and his wife. His
mother's desire for the typical big wedding
had been eclipsed by Daisy's request, and
he knew Grace was relieved since, short
notice aside, she'd been through that kind
of very public event before and had no
interest in doing it again. He also knew she
would've preferred more time . . . Still, to
her credit, she embraced the idea of small
children running amok and causing general
mayhem on her wedding day.

He didn't care one way or the other. He
just wanted Grace Emery to become Grace
Carson.

She looked incredibly beautiful.

His brothers were acting ridiculous. If they
weren't unmistakably kin, he'd disown them
both. They grabbed her away from Red and
kissed her soundly before the ceremony had
even started, undoubtedly to irk him.

"Sorry," he told Grace as they joined
hands in front of the preacher once the
shenanigans were over. "They have a . . .
quirky sense of humor."

Drake merely smiled as he took his place
next to Slater. With his dogs, for heaven's
sake. Harold and Violet just sat politely, ears
forward.

Mace winked at Grace. Ryder grinned.

She was laughing, with that lovely telltale blush on her cheeks. She squeezed his hand. "Your problem is you don't think you have an expressive face, but you do. They know how to get to you. Now, if this makes you feel better, they came to me individually and said I'm the luckiest girl on earth to be marrying you."

His brothers looked at each other accusingly. Drake said, "You did something that sappy?"

Mace countered, "Apparently, so did you."

Standing beside Grace, Daisy piped up. "Uncle Drake, Uncle Mace, I win! I told her first."

One of the most touching moments in his life was when Daisy had said on the day she heard about the engagement that she thought Grace was making a "perfect" decision.

From the mouths of babes . . .

Except that she was eleven now, today, so not a baby anymore. She'd become a wise little girl.

Grace pointed out, "Maybe we should get this started. It might not be the most orthodox wedding ever, but it's still a wedding."

He couldn't agree more.

And after the ceremony and the celebration came the wedding night . . . Enough said. The minister spoke, and Slater was fairly sure he repeated the right words, but if he didn't, not one person called him on it. Finally he heard the magic phrase. *You may kiss the bride.*

He leaned down and threaded his fingers through her hair, looked at her luscious mouth, and then, just to tease her, kissed her forehead.

A nice kiss. Soft and affectionate, but he knew Grace, and she wasn't having that.

"No way, Carson." She caught his tie and pulled him down for the real deal, and then they were both laughing. He picked her up to the cheers of a group of eleven-year-olds and the enthusiastic guests, all applauding as he carried her out of the room. Even Ryder was clapping.

"*Yes* way, Carson," he said as he headed for the front door. "We have a date at the finest suite in a certain resort right here in Bliss County. I'm going to fill out the satisfaction questionnaire afterward, by the way. Just giving you fair warning."

She tossed back all that gorgeous hair and gave him a sultry stare as he carried her to the truck. "I'm expecting to get an A-plus rating."

She did.

ABOUT THE AUTHOR

The daughter of a town marshal, **Linda Lael Miller** is the author of more than 100 historical and contemporary novels. Now living in Spokane, Washington, the "First Lady of the West" hit a career high when all three of her 2011 Creed Cowboy books debuted at #1 on the *New York Times* list. In 2007, the Romance Writers of America presented her their Lifetime Achievement Award. She personally funds her Linda Lael Miller Scholarships for Women. Visit her at www.lindalaelmiller.com.